MOVED TO MURDER

Stephanie,
 From one Cali girl to another: Hope you enjoy this!

ALSO BY GIANETTA MURRAY

Spring Paths: "As Flies to Wanton Boys"
A Supernatural Shindig: Amusing Tales of
Paranormal Pranks

MOVED TO MURDER

A VIVIEN BRANDT MYSTERY

G. Murray

GIANETTA MURRAY

Copyright © 2024 Gianetta Murray

The moral right of the author has been asserted.

Apart from any fair dealing for the purposes of research or private study, or criticism or review, as permitted under the Copyright, Designs and Patents Act 1988, this publication may only be reproduced, stored or transmitted, in any form or by any means, with the prior permission in writing of the publishers, or in the case of reprographic reproduction in accordance with the terms of licences issued by the Copyright Licensing Agency. Enquiries concerning reproduction outside those terms should be sent to the publishers.

This is a work of fiction. Names, characters, businesses, places, events and incidents are either the products of the author's imagination or used in a fictitious manner. Any resemblance to actual persons, living or dead, or actual events is purely coincidental.

The villages and people described in this story are fictional (although Doncaster is real) and are not meant to resemble anyone living or dead. At least, not entirely accurately.

Troubador Publishing Ltd
Unit E2 Airfield Business Park,
Harrison Road, Market Harborough,
Leicestershire LE16 7UL
Tel: 0116 279 2299
Email: books@troubador.co.uk
Web: www.troubador.co.uk

ISBN 978 1 80514 389 5

British Library Cataloguing in Publication Data.
A catalogue record for this book is available from the British Library.

Printed and bound in Great Britain by 4edge Limited
Typeset in 11pt Minion Pro by Troubador Publishing Ltd, Leicester, UK

My eternal thanks to my husband Chris for his multifaceted support during the creation of this work. I hope you are pleased with the result.

Also to my two cats, Winifred and Cordelia, for relieving my stress by constantly reminding me there are more important things than my literary pretentions: namely, their meals.

PROLOGUE

Two Years Earlier

I really don't want to think about what I've just seen, but it keeps replaying in my mind in horrific detail. Deep down I guess I've always known something like this would happen.

Still, it was a shock. I turned and ran like the coward I am, all the way to the park. I remember stumbling, the feel of cold, wet grass on my hands and soaking through the knees of my trousers as I struggled to catch my breath. Can't believe I'm so out of shape.

I'm pretty sure they didn't know I was there. Well, they were obviously busy, weren't they!

What could they have been thinking? What if I had been somebody else, somebody who could have ruined everything?

I wish there was someone I could talk to, someone who could help me decide what to do. But I've been racking my brain and there simply isn't anyone I can trust. Not with this.

So that's it, I guess. I'm just going to have to keep it to myself and hope no one ever finds out. God! Like this is what I needed, on top of everything else in my disaster of a life. As if being a teenager in this bloody, boring village wasn't torture enough.

1

"I had the urge to examine my life in another
culture and move beyond what I knew."
— Frances Mayes, *Under the Tuscan Sun*

Wordsworth, Mary Queen of Scots, Churchill, Jack the Ripper.

Vivien Brandt simply adored all things British. The love affair started when she saw *Upstairs, Downstairs* at the impressionable age of ten and blossomed steadily over the years, fueled by daydreams about what her life would be like in the country she cherished.

Now her dreams were finally coming true.

She wiped the last streaks off the front window and stepped back to enjoy the sight of her new home, a two-story redbrick situated in the South Yorkshire village of Nether Chatby. It was absolutely perfect and she sighed with happiness.

No one had been surprised when Vivien announced she was moving to England. They only wondered that it had taken her so long. But a moderately successful career, marriage, and the love of friends and family had all provided valid excuses for her inertia.

Instead, she survived for decades on mere glimpses of Britain, making the long flight over whenever she could save up enough money and vacation time, starting with her first trip after college graduation. She'd been thrilled to find the country exceeded the promise of her beloved Victorian dramas. The gardens were stunning, the food wasn't nearly as bad as rumored, and she suspected plumbing had greatly improved since the nineteenth century. She enjoyed being called "ginger" instead of "redhead", although she considered herself more titian-haired, like Nancy Drew.

When Charlie, her charmingly irresponsible first husband, arrived in her life, the dream came dangerously close to being suffocated. But after his gambling addiction finally put an end to their twelve-year marriage, Vivien began to rebuild her bank account and revived thoughts of moving to London, where she hoped her Silicon Valley tech-writing experience might snag her a job. She'd been exploring interior design—even taking night classes—but knew there wasn't a living to be made as a novice in a brand-new country.

So she continued to work at increasingly unfulfilling jobs, saving and planning for the future, and relied on visits across The Pond to keep the dream alive.

Pulling her thoughts back to the present, Vivien noted the ivy growing up the left corner of the house to curl ever so gracefully around an upstairs window frame. She'd either need a very tall ladder or a regular gardener to keep it in check, but it looked so lovely and…well…British. Visiting Americans would be impressed by the house, especially the ones naive enough to believe Geoffrey's sardonic assurances that Shakespeare once slept there. Vivien found most of her friends couldn't name the countries that made up the United Kingdom, much less which century gave birth to the greatest-ever English playwright. She'd given up trying to explain devolved parliaments, or why Andy Murray was British when he won a tennis grand slam and Scottish when he lost.

She shivered in her short-sleeved shirt and black jeans, clothing that would have been appropriate at this time of year in her native California, but which was unequal to the chill of northern England in October. A few houses up the road a door slammed and she watched a tow-headed teenager dressed entirely in black stalk away from her toward the village center, his body stiff and his fists clenched. *Probably disgusted with his parents*, she mused with a wry smile. Some rites of passage were universal and she suspected teen rebellion was one of them.

Her gaze landed on the house next door, with its dark windows and empty driveway. No one had come or gone since she and Geoffrey had moved in a couple of days ago, but there was no To Let or For Sale sign, so she assumed the owners were simply on vacation. Or holiday, as they said here.

Or maybe they're all lying dead inside and we won't know until the smell escapes. Vivien chuckled at her overactive imagination. She really needed to stop reading so many murder mysteries.

She noticed a missed spot on one of the many panes and attacked it with purpose, her mind continuing to reminisce as the sun broke through the clouds and a welcome warmth caressed her shoulders.

Now where was I? Ah yes, Geoffrey. Vivien never imagined it would be love that finally made her get off her butt and move to England. As an emancipated woman, it was somewhat embarrassing. Her membership in the Power Chicks Club would be rescinded, if such a thing actually existed.

It wasn't that she was against love. Of course she'd fantasized that someday, when she'd grown tired of her hectic London life as a famous interior designer, she'd accept a commission from an irascible-yet-handsome duke or earl. The two of them would trade verbal barbs for a few days after being trapped in his stately home by a freak storm, then suddenly realize they were madly in love. A fabulous society wedding would ensue, followed by a dazzling career in charity work (for which she would be made a Dame), and evening strolls with their three West Highland terriers: Lancelot, Galahad, and Percival. There might even be casual gatherings with royalty, necessitating the purchase of amazing designer hats. After all, that kind of thing happened quite often in Hallmark movies.

But Vivien knew deep down this course of events was highly unlikely, and her practical, well-laid plans did not require men, marriage, or monsoons.

Fortunately for her, Fate didn't give a fig about her plans, somewhat literally upending them during a tour of the Tower of London on yet another British vacation.

Starting the climb up the White Tower (where Anne Boleyn had been imprisoned and reportedly still haunted, presumably for lack of anything better to do), Vivien slipped on an uneven stair and catapulted forward into the firm-yet-unhelpful posterior of the man in front of her. Her finger snagged the back pocket of his jeans even as the rest of her body recoiled in horror at this unintended intimacy, and she ended up pulling him with her as they careened down the few steps to the landing.

Vivien's whole romantic fantasy might still have come to fruition if she'd merely broken a nail and sat crying prettily (no running mascara) while the handsome doctor/lawyer/playboy attended to her.

Instead, she sat there stunned, legs akimbo, as her unwilling companion emitted a startled grunt followed by some heartfelt cursing. Even in her dazed state, Vivien couldn't help thinking how charming British swear words sounded. It was the way they said "bollocks" in that clipped, slightly annoyed tone.

"Oh my God, I'm so sorry!" she exclaimed as they disentangled themselves. "I tripped. I didn't mean to grab you. Are you all right?"

"Nothing broken, I think. And it's good to know you don't purposely go around lurching at people's backsides," he groused, slapping dust from the knees of his blue jeans and out of his adorably mussed fair hair.

"Well, I was reaching for a banister or something. Your ass wasn't really meant to be part of the program."

The man looked at her and sighed. "You are American, I see. Or hear, rather. Well, madam, I'm not a doctor, but that cut on your leg looks like it requires attention. You must have scraped it on the stair. I suggest we find you a plaster."

"A plasterer? Why, did I crack the wall?"

There was a momentary pause during which Vivien could almost taste the man's exasperation.

"I believe you call them Band-Aids." He stood and gestured toward a door with one well-manicured hand while offering the other to help her up. "After you."

One hour, one plaster, and a couple of pints of lager later in a nearby pub, Vivien gazed somewhat blearily at her new acquaintance. Her eyes eventually focused on his, which were a lovely shade of blue. Not the light, watery kind, like those of the high school boyfriend who had dumped her the second he realized he had the chance to date a cheerleader. No, these were a deep, azure blue, like the twilight sky after a warm summer day.

He was six gorgeous feet of well-dressed Brit with skin that looked like it would tan easily if there was sunshine. He told her his name was Geoffrey Wooster (as in *Jeeves and*), he was fifty-three, and he worked in pharmacological research. He was also making Vivien's heart go pitter-pat in a completely new and exciting way (though it dimly occurred to her that might be the lager).

Drinks led to lunch, which led to dinner, or "tea" as he confusingly called it. This led in turn to evening walks along the Thames and, by the end of Vivien's vacation, to some quite steamy nights. Following her return to the States, there were online discussions about music, sports, and the television shows that had shaped them (*Buffy the Vampire Slayer* for her, *Doctor Who* for him). Love grew almost as quickly as her frequent flyer miles thanks to romantic weekends in New York, a couple of long-distance hauls to meet each other's families, and eventually an English wedding.

It wasn't the grand ducal affair of her fantasies, but it was a lovely ceremony in a fourteenth-century manor house turned hotel, and enough of Vivien's friends and family were able to fly over to make it truly memorable. Her Aunt Jenny was particularly delighted to discover the Beatles had once stayed at the hotel and constantly wondered aloud which bed George Harrison had slept in, until Geoffrey's Uncle Max drily assured her it didn't really matter as the sheets had undoubtedly been changed since then.

Vivien's mother, having long tolerated her daughter's Anglophilia, required reassurance before the wedding that Vivien wasn't marrying Geoffrey just to get free room and board in her favorite country. Geoffrey's twenty-three-year-old daughter Sara likewise asked her father if he was doing it for the companionship. Or the sex.

But with assurances given, the day went beautifully and everyone danced late into the night despite the jet lag.

After a short honeymoon in Edinburgh, Vivien returned to California to sell off most of her worldly goods, apply for a spousal visa, and prepare her Siamese, Sydney, for the big move.

And that was how she came to be here, a forty-eight-year-old newlywed arriving with an exceptionally large suitcase and a very disgruntled cat, praying that the heartfelt pitter-pat of that first meeting wasn't going to peter out when faced with the reality of cohabitation.

But what the heck, she thought, *even if we don't live happily ever after, I will always have the memory of that weak-in-the-knees feeling I get when Geoffrey looks at me. Life is too short not to take risks. Nothing ventured, nothing gained, yada yada yada, don't spit into the wind.*

Vivien tried to come up with more hackneyed advice to give herself, but the well was dry. She once again took a few steps back, bringing her to the edge of the street, and ran a hand through her short bob of hair. It had surprised her that many new English houses lacked the fenced-in, spacious front yards she was used to in California. It felt a little like living in a fishbowl when people walked by. But she nevertheless felt immensely satisfied as she once again admired their new home.

Having been thus-far limited to practicing her budding interior design skills on her little California condominium and doing up a few rooms for friends, she looked forward to decorating an entire house. She would create something that showed everyone what could be done with imagination, taste, and a disdain for beige. All of Geoffrey's friends would be asking for her help in no time, and then, armed with a stunning portfolio and a reputation for creative genius, she would take Britain by storm, no doubt ending up with an invitation to decorate Windsor Castle or Number 10 Downing Street. After that, the world.

Vivien still tended to dream big.

In the meantime, she had a Library Science degree she could put to good use while she got to know the British in all their *Masterpiece Theatre* glory (minus the overworked servants and dodgy Victorian medical practices).

Vivien turned to survey the neighborhood. Nether Chatby was a smallish village, but around its main street branched various "planned estates", including the one she now lived in.

The curvy lanes were lined with the same sort of Edwardian-inspired homes, differentiated only by minor alterations in trim and floorplan. The architectural consistency provided a comforting symmetry that enhanced the village feel. Next to their house, which was at the end of a cul-de-sac, there was an entrance to a grassy field complete with a meandering pathway and a lamppost that would have fit neatly into Narnia. Vivien thought it would be perfect for walking her future Westie. (She'd decided it would be better to stick to one dog instead of three, since she no longer had access to her imaginary duke's vast expanse of stately gardens, not to mention his canine-loving housekeeper to provide care and feeding for the pampered pups.)

Yes, she mused, "Galahad" would be an ideal companion for Sydney, who had loudly objected to having a chip put in his head just so he could be transported in a dark space for twelve hours to start a new life he in no way asked for. He was still ignoring Vivien, except at mealtimes.

A dog would cheer him up no end, she thought with a pinch of sadism.

As Vivien scanned the house across the road, she saw the twitch of a lace curtain. *How quaint, a nosy neighbor. It's all so very Agatha Christie.* But then, she probably did look pretty dorky just standing there admiring a perfectly ordinary house. She smiled and turned to walk the few steps to her front door.

Entering the hallway, she stopped to take a deep breath, getting used to the smell that would soon represent home. Vivien had a keen olfactory sense and knew she would miss the dry, sun-warmed-redwood scent of California, but she was determined to make new memories in her adopted country. At the moment, though, the house smelled overwhelmingly of fresh paint.

She found Geoffrey organizing stereo equipment in his self-identified "man cave". Vivien had banished the most hideous of her husband's bachelor pieces to this space—including a truly ugly green-checked sofa and a couple of neon-colored beanbags—to avoid having to look at them regularly. Watching him bend over to untangle some electrical cords, she was glad to find her heart's pitter-pat was still very much in working order. The man was just gorgeous.

"Honestly, hon, do you really think that's a priority?" she purred, lifting her eyebrows suggestively.

Geoffrey stopped fiddling with the cords long enough to straighten up and consider his wife standing in the doorway. Her Rubenesque figure was alluring, even clothed in a white T-shirt featuring a cat's butt. It was, after all, Rudyard Kipling's Cat That Walks Alone, which gave it unexpected gravitas for leisure wear. Her hazel eyes were full of the humor that had attracted him from the start. Well, almost the start.

"It depends on whose priorities we're talking about," he replied. "I'm sure I will soon need a place to flee from your constant demands and visiting in-laws. But since we are recently married and still therefore in the honeymoon phase, I'll do the polite thing and ask: What would you rather I do?"

And since they *were* still in the honeymoon phase, Vivien suggested they set up the bed, which they did, after which unpacking stopped for a while and she forgot all about twitching curtains, angry youths, and thinking of England.

2

"Indeed, in many respects, she was quite English, and was an excellent example of the fact that we have really everything in common with America nowadays, except, of course, language."
— Oscar Wilde, *The Canterville Ghost*

The next day, with Geoffrey safely off to work, Vivien headed for the nearest supermarket to stock up the kitchen. Passing by little villages on the way, she noted how the houses were often built around a village green, with shops and services fitted in between country cottages that backed onto fields. She wondered if she would ever get over the beauty of the English countryside. Sure, it required constant rain to keep it green and beautiful, but what a small price to pay come spring when the whole country burst into bloom and nature resembled a bounteous mother rather than Tennyson's "red in tooth and claw". In all the years Vivien had visited England, she hadn't found a season that didn't charm her in one way or another. She was looking forward to actually experiencing it year-round, seeing if its beauty would become ordinary with familiarity. She hoped not.

One thing was certain, supermarkets didn't differ that much from country to country, although here they were often banished far from the villages to save local shops and preserve the village feel. This meant you needed a car to access them, and as she drove into a packed parking lot—*did they saying parking lot here? Car park? Automobile containment area?*—she was made slightly nervous by the people walking right in front of her bright blue Toyota Prius, blithely unaware of her dodgy driving record and her confusion about which side of the road she should be on. At least there were fewer SUVs to deal with, she noted, and most of the cars were smaller than she was used to in America, thanks to the relatively expensive cost of gas in Britain. (*It's petrol now*, she reminded herself.)

Once parked, Vivien commandeered a cart (*trolley!*, she corrected) and started cruising the aisles. Her favorite was the 'World Foods' section, which thankfully included the ingredients for the Mexican food she knew she couldn't live without. She was disappointed to find only pre-shaped corn taco shells, though, as she preferred to fry her own. She'd have to look up a recipe for making them if she couldn't find them somewhere. Blue cheese salad dressing also turned out to be elusive, with most of the 'Dressings' section taken up by jars of the dreaded salad cream that for years had been England's only choice for salad topping. Thank goodness they'd eventually discovered the joys of balsamic vinegar and honey mustard.

She did manage to get most of the items on her list before finding herself stymied in the vegetable aisle. Cornering a member of staff, she put to him what she thought was a straightforward question.

"Can you tell me where to find the zucchini?"

She was rewarded with a blank look, a shrug, and a mumbled apology as the young man turned and fled to a safer location, away from babbling Americans. From behind her came a gently feminine chuckle, and Vivien turned to view one of the most wonderfully dressed women she'd ever seen. The kitten-heeled leather pumps, pastel-green Chanel skirt suit, and simple-but-expensive matching gold necklace and earrings all suggested their wearer was a lady of immense wealth and taste. *This woman dresses better to shop for groceries than I did to get married*, Vivien marveled. With her ice-blonde hair done up in a neat chignon that left exposed a pair of cool blue eyes, high cheekbones, and classically even features enhanced with the perfect amount of makeup, the apparition was a magical combination of Donna Reed and Cate Blanchett. Vivien was intimidated before a word was spoken.

"I'm sorry," said the vision, in a honeyed tone that in no way lessened the intimidation factor. "I was just amused by the look of dismay on that poor boy's face. In England, we call them 'courgettes', which is probably why he hadn't the faintest idea what you meant. Let me show you where they are."

She turned elegantly on the ball of her (probably Prada) shoe and Vivien dutifully followed her into the next aisle like a fourteen-year-old girl in the throes of a first crush. The woman handed her a zucchini with one hand and proffered the other to shake. Vivien crossed her arms to accept both, feeling as if she was getting some sort of diploma, and received a glossy smile in return. No smeared lipstick marred the perfectly white and even teeth. It wouldn't dare. Vivien caught a whiff of a Chanel-numbered perfume.

"I'm Rachel Bonner. And you're Vivien. I saw you and your husband moving in a couple of doors down from us. My husband is Archibald Bonner, your MP. He likes to keep track of new voters in the neighborhood." Rachel gave a subtle wink, as if to reassure Vivien that she was joking because all constituents meant so much more than that to her husband, who might even be willing to be godfather to their future children.

"W-wow," stuttered Vivien. "Of course, I can't vote yet, but I certainly look forward to meeting your husband. Oh, and if your house is the one with the pillars in front, I think I saw your son the other day. The young man in black?"

"Sebastian. Yes, he's going through a bit of a phase at the moment. Don't they all?" Rachel's smile suggested Vivien of course knew all about the challenges of childraising, and it made Vivien desperately want to agree.

"He's our pride and joy, of course," Rachel continued. "An excellent student. But please, come and meet all of us, if you feel up to it. Archie and I are having some people over Friday night, just a local thing. We'd love it if you and your husband would stop by, say around seven? Then we can introduce you to everyone properly and get you settled in the village."

"That would be wonderful," Vivien replied. She couldn't believe it was going to be this easy to join the "in" crowd. She'd thought the English were supposed to be somewhat reclusive, but here she was being invited to party with them her first week in town. Not bad.

"Well, I'd best get shopping, then, if the family is going to have anything to eat for dinner tonight," said Rachel, gracefully waving a few fingers. The kitten heels clicked crisply as she walked away, all polish and niceness and politician's wifeness. Vivien felt as if she'd been through some sort of recruitment interview and wandered around the market in a daze as she searched out the final items on her list, minus the unfindable blue cheese dressing. She waded through the checkout lost in her daydream, forgetting yet again that she had to bag her own groceries until she suddenly registered the glare from the woman on the cash register (*Till! It's a till, now!*) and started bagging madly.

3

"Kindred spirits are not so scarce as I used to think. It's splendid to find out there are so many of them in the world."

— L. M. Montgomery, *Anne of Green Gables*

Tuesday dawned bright and sunny, which might have caused Vivien to doubt all the horror stories about English weather if she hadn't been there quite so much over the years. She knew from her many visits that the weather could turn dark and rainy in the blink of an eye, so she decided to go for a run before the inevitable happened.

Donning a matching pink sports bra and leggings trimmed with flashy neon aqua stripes down the sides, she did some limbering up in the driveway and then set out at a brisk pace through the village. She passed all three of Nether Chatby's churches (Methodist, Catholic, Church of England), the pub, a hair salon, a veterinarian and a cattery (*handy!*), something called the Mill Shop, which resembled a 7-Eleven in America, and two very large cemeteries. She supposed it was probably tricky to find places to bury people after hundreds of years of habitation, remembering the time she'd spent several afternoons reading in a park in Leeds before realizing the pathways were made of headstones. Vivien sometimes wondered if having reminders of death all around made the British more blasé about it but the extravagance of Victorian funerals seemed to argue the opposite, and she still occasionally saw processions led by a coach and horses along with a black-hatted funeral director setting the somber pace.

She herself moved considerably faster, and a pleasant two miles later she was approaching home when she noticed a petite, dark-haired young woman standing on the pavement outside the house across the street from her own—the house of Sunday's twitching curtain. The woman's back was to her as she watered a fading flower border, but Vivien's eye was caught by her outfit, a riotous combination of rainbow-striped sweater, green tartan trousers, and pink, flowered wellingtons. Not wanting to appear rude by jogging past without saying a word, Vivien walked up to the curb next to the woman and raised her voice slightly so she could be heard over the hosepipe.

"Hello! I'm Vivien Brandt. My husband and I just moved in across the street."

Her words were met with absolute silence. No acknowledgement, not a turn of the head or a sideways glance, nothing. The woman continued to water as if it were the most important task in the world and allowed her no time for dealing with upstart newcomers to the neighborhood.

This does not bode well, thought Vivien. She realized Americans were not the most beloved people on the planet—often ranking only slightly above politicians who sell used cars and steal candy from babies—but she felt she was owed at least a verbal snub. Stepping sideways to forcibly catch her neighbor's eye, she was quite unprepared when the woman screamed and dropped the hose, dousing Vivien in the process.

The woman quickly reached down to recapture the flopping hose, then straightened up and said, "I'm sorry, I didn't see you there. I guess I was just lost in thought and didn't notice you approach." A slight lisp in her speech was explained when she pointed to her ear with the non-hose-holding hand. "I'm deaf, so I wouldn't have heard if you said something."

Holding up a finger to request Vivien wait a moment, the woman carried the hose to the side of the house and turned off the faucet before returning to the pavement. "Can I help you?" she politely enquired.

Vivien slowly and loudly mouthed, "I was just saying hello. My name is Vivien, I'm your new neighbor." She pointed out her house.

The woman smiled. "You can talk normally. I read lips very well, I just need to be able to see you. My name is Hayley. Hayley Mason. You're American, aren't you?"

Vivien looked perplexed. "How can you tell that if you can't hear me?"

Hayley pointed at her jogging outfit. "Only Americans dress like that for sweating. Would you like to come in for a cup of tea?"

Vivien thought about pretending to be insulted by this diminutive twenty-something person, upon whom mismatched clothes looked adorable, but she decided it would take too much energy to create a proper huff and she was already tired from her run. So she smiled instead and accepted the offer of tea.

Vivien had learned early in her travels that the English

view tea (and more recently coffee) as a universal courtesy, and that it was not to be refused lightly. The occasional "Oh, I don't want to be a bother!" was perfectly appropriate but would inevitably be followed by assurances tea was being served imminently anyway, so it was no bother at all. This was a delicate dance of politeness that Vivien had yet to fully master. Her failure to offer refreshments to the moving men had incurred their subtle displeasure until Geoffrey informed them his wife was American and proceeded to heal the rift before any of her treasures were "accidentally" broken.

The two women made their way to the kitchen where Hayley got her guest a towel and began to set out tea things. Vivien looked around the house with interest as she dried herself off. The decor was bright and cheerful, made cozy by a scattering of colorful knitted blankets and embroidered pillows. Unlike in her own house, here the kitchen was open to the dining room with a fireplace in the middle of the long wall serving both areas. It made for a more informal and friendly living space and allowed sunshine to beam freely throughout. Vivien mentally vowed to pursue a similar floor plan in her next move, and then felt guilty for being unfaithful to her new abode.

"The architects were really very creative in coming up with the different floor plans and little touches to distinguish these houses, weren't they?" she remarked.

Glancing back, Hayley shook her head. "Sorry, I only caught the end of that. I can sometimes hear slight whispers of sound when people are talking, but little that is discernible. Hold on until we can sit down for a minute."

This woman will certainly put the kibosh on my habit of random piffling, mused Vivien. It was something

Geoffrey never got used to, Vivien's need to fill pauses with conversation. But Vivien had grown up with a noisy extended family where you had to talk constantly and loudly to be heard at all. Silence was surrender.

Vivien approached the breakfast bar bordering the kitchen and took a moment to admire a polished oak bar chair with a back sinuously carved to resemble three stems topped by connected tulips. She settled into it, finding it was as comfortable as it was beautiful. As Hayley turned and placed two cups of tea on the counter between them, Vivien decided to stick to her conversational strengths by jumping right in with personal questions.

"Have you lived here long?"

"About eight years. My husband has lived here most of his life, he's a joiner. He made that chair you're sitting on."

"Did he? It's absolutely gorgeous. It must be wonderful to have that kind of talent. I may need to commission him to do some pieces for our house."

Hayley paused to take a sip of tea and then appraised her guest with avid interest. "Vivien is an unusual name these days. Is it something that runs in the family?"

"Not really, not like insanity does. Although my father insists we're not insane ourselves, just carriers. My mother is a huge fan of *Gone with the Wind*, so I'm named after Vivien Leigh."

"I suppose it could have been worse, she could have named you after the main character!" Hayley chuckled. Then her smile faded as she noted the wry look on Vivien's face. "No! Really?"

Vivien made a slight bow from her seated position. "Vivien Scarlett Brandt, at your service."

"Huh."

Vivien waited through the ensuing pause she had learned to expect when telling this story, as the full implications were absorbed by her audience. "Wait," Hayley continued eventually, "do you have siblings? Oh please, don't tell me there's some poor sod in America who's had to live his life as Clark Rhett Brandt?"

It was Vivien's turn to laugh. "No, just a sister, Olivia Melanie O'Connor. She prefers to go by Mel and she lives in San Antonio with her high-flying attorney husband and her higher-flying three children, all of whom have solid biblical monikers."

"Didn't your father have any say in your naming?" she asked.

"Oh, indeed he did. It's the reason Scarlett is my middle name instead of my first, thank goodness."

Hayley gave her a sympathetic smile. "What part of the United States are you from, then?"

"Californian born and raised." Vivien waited again, this time for the usual expressions of surprise, the query about why she would move to England from such a summer wonderland. But Hayley merely nodded and sipped her tea, leaving her new acquaintance oddly disappointed. Vivien was used to indulging in a bit of bragging about sunshine and Silicon Valley, but apparently her neighbor was going to be harder to impress. Hayley's close-cropped brown hair and total lack of makeup suggested a practical, no-nonsense attitude. Of course, Vivien thought jealously, she also had that lovely English rose complexion that British women carried well into their senior years. This particular one had a long way to go yet, Vivien guessed she was in her late twenties or early thirties. Add large green eyes in a heart-shaped face and the result resembled an adorable pixie, an impression that was enhanced by the bright, eclectic clothing.

"I moved here after I married an Englishman," Vivien resumed. "Geoffrey's a pharmacologist, mostly working in research for international drug manufacturers. He specializes in treatments for diabetes."

"Is your husband Geoffrey Wooster, then?" Now Hayley looked impressed. "He's done some marvellous work."

"Good heavens, how do you know that?" Vivien blurted. "Did I miss the announcement of his Nobel Prize or something?" *I'm only here five minutes*, she thought, *and already I'm the little woman to the big important science guy.* Her Power Chicks membership was definitely hanging by a thread.

Hayley grinned. "The man in charge of the pharmacy where I work heard your husband speak at a conference about the latest advancements in diabetes medication. He was quite impressed and told me all about it, and noted your husband was taking a job in Sheffield." She wagged a finger at Vivien. "You'll need to get used to village life, my dear. Everyone knows everything about everybody. Here's a tip for free: don't ever have an affair around here. Or anywhere within a ten-mile radius. It won't be a secret for long."

"Good to know," said Vivien, "although that wasn't on today's agenda. Is there anything else I should know about the neighborhood? Anyone to watch out for, like an axe-wielding gas man? Maybe a fire-and-brimstone preacher at the local church?"

Hayley considered the question. "There's the head of the local witches coven, who frequently leads sky-clad rituals when the moon is full," she calmly pronounced. Vivien glanced up in surprise only to see her neighbor burst into laughter, causing her to smile ruefully in response.

"Okay, I no doubt deserved that. I'll wait to meet the villagers myself."

"Probably best, although I wasn't entirely kidding about the coven," said Hayley with a wink.

A tall, solidly built man in his mid-thirties with a wide, friendly face entered the kitchen and peered into the refrigerator. Hayley introduced him as her husband, William. ("Will, please!" he interjected.) He was dressed in jeans and a blue-checked, short-sleeved dress shirt, untucked to give him the slightly scruffy look Geoffrey insisted was the mark of a true Englishman. With a wave, Will confessed to Vivien that he'd spotted her through the window the day before while waiting for a co-worker to pick him up, which explained the curtain twitch. Vivien complimented him on the bar chair, causing him to blush. He then wished them a good day and departed for work, banana and bottle of juice in hand.

Hayley offered Vivien a croissant, which was gratefully accepted.

"As a matter of fact, I have met one of the neighbors," Vivien continued. "I ran into Rachel Bonner at the supermarket yesterday."

"Ah, Rachel, our Lady Bountiful. She actually grew up here. Her father is a retired army colonel, a total sweetie, and her son Sebastian attends the local school. Of course, her husband is your MP, which I'm sure she mentioned."

"She did indeed, but I'm suddenly blanking on that acronym. Man of Property?" Vivien slurred, her mouth full of flaky goodness, and then had to repeat it so Hayley could understand.

Hayley laughed. "Member of Parliament, but basically the same thing."

"Ah, I did know that. She's invited us to a gathering later this week, so maybe I'll get to meet the whole family then."

Hayley took a moment to swallow her own overly ambitious bite before answering. "It depends if it's one of dear Papa's good days. Rachel likes to trot him out for the effect on military voters, but Colonel Jay can go on a bit with his army reminiscences, so she may not bother if there isn't anyone there she's trying to impress. Although there usually is at these hootenannies. Well, more a shindig or a gathering, I suppose, in the Buffy definition."

"You like *Buffy the Vampire Slayer*?" Vivien went a bit goggle-eyed with excitement. "I'm a huge fan! So then, Rachel's parties are definitely not a whole lotta hoot…"

"And a little bit o' nanny!" Hayley finished with a laugh. "No. But tell me, were the accents on that show as bad as everyone on the fan sites claimed? Angel's Irish came in for particular abuse. I was almost glad I couldn't hear it."

"Lucky you. But to be fair, his accent got better with time. And I still think Buffy loves him more than she loves Spike."

"Goes without saying," Hayley replied, unconsciously cementing their new friendship. "Are you a fan of all vampire shows, or just the good ones?"

"It's true not all vampires are equal, but I love anything with good writing, whether it's television, film, or book. Books are my drug of choice. In fact, my love of literature combined with having the delicate skin of your average redhead meant I was one of those kids who had to constantly be ordered to go play outside. I think my mother was concerned I might develop rickets."

Hayley paused while applying jam to her second croissant in order to point the butter knife at Vivien. "Ah ha, so is sun-sensitivity the reason for your move from California to moister climes, or are there darker forces at work? Scary family? Psychotic ex? Trouble with the law? Or maybe just a fool for love!"

Vivien laughed. "The family has the usual quirks, obviously, and the ex has moved on to greener pastures in the form of a thirty-year-old yoga instructor. And while my record of speeding tickets is impressive, I'd like to believe The Law has better things to do than pursue my entirely paid debt to society. I suppose it's mostly the last one, but it's not just the love of a good man, marvellous though that is. I've always felt Britain was my spiritual home. So when Geoffrey decided to move from London to accept a prestigious new job up here near his family, it made sense for me to ditch the Silicon Valley rat race after decades of working in underfunded libraries and writing technical manuals. Although at least the latter did pay well enough to fund my traveling."

"Do you plan to find work now that you are here, then?"

"Absolutely. I thought I'd check with the libraries around here to get started, but longer term I'm hoping to get an interior design qualification. I've had some training—university extension courses, mostly—but I need to learn about it from a British perspective."

"Ah, hence the admiration of the chair," Hayley nodded, then tilted her head slightly. "I believe Geoffrey was also married before?" Her solemn tone told Vivien she already knew at least the short answer to that question.

"Yes. Kathryn, his first wife, was killed in a car accident six years ago. Their daughter Sara recently graduated with a degree in archaeology and is taking a gap year before she puts her nose to the proverbial grindstone. Geoffrey tells me she's sporadically working her way around Australia as a bartender and lifeguard."

Hayley nodded. "I assume you've met her, though?"

"I only spent a couple of days before the wedding with her, but she seems lovely so hopefully I won't have to come over all evil stepmother. What about you? Any skeletons doing the Lambada in your wardrobe?"

"I wish," smiled Hayley. "I'm a country lass, raised in the wilds of Shropshire. I was born hearing, but lost it during a childhood illness, although as I said I can still hear some sounds, particularly those at high frequencies. And with the right floor and a reverberating bass, I can boogie with the best of them."

"I'm very impressed by your lip-reading skills, the few times I've tried to do it I hadn't the faintest idea what people were saying."

"It gets easier with practice, and without the distraction of sound. My father insisted on mainschooling me to ensure I could make my way in the world. It was quite challenging at times, but it made me resilient, for which I'm grateful. Then I met Will on a bus holiday in Ireland when I was a young, impressionable twenty-year-old, was charmed by his stories of house-building high jinks, and the rest is history. So I, too, moved for my man." Another head tilt. "Why does it so often happen that way? Seems to me we've not quite achieved that whole equality thing yet, at least when it comes to standing our home ground."

"I think if I hadn't wanted to move, Geoffrey would

have come to me. But I'm looking forward to enjoying the local culture and contributing to village life. And thanks to the miracle of streaming television, I can still get all my favorite shows and never have to miss an episode of *Murdoch Mysteries*. Plus, I get to see all the BBC series before my sister in America does, and then taunt her about it."

Hayley laughed. "Well, sibling taunting aside, I'm happy to watch an hour or twelve of *Murdoch* with you. It shares an actor with another favorite show of mine, about a deaf FBI agent."

Vivien's eyes widened. "You mean Yannick Bisson on *Sue Thomas: F.B.Eye*! Have you ever seen a man with such long, luxurious eyelashes?"

They both paused a moment to mentally swoon over the lushness of Yannick's eyelashes.

"I'm so glad you moved here," Hayley said after the moment was done and Vivien announced she needed to get home.

"Me too," Vivien replied. "It seems such a quiet, restful place. Although I'm sure once I'm settled I'll be dying for some excitement."

"There's always the coven," Hayley teased with a cheeky grin.

As she crossed the street carrying the slices of apple pie Hayley had offered as a housewarming gift, Vivien noticed the boy in black sitting on the front step of the house up the road, which she now knew belonged to the Bonners. *So that's Sebastian*, she mused. In addition to the all-black clothing, a leather wristband and the longish blond hair suggested Goth or possibly Emo tendencies, and Vivien placed his age at approximately sixteen.

She'd known several Goth types from her library work in America. They were usually sensitive, intelligent kids, acting out in the only ways they could control: through clothes, music, and attitude. They tended to be some of her best readers, so she had a soft spot for them.

This one, however, clearly didn't want to encourage conversation as he studiously avoided glancing her way. Vivien gave him the courtesy of privacy and entered her own front door just as the heavens opened and the rain came pelting down. She breathed a sigh of satisfaction at the thought of spending the rest of the day at home. Although obviously at some point she needed to go shopping for less-flashy running gear.

4

"There is nothing like staying at home for real comfort."
— Jane Austen

Back at home, Vivien addressed herself to hanging pictures and arranging knick-knacks on her recently arrived furniture. She'd learned from a few jet-setting acquaintances that moving companies say your things will get there in five weeks but in fact it's closer to three months, assuming all goes well with Customs.

Keeping this advice in mind, as soon as she and Geoffrey had their offer on the house accepted she'd shipped her most-loved things to a storage unit nearby so they could be easily and quickly retrieved when needed. The two of them then moved into a furnished apartment until the chain negotiations involved in house buying were complete and they could move in. Although it was actually the three of them, as Vivien recalled Sydney robustly communicating his feelings about being removed to a colder clime.

Now, looking around her, she was glad she'd taken the trouble to ship so many of her things, because it was nice to have a few beloved items to ease the pain of separation from her family and friends. There was her grandmother's china cabinet, a beautiful photograph of a river taken by her sister, and the funky teak coffee table she'd picked up for a song at a flea market.

Upstairs was the California King—sized bed that was so large she couldn't even buy sheets for it in England. Geoffrey had insisted she bring it after visiting her in America. He claimed, while waggling his eyebrows, that it offered possibilities. For what, she didn't know. Maybe orienteering. It had been purchased on a whim by her ex-husband, so she had no emotional attachment to it; the opposite, in fact. But apparently her husbands shared a fondness for large beds as well as for spirited wives.

So Vivien was pleased with her little bits of home away from home, and they warmed the house as new furniture never could. *Not that I won't also be buying new furniture, of course!*, she assured herself. An antique in every room, if she had her way, as she imagined the Edwardian and Georgian gems she'd be acquiring at auctions for a snippet of the price they'd go for in America. Thank goodness Geoffrey had little interest in interior design beyond the occasional purchase of some piece of Victorian sentimentality, usually featuring maudlin kittens. Although he did make her promise not to put a frightening African mask above the television to glare at him when he watched the football. By which he meant soccer.

Humming along to a Simon and Garfunkel tune, Vivien wandered upstairs into the guest room to do a bit of cleaning. She'd painted the room a lovely sunny yellow and decorated it with images of the Golden Gate Bridge to make her American guests feel at home amid the grey skies of Great

Britain. Already she suspected she would hang out there herself sometimes, just to bask in the memory of California warmth. She laughed when she noticed Sydney stretched out in a beam of sunlight on the bedspread. He'd obviously had the same idea and gave her a nasty look as she hauled in the vacuum cleaner. With an outraged yowl, he jumped down and went to seek another toasty spot.

As she vacuumed, Vivien thought about how weird it was that the English called it 'hoovering', as if Hoover was the only brand of vacuum available, until she remembered that Americans had Kleenex and Chapstick. And, of course, Band-Aids.

Vivien spent the rest of the afternoon preparing a pea and parmesan risotto for dinner (*supper? tea?* It was all so confusing!). Risotto was one of her favorite dishes to make, but she felt keenly the lack of access to her usual California wines as she substituted an unknown Sauvignon Blanc to flavor the arborio rice. She would have to search out some wine outlets where she could find a larger selection than what was available in the grocery stores. That was definitely something to look forward to.

Geoffrey seemed to enjoy the meal that evening, despite the dubious wine, expressing his usual amusement at her American pronunciation of "risotto". After dinner they settled on the sofa to watch a film. Sydney, traitor that he was, followed up his afternoon nap by curling happily next to Geoffrey for his evening nap.

Vivien was currently taking her husband through the Molly Ringwald oeuvre, and this evening featured a classic, *Pretty in Pink*. Geoffrey was thrilled with the slice of apple pie she presented for dessert, causing Vivien to confess it wasn't her own doing. Her husband professed himself delighted to hear she was making friends with the neighbors, especially ones who could share her love of American television. So much so that she deduced he wouldn't miss being the sole recipient of her vampire obsession, which was fair enough. Not everyone enjoyed theorizing about where vampires found barbers open at night, especially ones who could give them haircuts that looked great every evening without being able to check in a mirror.

"Will sounds a useful sort," Geoffrey remarked. "Particularly as we embark upon whatever improvement projects you've devised."

Vivien looked askance at him. "Here I thought I was the cynical one in this relationship. I hope you aren't going around the neighborhood evaluating who can be the most helpful. And I'll have you know, I have no major renovation plans at present beyond painting, furnishing, and hanging things on walls. All of which I can do with my own two little hands. Thank heavens the house is fairly modern and the tiles in the bathrooms and kitchen aren't hideous, as I have no desire to be inundated with plumbers and electricians."

"Your hands are capable as well as beautiful, and the house *is* looking wonderful," he complimented her as she put in the DVD and returned to the sofa. "Did you spend the whole day on it?"

"Other than my time next door, yes. And I forgot to mention I met another of our neighbors yesterday, Rachel Bonner. She's evidently the wife of our local representative, Archie."

"Ah yes, the up-and-coming *wunderkind* of British politics. I checked him out before we moved here. Seems a decent enough bloke, even though we don't agree on all things politically and I'm certainly not a fan of his party." Geoffrey paused and cocked his head in thought. "I think there was a suggestion of some personal scandal about him at one point, but it either died down or wasn't true to begin with, as so often happens. I can't remember anything about it now."

"Hmmm, I'm sure someone knows something. But speaking of parties, we've been invited to their house on Friday night for a soirée, a meet-the-neighbors sort of thing. I hope you don't mind, but I accepted for us. It would be helpful to get to know some of the people in the village, aside from their usefulness rating. They all seem to know about you already, of course, your fame precedes you."

"Well, that's what you get for marrying a pharmacological rock star, my darling," Geoffrey blandly replied.

Vivien slapped him playfully on the shoulder. "Watch that head swelling, mister. When I get my interior design business going, you won't be the only eminent expert in this family."

"I do not doubt it for a minute. Have you thought about how you might go about that, or is it too soon?"

Vivien pursed her lips as she considered. "I need to check out qualifications and learn more about British design. Although I hear, as with most everything, you've stolen quite a bit from the French."

Geoffrey snorted in protest at the idea that the French had anything worth stealing. Vivien was used to this, she'd learned the English and the French took pleasure in reliving their cultural battles long after the Hundred Years War, so she simply ignored him and continued outlining her plans.

"I might see if I can put my library experience to use and get some work as a contractor, in the meantime. I don't think I need retraining for that, I spotted a local teenager earlier who was dressed exactly like the kids who came into my library in America and looking every bit as surly. I gather he's part of the Bonner family, so maybe we'll see him at the party and I can talk to him about what kinds of things kids around here are interested in before I face them all in a library setting."

"I admire your optimism if you think you can get a teenage boy to confide in you on a first meeting," Geoffrey replied as he scanned the DVD case. "Now, let's see who Ms. Ringwald is going to pick for her happy ending this time. I see in addition to Mr. Cryer and Brat Packer Andrew McCarthy, James Spader also makes an appearance in this adventure. She will have her work cut out for her."

5

"Now is the time for all good men to come to the aid of the party."

— Typing drill created by Charles E. Weller

As she rang the Bonners' doorbell on Friday evening, looking at the pillared, porticoed entrance renewed Vivien's sense of awe and made her uncharacteristically nervous about her wardrobe selection. Was the velvet top too much? Would she have to take her shoes off, and if so, did her stockings have any holes? She glanced sideways at her husband, who looked debonair in tailored blue trousers and suit jacket, with a grey-striped dress shirt casually unbuttoned at the top. Geoffrey fit in anywhere. He even smelled good. He actually disliked socializing, but only Vivien knew this since he was always charming once thrown in and, unlike herself, he was able to calmly listen to the most ridiculous prattle.

Of course, he would then vent about it all once they were back at home. He'd informed her early on in their relationship that an English wife's main purpose was to listen to her husband complain about the state of the world. She'd foolishly assumed he was kidding.

But any venting about tonight was in the future. Right now, Vivien was trying to think of an excuse to run around the corner and check her stockings. Her time ran out when the door opened and they were greeted by a tall, very suave man in his fifties, sporting tan trousers and a light blue Oxford shirt. His wavy black hair was lightly salted with grey at the temples and his welcoming smile featured immaculately white and even teeth.

"Hello, I'm Archie, and you must be the Woosters," he said, stepping aside and inviting them in with a smooth gesture. "Do come in, we've been looking forward to your arrival."

For a moment, Vivien pictured all the guests standing around in silent anticipation staring at the front door, then she mentally shook herself and returned his smile. "It was so kind of your wife to invite us," she responded as she entered the hallway. She would wait until a little later in their acquaintance to straighten out the last-name issue. No one liked being corrected upon first acquaintance.

Behind her, Geoffrey and Archie did the male nod, grunt, and handshake ritual as Vivien made her way toward the murmur of cocktail chatter. She could tell from the outside that the Bonners' house was bigger than hers. (*Theirs!* she corrected herself. *Be nice, share.*) She was, however, unprepared for the grandeur of the living room she entered.

The front of the room extended up two stories, and a huge, glittering chandelier claimed most of the space near the top. The rest of the room was a Hollywood starlet's dream, all white, taupe, and silver with lots of reflective surfaces. It should have looked tacky, but it was livened by colorful modern paintings hung prominently on three of the walls, making the room into an elite art gallery.

The other end of the room, delineated by a lower ceiling, was obviously the dining area as it housed a circular glass table big enough to accommodate the Last Supper plus Mary Magdalene and her gal pals. Held up by a central column of copper that extended into sinuously twisting vines of the same metal, the table was piled high with hors d'oeuvres that were works of art in their own right, and which seemed to float atop the gleaming glass. This sense of overflowing plenty was enhanced by a giant arrangement of hothouse flowers in the center of the table. A delicately muted scent of gardenia tantalized the nose, hinting of tropical climes but not strong enough to interfere with the taste of the food. The counter that separated the dining room from the kitchen was set up as a bar and here at last was the help, an immaculately bow-tied bartender calmly shaking a cocktail mixer.

Around the edges of the two rooms, people were gathered in groups of three, four or five. Vivien noted with relief that many of the women wore traces of silk or velvet, and shoes were firmly ensconced on feet despite the white shag area rug spread over the middle of the shining oak floor.

Rachel spotted them at that moment and headed their way. Her lovely figure was wrapped in a long rose-silk gown, accented with pink diamond earrings and a matching solitaire necklace. The half-slit up the side of her skirt tastefully revealed a glimpse of toned calf and thigh, and Vivien had to quickly imagine the woman unattractively sweating through a treadmill workout to counter a flash of awe-tinged envy. It was her twist on picturing people in their underwear. *How*, Vivien wondered, *does this woman stay in such excellent shape when I put on a pound at the mere thought of corn chips? Or are they corn crisps now? And I wonder if there are any on that buffet...*

Vivien wrenched her gaze and thoughts away from the food as Rachel reached them, all smiles. "How lovely to see you! I'm so glad you could make it. And this incredibly handsome man must be Geoffrey." Rachel reached past Vivien to offer a manicured hand to her husband.

"Very nice to meet you, Rachel," Geoffrey replied, in what Vivien jokingly referred to as his caramel company voice, since it sounded like a smooth pour of maple syrup over light, fluffy pancakes. "It was kind of you to invite us to your lovely soirée at such short notice."

"That's my Rachel," Archie chimed in from the doorway. "The more the merrier." He gave them an apologetic glance as the doorbell rang again and he turned away to answer it. It was nice, thought Rachel, that he greeted all the guests at the door. She wouldn't have been surprised to find they'd rented a butler for the evening. Or maybe she'd just been watching too much *Downton Abbey* lately.

Rachel beckoned them to follow her as she made for the nearest clutch of people, asking for their drink preferences on the way and nodding at the bartender who replied in kind to indicate he'd heard the order and would get right to it.

"Geoffrey and Vivien, I'd like you to meet Kartik and Susan Ramakrishnan, who run the local shop, and James and Beth Frederick, who own the cattery. Everyone, these are our newest neighbors. Vivien is American."

Was it Vivien's imagination, or did that last part sound suspiciously like some sort of warning? She smiled and turned toward the cattery owners.

"Do you by any chance live in the house with the cat design on the gates?" she asked. "I noticed it during my run yesterday."

"Yes, that's us," Beth replied. She was an attractively plump woman in her sixties, Vivien guessed, and you could immediately sense a soothing aura about her that would make animals relax. Her dress, composed of layers of floating pastel chiffon that gave her a somewhat ethereal air, was obviously only for wearing outside the cattery as Vivien imagined it would prove irresistible to curious claws. She also sported silver, dangling cat earrings and her scarf was pinned with a pewter brooch in the shape of a heart with a cat sleeping on it, leaving the casual observer in no doubt this was a woman who really loved cats.

"We've just won England's Cattery of the Year award, so we're in a celebratory mood tonight," Beth said. "Do you like cats?"

"I'm owned by one," admitted Vivien. "A Siamese named Sydney." She turned to accept their drinks from the bartender—Chardonnay for her and a gin and tonic for Geoffrey—handing the latter to her husband before resuming the conversation. "He's a handful, but I hope you'll take him on when we go on vacation. Sorry, I mean holiday. It will be such a comfort to know he's somewhere nice."

"We'll be glad to," said James, who looked to be about a decade older than Beth, his white hair and thin build making him seem slightly frail. But he had lovely brown eyes and a gentle smile that brought his face to life. "Just do let us know a couple of months in advance of your planned vacation-slash-holiday. Beth's success has made the place quite popular, and this award won't slow things down any. We'd hate to miss the chance to meet your feline. You might want to arrange for a tour of the cattery before then, we'd love to show you how we'll spoil your cat. Has Sydney got the Siamese howl?"

"Down pat," Vivien assured him. "If the dead were wakeable, we'd know it by now."

Kartik, tall, dark, and slender with a well-trimmed beard, broke in at this point. "Susan and I are often the last ones awake in the village since the shop doesn't close until midnight, and I promise you we've not seen a single zombie wandering the streets."

Susan, a brunette, blue-eyed beauty, merely nodded her agreement as she sipped a pink concoction in an old-fashioned martini glass. A tailored trouser suit in off-white satin showed off her golden tan to perfection, and Vivien wondered if there was something in the town water that produced good-looking women, or maybe there was a pill like in that old *Star Trek* episode about the settlers who bought artificially gorgeous wives.

She was reassured when, after a bit more polite chatter, they were introduced to another group, and then another, including several quite ordinary-looking people, until Rachel left them to attend to the restocking of the food table. Vivien politely separated herself from the local vicar (far from the fire-and-brimstone variety, this one seemed more of a kindly older brother and had the most gorgeous brown eyes) and followed her hostess to grab a small plate and salvage a few delicious-looking tidbits before they were carted off to the kitchen to be refilled with newer delicious-looking tidbits. Vivien wasn't usually a fan of seafood but the selection here was stunning, ranging from bacon-wrapped prawns to bite-sized crab cakes accompanied by fruit carved in flowery shapes. Some delicacies weren't recognizable to Vivien at all, probably because she was more from the 'burned water' school of cookery unless she was making one of her much-practiced dishes. She noted Hayley and Will weren't present and thought how remiss she'd been not to have asked if they were going. She lifted a bubbly cocktail off a passing silver tray before realizing she was already a bit overly full of liquid.

Placing her glass on a side table, she wandered down the nearest hallway in search of a bathroom. (*Toilet!* She must learn to say that word without being embarrassed. Or maybe she could just resort to "loo".) She glimpsed books as she passed a softly lit room on her left and couldn't resist a peek inside. What she saw set her librarian heart beating and her decorator soul singing.

Having just finished setting up a smallish library in her own home that day using a few basic IKEA shelves, Vivien was swamped with envy as she viewed the richly carved mahogany ones built into three walls of this much grander room. A large rosewood desk took up floor space at one end and the remaining wall featured a grand marble fireplace. French doors across from where she stood opened onto a dusk-darkened garden. Vivien knew she was snooping, but it was a beautiful room, and she took another step inside to have a better look.

Green leather wingback chairs were placed on either side of the fireplace, and it was from the depths of one of these that a gruff voice said, "Come in, my dear."

This was followed by the appearance of a face around one side of the chair. The face had a ruddy complexion and sideburns that Vivien just knew would be called mutton chops if fashion allowed. These were paired with a handsome moustache that curled slightly up at each end. Vivien realized she must be looking at Rachel's father, the army... uh...captain?

"I'm sorry, I didn't mean to disturb you, I was just admiring the room," she said.

"Nonsense, you're not disturbing me at all," the man replied. "Hmmm, I thought I knew all the beautiful women in these parts, but I see I was mistaken, and a benevolent God has saved me the best for last. Do come sit and tell me who you are and where you've been all my life. I'm Jeremy Hardwick, commonly—but respectfully—referred to as Colonel Jay."

Vivien cautiously walked across and seated herself on the edge of the other wing chair. She'd have to be careful, this one was turning on all the charm, although he had to be in his eighties. He was dressed in grey wool trousers with a knife-edge pleat, a white shirt, and what could only be described as a burgundy smoking jacket complete with a gold-tasselled belt tie. As if this wasn't enough to suggest he was relaxing after hunting tigers with the Raj, she glimpsed a volume of Kipling's *Just So Stories* open on his lap. She surmised there was no one at the party who would be impressed by a military past, hence dear Papa had been instructed to amuse himself in the library.

"I'm Vivien Brandt, commonly—and rarely respectfully—known as the American. We just moved into the neighborhood. Pleased to meet you."

"Brandt? Thought for sure the name I heard was Wooster. Not married yet, then? Is there hope for me?" Colonel Jay tried for a rakish grin, which was somewhat marred by a couple of missing teeth but was a game attempt, nevertheless.

She thought he was probably going for an "eligible mature bachelor" look, but in Vivien's view he came across more as "randy great-uncle".

"Sorry, no," she replied. "I am married to the Wooster fellow. I kept my name."

"Silly nonsense. Woman shares a man's bed, she should share his name. Tradition and all."

"Well, it's actually my bed, so if anything, Geoffrey should be taking my name in that case. And I hope you don't mind me saying, but tradition has been an excuse for all kinds of horrors throughout history, so I'm afraid it carries no water with me. However, I hope this doesn't mean we can't be friends."

Colonel Jay chuckled. "Shouldn't think so. Small village, too difficult to be making enemies over trifles. Got enough already. Enemies, not trifles. Nice trifle wouldn't go amiss right now."

He really should be puffing on a meerschaum pipe with a brandy glass in hand, thought Vivien. His act cried out for it, even if he was too young to have served in India. Then she noticed a whisky glass on the cherrywood table next to his chair and smiled. Close enough. She could tell it was a strong whisky because she smelled the peatiness from over a foot away.

"Would you like me to get you a plate of food, Colonel?" she asked. "I didn't see any trifles, but there's a kitchen full of cooks and I'm sure you can have whatever you want in your own house."

"My house?" The colonel gave a bark of laughter. "My pension doesn't rate this level of luxury," he proclaimed, waving a hand in the direction of an excellent print of Dante

Gabriel Rossetti's *Lady Lilith* hanging over the fireplace in a beautiful gilt frame. "Besides, except for the boy, I prefer the company of my neighbors over in The Meadows, which is where they stash retired relatives around here. No, I'm well aware the children only invite me to these do's in case they need a military title to influence votes. But I get to eat well and enjoy the company of lovely ladies such as yourself, so you won't hear me complain. Much."

Colonel Jay grunted happily at his own wittiness before re-focusing slightly rheumy eyes on Vivien. "Now, let's talk about how that bed-stealing husband of yours doesn't deserve you and why I do."

The sound of a heavy sigh caused Vivien to look over her shoulder as her hostess walked into the room.

"Father! What are you doing monopolizing my new guest?" Rachel demanded before turning toward said guest. "I'm sorry, Vivien, I shouldn't have left you on your own, my father tends to pounce on those separated from the pack." She threw the Colonel a look that combined exasperation and forbearance, which he ignored entirely.

"Not at all," said Vivien. "He's been delightful. I was actually on my way to the bathroom…uh, loo…when I was distracted by your excellent taste in interior design—that William Morris wallpaper is to die for—and your father was kind enough to forgive my interruption."

There was a disparaging harrumph from the chair, although it was hard to tell whether it was aimed at his daughter's interior design skills or Vivien's shameless flattery. "Down the hall, next door on the right," he muttered, returning to his book.

Vivien rose, resisting the urge to salute. She tossed a

slightly apologetic look toward Rachel and proceeded to the bathroom, taking an extra few minutes to compose herself and check her makeup. Rachel might make being a politician's wife seem effortless, but Vivien bet she had her hands full with her father. Still, it was nice that the colonel felt so comfortable in his daughter's house, despite being occasionally trotted out as a political device. Maybe that was part of the draw, the man obviously liked attention.

Her thoughts were interrupted by a giant crash from the front of the house. She exited the bathroom and quickly retraced her steps down the hallway.

A chaotic sight greeted her when she re-entered the dining room. The table of food was tipped over and next to it, covered in frosting, prawns, and Marie Rose sauce, was a black lump of unmoving person.

Rachel was standing nearby with her hands to her cheeks, her mouth open in dismay. The rest of the guests seemed equally stunned, until Geoffrey finally approached and knelt down next to the body. A nudge on its shoulder elicited a faint moan, and the lump resolved itself into a boy, presumably the Bonner offspring, which was confirmed when Rachel recovered and rushed up to him.

"Are you all right, Sebastian? What happened?"

Sebastian shook his head to clear his eyes of sauce-covered hair before replying.

"Sorry, Mum, I was trying to nab a fairy cake at the top of the table. Had to lean hard to get it, and I guess that was a bad idea. The whole thing just fell over." His words were slightly slurred.

Archie appeared at the back of the crowd and took in what had happened with a quick glance. Gently manoeuvring through his guests, he stood next to the boy, then lowered himself onto his haunches and assessed his son's condition.

"That's all right, Sebastian. Let's get you to your room where you can clean up. No harm done, I'm sure your mother has plenty more food." He stood up, then reached down a hand to help Sebastian get to his feet.

"Through the kitchen, please," Rachel added. "It will save cleaning more food out of the carpet." Now that she knew her son wasn't injured, Rachel the hostess had re-emerged and was managing the situation. Vivien thought the woman and her husband made a formidable power couple, although she had to wonder how the son took to having two such strong personalities as parents. But the boy seemed placid enough as he plodded off through the kitchen, and everyone else gradually resumed their conversations. A couple of caterers emerged and started cleaning up the mess on the floor. Others followed bringing out more desserts to place on the swiftly righted and wiped table.

Geoffrey appeared at Vivien's side with a couple of fresh drinks and offered her one. "Better imbibe while you can," he said, "before Junior gets back to the drinks table."

"Are you implying what I think you're implying, sir?" Vivien responded.

Geoffrey nodded. "Soused, he is," he intoned in his best Yoda voice.

Well then, Vivien mused, *maybe a certain someone wasn't happy being managed by his perfect parents.* She turned in time to glimpse Colonel Jay in the hall doorway, a thoughtful look on his face. He caught her gazing at him and slowly winked before returning to the library and his tales of foreign lands.

6

"City people. They may know how to street fight but they don't know how to wade through manure."
— Melina Marchetta, *On the Jellicoe Road*

The following Sunday, Geoffrey and Vivien took the elderly Mrs. Wooster out to lunch, along with Geoffrey's younger sister, Beth, and Beth's ten-year-old son, Ian. Sunday lunches were one of Vivien's favorite things in her new country; it was like having a Thanksgiving meal every week, and they used the occasion a couple of times a month to catch up with family. Geoffrey's mother ("call me Pauline, dear") was equally fond of a traditional pub lunch and diplomatically ignored suggestions of substituting Thai food or sushi ("Regular English food has always been good enough for my family!") and Beth, newly divorced and moved back into the family home with Ian, was grateful for the chance to relax without worrying about cooking or cleaning up. Ian, stuck with a table of adults instead of playing outside with his mates, tended to fidget, for which Vivien could hardly blame him.

After listening respectfully to her new mother-in-law for the few hours required, Vivien and Geoffrey were on their way home, with Vivien looking forward to catching the last bit of *Bargain Hunt*.

As Geoffrey turned the car into their street, she saw Archie Bonner up ahead, standing in front of his house and listening to a somewhat scruffy man in a typical Yorkshire flat cap. A few feet away, Sebastian and a Hispanic-looking teenage boy were casting worried looks at the two men who, based on the wild waving of the older one and Archie's arms being crossed in front of his chest, appeared to be arguing.

With a final shout, the older man turned and, without looking, stepped into the street right in front of Geoffrey's moving car.

"Bloody hell!" Geoffrey yelled as he hit the brakes, causing both him and Vivien to be thrown forward into their seatbelts and then back as the car came to a shuddering halt mere inches from the man's leg. The man neither paused nor looked up, just flipped them a middle finger as he marched across the remainder of the street and continued on toward the center of the village.

They both sat there, stunned, as they considered how close to tragedy they had just come.

"Someone isn't long for this life if that's his idea of road safety," Geoffrey finally remarked. His voice was hard and Vivien could still see the anger in his eyes, but she could tell he was purposefully calming his breathing as her own heart rate gradually settled down.

"Who was he, do you know?" she asked him.

"I didn't get a good look thanks to the cap, but I don't think I've seen him before." Geoffrey looked past Vivien to check the pavement where the man had stepped off. "Looks like we can't ask our Mr. Bonner either, as he appears to have gone inside. How odd. You'd think he'd at least check to ensure we're okay. Those two kids are gone as well."

Vivien thought back to the fleeting glimpse she'd had of the heated conversation on the pavement. "They seemed to be arguing pretty vociferously. Maybe it's an unhappy constituent, and Archie doesn't want to break privacy rules by discussing it with us."

She caught Geoffrey's doubtful look and laughed, her equanimity restored. "Yeah, I don't think it's a good excuse either, but I like Archie, so I'm willing to give him the benefit of the doubt. Still, it worries me that every time we come across his son the situation seems to be fraught with tension. That doesn't appear to be the happiest of families. I wonder why."

Geoffrey resumed driving the short distance to their home and pulled into the driveway.

"You know what Tolstoy said, my darling. 'Happy families are all the same, but unhappy families are all unhappy in different ways.' Or something like that. Don't quote me."

Vivien smiled at him. "Cease your worry, my love. I seldom do."

7

"A circulating library in a town is as an evergreen tree of diabolical knowledge."

— Richard Brinsley Sheridan

It was two weeks since the party, and Vivien was starting to feel part of the village. Upon application to the local council, she was told there would be permanent library jobs coming up, but in the meantime, would she be willing to do temporary work to help out?

She certainly would, she informed them, and after submitting to an interview and the appropriate background checks, today was her first day working in a local branch library in Bickford, the next village over from Nether Chatby, where one of the regular staff was on maternity leave. As it was raining she decided to take the car, even though the library was only a mile or so from home.

Vivien, used to having a couple of libraries to serve large cities in the US, was delighted to discover the English version featured lots of small community libraries, often housed in buildings with other businesses. This one was just a single room attached to a larger medical center (or surgery, she learned they were called, although bizarrely it seemed very little surgery was done there). The shelving divided the room into sections for children and adults, with the latter being split again into fiction and non-fiction. It was a fairly new building, with one wall containing large windows that made the library bright and inviting. Most of the books were also new and shiny, their pages notably clear of bodily fluids and smashed bugs, and there were half a dozen computers spread around the edges of the room.

She introduced herself to the remaining librarian: a gentle, older woman called Becky, whose Westie-patterned sweater marked her out as a dog lover. She gave Vivien a quick tour of the stacks as well as instructions on how to check out books and take in fines. Becky was delighted to find that Vivien had done it all before, enough so that she felt able to leave her alone for a few minutes while she went into the back room to get them some tea.

As soon as she left, Vivien's first customer arrived in the form of Nether Chatby's Church of England vicar, whom she had already met at the Bonners' party. The man's dog collar probably indicated he'd come from some service or clerical duty and Vivien was again struck by the combination of competence and boyish charm he exuded—despite a slight receding hairline—thanks to those melting brown eyes and lips that were perhaps a touch fuller and more sensual than one expected in a vicar. He couldn't have been more than forty, but he was obviously leading a life that suited his talents and desires, and she had no doubt there was competition among the village ladies, especially the single ones, to help with services. She smiled at him as he approached the checkout desk.

"Reverend Edwards, isn't it? I don't know if you remember, but we met at the Bonners' party. I'm Vivien."

"Yes, of course I remember, it's not often we get Americans in our little hamlet. It's lovely to see you again. And please call me Jonathan. I've got some books to bring back, if you'd be so kind," he said as he handed them to her.

"Sure, let me just check these in." Vivien scanned the barcodes on the books, then paused. "I may be reading this wrong, being new and all, but I think the system is telling me these are two days late, and therefore there's a fine." She frowned at him in sympathy. "It'll be £1.20 to get this off your record. I hope you had a good offering this week," she said with a conspiratorial wink.

Reverend Edwards looked momentarily taken aback, but quickly recovered and smiled at her.

"Couldn't we just forget about the fine?" he said. "After all, in my line of work, forgiveness is essential." He winked back.

Vivien did her best to look shocked. "Well, maybe your boss isn't picky about the receipts balancing, but in the library world, not paying your fines is the eighth deadly sin. I wouldn't want to 'disappear' for insubordination on my first day."

She heard Becky gasp as the latter came through the doorway carrying the tea tray in time to overhear the end of this exchange. Jonathan merely laughed and handed over the money. He was indeed a mild-mannered, unassuming fellow, and Vivien was pleased to find he had a slightly naughty sense of humor. It must make his job easier. She resolved to try to go to church on Sunday, even though she didn't regularly attend back in the States.

After the vicar left there was a steady flow of customers, mostly elderly, and they all stopped to have a chat with each other and with Becky. The topics seemed to regularly revolve around everyone's latest medical operation, which Vivien supposed was natural as they were often there for doctor appointments as well as visiting the library. The morning passed pleasantly enough, and during her lunch break Vivien discovered a wonderful little neighborhood deli that provided her with a freshly made sandwich before she returned for the afternoon shift.

Which proved to be a different kettle of fish.

Shortly before three o'clock, the children started to arrive as schools let out. These were mostly teenagers, and Vivien saw Becky's mouth tighten as they poured in. She figured there must be history there, and it probably wasn't good.

Vivien understood her co-worker's hesitation based on her own experience. Teenagers were always a librarian's challenge. They wanted a warm place to be with their friends, but books were seldom on the agenda, except for those rare, longed-for months when something came out to interest them, like a Harry Potter-type book or an R. L. Stine horror story. Even then, there were limited copies to keep them happy. Mostly they just wanted to play games on the computers, make fun of each other, and flirt, all of which resulted in loud voices and the occasional shriek.

The kids landed boisterously on the sofas and chairs in the children's area, which due to a very bad floor plan was just out of sight of the circulation desk. Vivien listened to Becky valiantly trying to get them to dampen their exuberance with a few classic shushes, but she was predictably ignored. Fortunately, Becky didn't take this personally, leaving the kids to their fun but keeping a wary eye out so she could at least try and prevent physical damage to the furniture.

After another fifteen minutes of chatter punctuated by the occasional scream of either laughter or protest, Vivien wandered over to where the children were sitting and settled herself cross-legged in the middle of the floor.

Faced with an unknown adult, and one wearing pink studded cowboy boots besides, an immediate hush fell. Finally, one of the older girls dared to challenge the interloper.

"Who're you?" she glared, adding the coolest of hair tosses. She was well equipped for this, possessing a mane of long and shiny black hair. Her lightly tanned complexion and golden-brown eyes made her a stunner, even in a carefully faded yellow T-shirt and trendily ripped blue jeans.

"My name's Vivien. What's yours?"

There was a moment of evaluation on the part of the alpha girl. "Sam. Short for Samantha."

This seemed to be all the information Sam was willing to give up at this point in time. Question asked and answered. But as Vivien remained silently seated, eventually curiosity got the better of the girl, as Vivien had hoped it would, and she upped the ante.

"You're not from here," she stated, eyes slitted.

"Nope," Vivien responded, popping the 'p' for emphasis to show her lips were truly sealed.

There was another minute of silence. Then one of the younger boys, all freckles and tousled brown hair, could take it no more.

"Where are you from?" he queried.

"Can you guess?" she challenged them with a quirk of an eyebrow.

"Australia?" guessed another girl, this one wearing tortoiseshell glasses and still in her school uniform of limp grey cardigan and dark skirt. The group brain, no doubt. Vivien stored the knowledge for later, thinking she might have found her first reader.

"Nuh uh," she gave out with a solemn shake of her head.

"Say 'Kangaroo in a tree,'" one of the other boys demanded. Vivien took note of that, too. He was definitely NOT the group brain.

"Why in the world would I want to say that? As I said, I'm not from Australia, and anyway kangaroos don't live in trees. I've got a book on them if you want proof," she tossed back.

"Barnsley!" yelled one of the older boys in triumph. Vivien gave him a serious look. She knew Barnsley was no more than twenty miles from where they sat, but evidently that was enough to make it foreign to these children.

"Have you ever been to Barnsley?" she asked him.

"Naw, why would I wanna go there?" was the response.

Samantha was gazing steadily at Vivien. "Canada," she said.

"Now you are getting much closer," said Vivien. "Correct continent, at any rate."

"Right," said the blond young man next to Sam. He punched Sam's shoulder with a sense of familiarity that told Vivien they were probably a couple. "American, then."

"You got it," Vivien smiled. "Come back tomorrow and you get a candy bar. As I said before, my name is Vivien. I moved here from California, and my favorite superhero is Wonder Woman."

"I'm Thomas," said the one with freckles, "and Wonder Woman can't be a superhero cause she's a girl. Although she's got really great boobs." This elicited giggles from the younger boys, open mouths from the younger girls, and a look of disgust from Samantha.

"Well, Thomas," Vivien replied patiently, "she has superpowers and an invisible plane, and she uses them for good, so I say she's in the club. She's certainly got it all over Batman, who doesn't have much without his money, the Batmobile, and Alfred. Not to mention his lack of great boobs."

Facing unexpected opposition in the form of an adult who didn't hesitate to use the word boobs, Thomas started going red in the face, but Vivien got support from the girl on Thomas's right, whose beautiful curly blonde hair was no doubt the bane of her existence.

"I'm Paris, and I think Wonder Woman is definitely a superhero, but Batman is okay, too, and kind of hot in a dark, broody way."

"Ah, which Batman would we be thinking of, then?" Vivien asked. "As played by Christian Bale? George Clooney? Val Kilmer? The best, and my personal favorite, Michael Keaton?"

"Christian Bale, of course," said Paris. "Do you live in Hollywood? Have you ever met him?"

"No, I'm from San Francisco. Although I have been to lots of science fiction conventions in Los Angeles, and I've met most of the actors from *Buffy the Vampire Slayer* and *Firefly*. Have any of you seen those?" She got a couple of nods of interest. "What about Harry Styles?" she asked innocently.

Several of the children looked excited. "You met him?" Paris asked breathlessly.

"No," said Vivien. "But I bet I could find you an address

where you could write and ask for his autograph. As a matter of fact, if you all want to tell me who your favorite actors or musicians are, I will get you addresses to write to. Or email."

Most of the kids considered this offer for a moment, then nodded. Vivien had proven acceptable, and they spent the next hour looking up fan mail addresses. The kids remained in discussion about popular actors and superheroes until it was almost closing time, when Vivien looked up to see Sebastian Bonner saunter in, clothed in his habitual black and accompanied by the same young man she'd glimpsed the day of their near auto accident. The latter wore a brightly colored shirt and blue jeans and looked around the library with shy curiosity. Sebastian threw Vivien a hesitant smile of recognition as they headed for the non-fiction section, pulled out a book on the history of Bonfire Night and sat on the floor next to each other. Over in the children's section, Vivien noticed the other kids had gone silent again, and some of them were watching Sebastian and his friend with narrowed eyes.

Vivien could feel trouble brewing but wasn't sure of the cause. She continued stamping check-out labels with the library name and kept an eye on the situation. It didn't take long for her fears to be realized.

The older boy who'd guessed her nationality—she'd heard the others call him Justin—rose and walked up behind Sebastian and his friend. Lightly nudging Sebastian's leg with his foot, he lifted his chin and said, "What are you two doing here? Don't you have something more gay to be doing?"

Samantha spoke up from the sofa. "Leave them alone, Justin. They're not doing anything."

Justin never took his eyes off the two in front of him as he replied to his girlfriend. "I think they're doing plenty. That's the problem, it's disgusting."

Okay, thought Vivien, *now that I know what's up, it's time to nip this in the bud.* She walked casually over to the children's area.

"It's time for us to close up the library. Everybody out."

The smaller kids began to obey, with most of the older ones slowly following as if it couldn't have mattered less that they were being kicked out. But the three boys didn't move. Sebastian and his friend were still paging through the book, with a tight-lipped Justin staring down at them. Vivien went over to the little group, her stomach twisting a bit as she felt the tension around them.

"That means you, Justin. All ashore who are going ashore."

She moved around to view the faces of the other two, who steadfastly kept their eyes on their book. "Sebastian, I'm headed home. Would you and your friend like to wait in the back room and I'll give you a lift?" There was no way she was letting them go outside with the rest of the kids to get their butts kicked as soon as there were no adults present.

Sebastian glanced up at her and nodded almost imperceptibly. He had a cowlick at the back of his hair parting that stuck straight up, making him look younger than he was and no doubt inviting schoolboy ridicule. As if he needed more. Vivien returned her attention to Justin, staring him down until he shrugged his shoulders and ambled toward the door where Samantha was examining her fingernails as she waited for him.

Vivien let go a sigh of relief. Armageddon avoided for today. She lowered the steel door over the library entrance, then beckoned to the boys as she headed for the back room. "What's your friend's name?" she asked over her shoulder as she walked.

"Lucius," came the gruff answer from Sebastian. Lucius silently confirmed this with a nod.

"Well, guys, if you want to just have a seat in the back here, Becky and I will close up, and we'll go out the staff door," she said. The boys settled themselves into two chairs that were some council worker's idea of trendy, being covered in burnt orange, nubbly upholstery, and which were comfortable to exactly no one's backside. Vivien suspected it was probably the same genius responsible for the impractical floor plan.

She returned to the front desk where Becky was clearing out the cash register to place the day's takings in the small safe in the back office.

"They won't let up, you know," she muttered *sotto voce* to Vivien. "Ever since school started, they've been annoying those two young men. Parents have been called, but it doesn't seem to do any good."

"Justin's parents are not the liberal, tolerant types, then?" Vivien hazarded a guess.

"Father's moved on, mother's uneducated, out of work, has a drug problem and her own temper issues. He lives with an aunt who is very old-fashioned, and I suspect she mostly ignores the boy."

"And how have Sebastian's parents responded?"

"Father's an up-and-coming MP, butter wouldn't melt in mother's mouth. Very proper. Said their son is being maligned and threatened, and they'll take it up with the police if it doesn't stop. Although I doubt they would. I don't think Mr. Bonner wants that kind of attention right now, with an election about to be called at any time."

"Hmmm. Well, this will be a challenge, then," said Vivien, her mind already on the conversation she would have with Geoffrey about it. It seemed prejudice and intolerance were not solely traits of the American education system. And she suspected she'd just seen another of the reasons behind the secret binge drinking. Certainly, neither Sebastian nor his persecutor was having an idyllic childhood.

8

"I take to the open road, healthy, free, the world before me."

— Walt Whitman

Although Vivien was allowed to drive for a year on her US driving license (*spelled licence now!*) before she had to apply for a British one, she decided it would be prudent to become proficient as soon as possible. Having obtained the name of a local instructor from cattery owners James and Beth Roberts, whose daughter had recently left for university with license in hand, Vivien quickly arranged for some lessons.

Based on his Yorkshire accent over the phone, Vivien didn't expect her new instructor to be Hugh Grant, but she had hopes of maybe a Sean Bean or Dominic West. Instead, she got Tony, a stout, swarthy middle-aged man who sported a heavy gold chain necklace long enough to nestle in the substantial patch of chest hair that overflowed the vee neck of his white T-shirt. Except for the accent, Tony was almost a comedic caricature of a New York Italian. But Vivien soon learned he didn't joke about driving.

Ever.

His knowledge of the driving code was unchallengeable, and he soon had her taking roundabouts with ease, especially after pounding on the dashboard the first couple of times she looked the wrong way for oncoming traffic.

Today was her second lesson and she was trying to get used to handling the gear stick with her left hand, which too often resulted in a nasty grinding noise. She slowed as they approached a stoplight. "Are you allowed to make a left turn on a red light?" she asked.

"No," Tony snapped. "Why? Have you been doing that?"

"Absolutely not!" Vivien did her best to look appalled, but she didn't think he was buying it. "I just wanted to know in case I need to one day. We're allowed to turn right on a red in California, so I wasn't sure."

"Hmmph," Tony grunted. "I'm sure you're allowed to do lots of things in California. Let's practice some *three-point turns*."

Vivien had explained that three-point turns were called Y turns in America, which hadn't made Tony any happier about her grinding the gears of his car while she performed them. She decided to skip telling him that indicators were called signals.

During Vivien's third attempt at the turn, a dark shape bolted behind the car, causing her to brake suddenly. Looking in the rear-view mirror she recognized Sebastian's friend Lucius, his body hunched in misery. Having halted at the squeal of brakes, the boy shook his head and rapidly continued down the street while Vivien carefully parked Tony's car on the side of the road and handed the keys to him.

"I need to talk to that young man. I'm close enough here, I'll walk home. See you next Tuesday?"

Tony nodded, then got out and circled round to the driver's seat before executing a perfect three-point turn with no clutch-grinding. *Maddening.*

Vivien set a brisk pace to catch up with Lucius, who she could just see rounding the corner ahead. When she came to it herself, she saw him sitting on a bench at the edge of the spacious village park, his shoulders heaving as he sobbed quietly.

Vivien stood next to him and laid a gentle hand on his shoulder. "I'm sorry. Is it anything you want to talk about? I promise, it will just be between us."

Lucius shook his head but moved over slightly to allow room for Vivien to sit, which she did, impressed by his ingrained politeness. Today the boy was dressed in khaki trousers and a white polo shirt, but the neatness she'd noted at the library had been replaced by a wrinkled, slapdash look, one of the laces of his military boots untied and ignored.

Vivien sat in silence with him for a few minutes, until his sobs began to subside. As they petered out, she softly enquired, "Is it to do with Sebastian?"

Lucius gave a lopsided smile, tears still clinging to his cheeks. "He hates his name. It's such a mouthful, but he doesn't like any of the ways to shorten it either."

Vivien smiled. "I know how he feels. And I don't imagine Lucius lends itself to macho nicknames come to that."

Lucius snorted in response before recalling his previous sadness and relapsing into silence. After another minute, he reluctantly began to speak, though he still stared resolutely at the ground.

"Seb says we can't hang out anymore," he moaned, ignoring his friend's name issues. "He says it causes too much trouble. For his parents, at school, everywhere."

"Have you two known each other long, then?" she asked.

Lucius shook his head. "Not really. My mother is English and we lived in this country until I was seven years old, then my father moved us to Spain. But my father lost his job there six months ago—he's a bricklayer—and couldn't find work. Mama missed her home, so we moved hoping to do better here, near her family. She has always made sure we spoke English, hoping we would come back one day. Seb's pretty much the only friend I've made since we moved." He paused and scraped a boot against the sidewalk. (*Pavement*, Vivien corrected in her head, and then felt bad for allowing herself to be distracted.) "I could tell right away that he liked the same things I did, and we've been hanging out ever since."

The boy's eyes once again filled with tears as he was reminded of his predicament. Whether the two were gay or not, or had even acknowledged the possibility to each other, it was obvious to Vivien the friendship ran deep.

"Tell you what," she offered hesitantly, knowing what she was about to suggest would most likely be refused, "let me have a talk with Sebastian and see if there's anything to be done. Sometimes a stranger's perspective can help. If you see him, will you ask if he'll talk to me? I have lots of experience in this area, being a godmother and honorary aunt many times over." She thought it best not to mention the training in child psychology that had come as part of her library education. That would only scare them off.

"And who knows," she continued, "maybe I can help with the parent thing as well, being old and all. Sebastian can come to my house or catch me at the library when I'm there, whichever he prefers."

Vivien was surprised when Lucius nodded, sniffling. He must really be desperate, she thought, most kids would have shunned an offer of help from an unknown adult. With a pat on the arm, she rose and started to walk home. It was probably the wrong thing to do, sticking her nose into this, but she never could stand to see animals or children in pain. If there was something she could do to help, she had to try.

9

"Each player must accept the cards life deals him or her:
but once they are in hand, he or she alone must decide
how to play the cards in order to win the game."

— Voltaire

A couple of days went by before Vivien chanced upon Sebastian on his own and was able to follow up on her promise to Lucius. She'd been keeping an eye out at the library to no avail. On an afternoon off, however, she spied him sitting on the front step of his house, dressed as always in his beloved black. She walked over, causing him to look up when her shadow fell on the graphic novel he was perusing. Vivien tilted her head to read the title.

"Ah, *Bleach*. Good stuff. The whole 'I see dead people' of the Manga world."

"You like Manga?" Sebastian shaded his eyes from the sun as he looked up at her.

"Some of it's pretty cool. I liked *Fruits Basket*, except I know if I turned into a sign of the zodiac every time a guy touched me, it would never be a centaur or a bull or something fab like that. No, I'd probably be the scales."

"Could be the twins. Then you could talk to yourself all the time and it wouldn't look weird." He smiled, and though he still had a bit of baby fat on him, Vivien thought he'd probably grow up to be quite a good-looking man. He certainly had the genes for it if his mother and father were any indication. The blond cowlick was still standing at full attention, though charming for all that.

Vivien, unsurprisingly, decided against beating around the bush. "Hey, have you talked to Lucius lately?" she asked.

Sebastian's lip quirked at her lack of finesse. "Yeah, he called me the other day, told me about his chat with you. He seems to think you rate. But I'm telling you right now, there's nothing to talk about, so I hope you haven't spent a lot of late nights thinking about how to get me to open up or go all Jeremy Kyle. I'm not big on sharing deepest thoughts."

"Course you aren't. Your family's in politics. Deep thoughts must be kept hidden at all costs. There's just no way to create snappy soundbites out of them."

Sebastian snorted. "True enough. And I'm sorry Lucius is having such a bad time with this. He just doesn't get what would happen if we're always seen together."

"And what would that be? Getting your ass kicked by the school bullies? Embarrassing your mother? Endangering your father's chances of re-election? And all of it leading to the end of the universe as we know it?" Vivien cocked an eyebrow. She could only ever cock the left one but figured side probably didn't matter.

"You don't know the half of it," Sebastian replied. "You saw the argument my father had with that old man the other day. Came to complain about the drains but couldn't resist calling us names at the same time. Dad tries to defend me, but I know it's a worry for him, so I made a deal with his campaign manager that I didn't have to do too much of the happy families BS if I keep a low profile until the election. Hence me and Lucius trying to keep out of their way."

"Can't you hang out in private at Lucius's house?"

Sebastian shook his head. "There's nothing private about his house. It's pretty small. He's got two older sisters constantly breaking the sound barrier, and his mum hovers."

"So what happens after the election, then?" Vivien queried. "Do you get to fly your freak flag every day of the year?"

Sebastian gave her a calculating look, probably assessing the chances this adult who spoke like a kid could actually understand his situation. He scooched over and waved a semi-gracious hand inviting her to sit down on the step, somehow resembling his mother and Lucius simultaneously. Vivien lowered herself down, reminded by the ache in her knees that she might be able to talk like a kid but she really wasn't one, as Sebastian answered her question.

"Doubtful, I suppose. But hey, another few months and I'm done with school and can move out of this hole and lose myself in a foreign country somewhere."

"Your parents are okay with that? And what about Lucius?"

"Mum and Dad probably want me to go to university and learn something respectable, but I'll be eighteen by that time, so I can do what I want. Besides, they'll probably be glad I'm gone." Sebastian sighed and shoved the toe of his tennis shoe into the pavement. "Lucius wants to go to university and become an architect. More power to him. He's better off doing that than bumming around third-world countries with me." His gaze flicked in the direction of Lucius's house half a mile away.

"You've given Lucius that choice, have you?" Vivien said.

The boy's face went from wistful to mulish. "No. He'd probably say he'll give up his dreams for me. But I can't let him do that. He's got a life planned. His family has saved up so he can be the first one of them to get a degree. And he's so smart, even in the short time he's been here he's got grants that will help make those dreams come true. No way I'm gonna get in the way of that and have him caught up in my crap. I mean, hell, we're only seventeen, he'll forget me soon enough."

Despite his youthful appearance, Vivien thought this boy was way too old and cynical for his years. *The price a political family pays, I suppose. It would be easier if he had siblings to share the burden. Or someplace to go away from the public eye.*

It suddenly occurred to Vivien she just might have a way to help them get through the school year without so much trauma.

"Tell you what," she said, "I need some help staining our shed and deck. What say I pay you and Lucius to do that, and if you happen to need a break during that work, you're welcome to hang out and watch a movie or two. As long as your parents approve, of course, and it doesn't negatively affect your schoolwork."

Sebastian tilted his head back against a pillar, watching her suspiciously from under half-closed eyelids. "Why would you do that?" he finally queried. "You don't even know us. We could steal something."

Vivien smiled. "You trusted me to talk to, so I choose to trust you in return. Besides, it's not like I'm letting Cecil B.

DeMille and a cast of thousands into my home. If something goes missing, I'll have a pretty good idea who took it, and I'm home most of the time anyway. But I've got a hunch you and Lucius are fairly sound citizens. Call it American optimism. We believe anyone could be president. And heck, some of our presidents prove it."

She paused to assume a more serious expression. "My only condition is that you have your phones on in case anyone is looking for you, you give me the numbers, and if your parents ask you where you are, you tell them. Oh, and weekdays after school only, I don't want my husband inconvenienced. And, of course, no football in the house or trying on my clothes."

Sebastian suddenly straightened up at the last comment, telling Vivien that there might also be gender fluidity issues at play here. Her heart ached for the kid, but she tried not to let her sympathy show, knowing it wouldn't be welcome this soon in their relationship.

"I'll make you a key so you can get in if I'm out for any reason, and we'll say £10 an hour, each." She stuck out her hand. "Deal?"

After a moment of consideration, Sebastian placed a slightly sweaty hand in hers, shook once and dropped it. "Deal. But I hope you know what you're getting into. This place is a hotbed of gossip with an undercurrent of ugly, you have no idea how they can warp the most innocent intentions."

Vivien stood and looked down at him, wondering who 'they' was. "I'll take my chances. We can't change things unless we try." She paused again, uncertain whether giving advice was a good idea, then decided to chance it.

"Do you have anyone you can talk to, Sebastian? Other than Lucius? What about Reverend Edwards, he seems to be a nice fellow."

Sebastian frowned and shook his head angrily. "No way. I definitely don't need any 'sins of the father' mumbo jumbo, particularly from that guy, so don't go confessing your worries about me to him. You say you want my trust? That's not the way to get it."

Vivien nodded. "Fair enough, and don't worry, he and I aren't besties. But I hope you know that I'm here to talk any time you feel the need, whether it's about school or home or the unadulterated magnificence of Eddie Izzard."

She heard another snort of laughter as she turned toward home and was glad she'd been able to make him laugh. And that, thought Vivien with satisfaction, was that. A job well done. Just like when the psychic in the film *Poltergeist* flipped her hair and declared "This house is clean."

Of course, in that case, nothing could have been further from the truth.

10

"When your children are teenagers, it's important to have a dog so that someone in the house is happy to see you."
— Nora Ephron, *I Feel Bad About My Neck: and Other Thoughts on Being a Woman*

Pleased as she was with the result of her talk with Sebastian, Vivien wouldn't have been human if she didn't have second thoughts about her impulsive generosity to the boys. Letting teenagers, and possibly teenagers in love, into your home alone required all kinds of second thoughts, and she had several during her short walk back home. But on the whole, she believed the circumstances justified a helping hand, and she was sure Geoffrey would agree when she told him about it later that evening. Plus, she wouldn't have to do the painting herself, which was a happy bonus as she suspected the shed was full of spiders. Vivien appreciated the genius and natural beauty of spiders but preferred to do so from a distance.

She saw Hayley coming through the field between their houses and invited her in for a cup of tea after their initial greetings, marveling anew at the woman's ability to combine clashing colors and patterns in ways that looked totally coordinated. Today her neighbor sported pink tartan trousers paired with a white T-shirt featuring a picture of a black and red matryoshka and the words "Russian Dolls. So full of themselves".

Hayley followed her into the kitchen, glancing around appreciatively. The room was big enough for a pedestal table and two chairs, as well as the large steel American fridge freezer that had been one of Vivien's requirements for moving to England. The walls were painted a warm peachy orange that matched the brightly colored towels embroidered with images of the Aztec god of mischief, Kokopelli. Hung on the walls were half a dozen gleaming copper pots that Vivien had collected over the years.

Settling in one of the chairs, Hayley enquired how things were going with the new job as Vivien turned on the kettle and got out the teacups.

"Well," said Vivien with mock seriousness, "amazing as it might seem, American and English kids seem to have more in common than they have differences."

"Yes, I imagine children are a powerful force that could bring nations together if given half a chance," Hayley laughed. "Or possibly just as easily rend them asunder. Which ones had the honor of opening your eyes to this life truth?"

"There was a whole group of them, but the leaders seem to be a couple called Samantha and Justin."

"Ah yes, the terrible twosome," said Hayley. "You've met Sam's parents, they own the shop. Justin, however, has a troubled history. Word on the street is that Social Services removed him from his parents about ten years ago, and since then he's been living with an elderly relative, an aunt or something. She's of the 'children should be seen but not heard' variety, and I'm not sure Justin has taken well to not being heard. You'll find he's known to the local constabulary, although not for anything too serious. Bit of vandalism, fighting in the streets. He's been cautioned by the police multiple times but it doesn't seem to matter, it just makes him cooler in the eyes of the other kids. Welcome to the neighborhood."

Vivien brought the tea to the table and poured, then they both took a sip as they watched Sydney wander in hoping for treats. Vivien popped open the jar she kept on the counter for this purpose and gave him a few, followed by a head scratch and then a firm look when he pointedly sat there waiting for more. After a couple of slow blinks, the cat decided the jig was up and wandered off to resume his nap.

"Word on the street seems awfully well informed. You must introduce me." Vivien sipped her own tea while she considered this expansion on what Becky had told her. "I guess being raised by an ageing aunt explains the old-fashioned attitude to homosexuality. He tried to pick a fight with Sebastian Bonner earlier, accusing him and his friend Lucius of the grievous sin of being gay."

Hayley winced. "I wish I could say Justin's aunt was the only one who feels that way, but Bickley is at heart an ex-mining village. You'll find arguments and prejudices run deep, accompanied by a resentment for authority—particularly government authority—as a result of the strikes in the 1980s. Check the market cross for the names of the fallen in world wars I and II and you'll recognize the same names in the current population. People have gone from birth to death in that village for decades, and they came to rely on each other and their traditions for almost everything. The sense of community remains strong, although any actual coal miners left around here tend to be upright citizens boggled by the younger generation's lack of commitment to hard work. Coal mining was a tough job, but the miners and their wives took pride in it, and in helping their neighbors."

Vivien nodded. She and Geoffrey had toured the coal mining museum in Wakefield during one of her visits to the area, and she'd been dismayed by the conditions the miners had endured, not to mention the pit ponies who were doomed to spend their lives underground.

Hayley continued. "Now that the mines are closed and unemployment has taken its toll, some of the younger generations have chosen to live on less rather than seek work. Not all, by any means, but some. So they have little money to spend on education as a way of raising living standards. But no matter their internal differences, the villagers are accustomed to sticking together against the world, and that makes it hard for outsiders who are different, like Sebastian and his friend Lucius."

Vivien sighed. "Different country, same problems. Human nature is what it is, I suppose. And at least here everyone gets healthcare."

"Which is only humane, of course. I've never understood how your country can claim to be progressive without it. And with the new football stadium, library, and college, as well as city status, Doncaster is doing its best to improve the lives of its inhabitants."

Hayley threw Vivien a smile. "But aside from discussing how to save the world, I really came over to ask if you and

Geoffrey would like to join us for a dinner out tonight. There's a new Turkish restaurant just opened in central Doncaster, allegedly complete with belly dancer, and Will is anxious to try it. Are you game?"

"Sounds good. Let me just check with Geoffrey to confirm, he's doing some errands for his mother. I need to have a couple of extra house keys made this afternoon, but I don't see how we can let a good belly dance go to waste. Do you mind, by the way, holding on to one of our extra keys? I have a bad habit of forgetting mine or losing it someplace, so I like to have other options."

Hayley shrugged. "No problem. Who else is getting one, just in case I'm not home and Will can't find it?"

"Well, the other is actually for Sebastian and Lucius. They need somewhere besides the library to hang out, away from prying eyes and prejudice. Evidently their own homes aren't viable, so I'm giving them a rare opportunity to do some maintenance work for me in the afternoons."

Hayley's eyebrows rose. "You're not worried about the wrath of Rachel or teenage sexual experimentation under your roof?"

"Well, I can't say I'd be happy about anyone using the house as a bordello, but I think forbidding such things outright will just inflame their teenage hormones all the more. Besides, I think these two are pretty responsible. I've warned Sebastian not to hide his whereabouts from his parents, although I should probably confirm with them just to be sure. Frankly, I can't just sit and watch him and Lucius get constantly hassled at the library, and it's not as if an English winter allows for outdoor meetings. They'd live in fear of discovery by bullies no matter where they went outside, anyway. These kids need a break, and my instinct is to trust them. Plus, I do need the shed and deck stained." Vivien gave a half-smile and a wink. "And if I'm wrong, I know where they live, so my revenge for any misbehaviour would be swift and thorough."

"You're a humanitarian and a gentleman, and possibly the Count of Monte Cristo considering your thirst for vengeance," Hayley grinned. "Let's hope they appreciate your generosity. And that none of this backfires on you."

11

"Trust your own instinct. Your mistakes might as well be your own, instead of someone else's."

— Billy Wilder

Vivien stretched luxuriously as the sun reached her side of the bed the next morning, pausing to marvel that Geoffrey had managed to get up so early after the somewhat raucous night of belly dancing, kebabs, and wine they'd enjoyed. Even considering the extra hour of sleep they'd gotten thanks to having to put the clocks back, she didn't feel ready to start the day. She made a mental note to remind her family about the time change for their regular call, since America didn't change for another two weeks.

When the smell of bacon and roasting coffee reached her nose, she realized that not only was her husband up, but that a full English breakfast would be delivered shortly. *Yes, I have indeed married well*, she mused, *even considering Geoffrey's inability to find the laundry hamper and his tendency to squeeze the toothpaste tube from the middle.*

Burrowing back into the bedclothes, Vivien dreamily

reviewed the activities of the previous evening. She desperately hoped no one they knew was at the restaurant when she and Will accepted the dancers' invitation to join in, their spouses smiling indulgently from the table. Her efforts had firmly convinced Vivien that a career in belly dancing was not on the cards, although Will had proven surprisingly lithe.

Thoroughly relaxed in her cozy bed, Vivien was drifting off once more to the dulcet tones of Aladdin singing "A Whole New World" in her head when Sydney interrupted her reverie by jumping on her stomach and howling piteously, causing pain in every muscle she'd so recently shaken. Fortunately, Geoffrey arrived with breakfast at that moment and she was able to satisfy her ferocious feline with bits of bacon. Or ham, as it was known in America. Vivien did miss Oscar Mayer streaky bacon, but it was next to impossible to find in England, along with her beloved honey barbeque corn twists. She made another mental note to remind her friends and family that the way to their host's heart was definitely through her stomach so they could pack the essentials before flying over to visit.

As it was a glorious day, once her appetite was sated Vivien rose, showered, and made ready to attack the garden. More used to outdoor spaces that heavily featured cacti, it never ceased to amaze her how fast things grew in England. She could tell the backyard had been carefully planned to introduce color at different times of the year, but it seemed the previous owners had been overzealous in their planting because the shrubs were now growing into each other and overhanging the lawn and the wooden deck.

Vivien was sure it was nothing a determined American

with a set of clippers couldn't sort out so, fuelled with food, she began to trim.

Two gruelling hours later, this particular determined American was dripping sweat and examining the blisters on her hands. There went a potential career in landscape designing as well. Call her Incapability Brown. This was obviously a job for the experts, and she would freely cede it to them.

As she started to return her tools to the shed, she heard a knock on the side gate into the garden. She opened it to reveal Sebastian and his friend Lucius, their eyes shyly lowered to the level of her mud-encrusted knees. Vivien smiled and said hello, then waited patiently for one of them to speak.

"Morning, miss," Sebastian finally ventured. "Sorry to interrupt, but I just wanted to ask about your offer of work. Is it still open?"

"Of course it is, Sebastian. I have an extra key for you just in case I'm not home when you finish school. Come on in and I'll give it to you, then I can show you what needs doing."

They followed her through the garden, politely wiping their feet before entering the conservatory and proceeding through the adjacent dining room and hallway into the kitchen, where Vivien retrieved the key from a drawer and handed it to her neighbor.

"I don't want to harp on about it, but I'm putting a lot of trust into you two," Vivien reminded them. "Please don't betray that, and I repeat, don't hide anything from your parents if they ask where you are."

"Don't worry," Sebastian said, "I've already mentioned it to my dad, he's cool with it."

"Good. You can come in if I'm not home to use the

facilities and raid the cookie jar, but I'd appreciate it if you don't mess anything up or eat our dinner. The television controls are on the table by the sofa if you need a break. Feel free to watch the pay channels but try to practice good taste, as some of them are on shared family licenses and I don't want my sister making fun of my sudden fondness for *Dude, Where's My Car?* Oh, and lastly, don't feed the cat, no matter what he tells you."

Vivien paused until both young men were looking at her. "Are we agreed?"

They nodded, so she took them outside to show them the shed and where she stored the cans of stain and the brushes. Then they exchanged mobile numbers with her (or "traded digits" as Sebastian called it) and took their leave with quiet thanks.

Vivien decided it was time to catch Geoffrey up with the latest events. She went into the lounge to find him at the window watching the boys leave as he finished a cup of coffee. He turned as she came into the room.

"Making friends, are we?"

"Well, starting to, anyway. I think. Those are the boys I told you about, the ones who were taking grief in the library. Thank you again for agreeing to help them. As we discussed, I've given Sebastian a key to the house so they can do some work in the back garden in the afternoons. I figure we know his parents and where he lives, and I just feel those boys desperately need a safe space to enjoy being kids. Oh, but I've asked them not to disturb us on the weekends, so they'll only be here on weekdays."

"That's fine, I guess, but considering my previous brush with young Sebastian I might just lock up the liquor. I hope your training in childhood development stands you in good stead and they don't do anything destructive. We both know teenagers are notoriously volatile."

"Ah well, so is our love, and we risked that, eh?" She gave him her sexiest smile, causing him to laugh before happily following her upstairs where they shared a shower and worked off the calories from Geoffrey's delicious breakfast fry-up. Then they spent a lazy afternoon watching old movies and worshipping the cat with treats and brushings, which Sydney felt was no more than his due.

12

"Tragedy is like strong acid – it dissolves away all but the very gold of truth."

— D. H. Lawrence

Vivien could hear rain pounding on the roof when she woke up Monday morning, so she shipped her husband off to work after a quick breakfast and went back to decorating. She'd come into an extensive art collection on a Caribbean cruise with her first husband some years before. Well, not so much "come into" as wandered—slightly tipsy from drinking too many Mai Tais at lunch—into an auction on the ship. She was told her purchases were tax free in international waters and proceeded to place multiple bids in between hiccupping like a dyspeptic chihuahua. As with most of her drunken purchases (a Cheshire Cat diamante brooch purchased at 2 a.m. during her bachelorette party in Disneyland came to mind), she ended up loving the various paintings. It led her to wonder if she had better taste when drunk than sober, although she certainly didn't have better control of her budget. But then, alcohol had also played a part in her initial attraction to Geoffrey, so like many things it obviously could be used for good or evil.

Hammer and nails in hand, Vivien placed various paintings near empty walls and pondered the suitability of their placement before making her decisions and proceeding to pound holes in the plaster. She also managed to pound her thumb while hanging the last picture, but all in all it was a good morning's work, and she could feel the house becoming more of a home thanks to having these familiar and beloved pieces around her.

After a quick shower she noticed the rain had stopped, so she decided to make a trip to the market and pick up some fresh fish and veg for dinner. It was another of the joys of England that many of its towns boasted regular market days, often held outdoors or in some Victorian marvel of architecture that was as much fun to look at as it was to shop in. Doncaster's market was in such a building, called the Corn Exchange, and it was one of the largest such markets left in England, containing an abundance of stalls overflowing with fresh produce, cheeses, fish, and meat. Vivien decided to dare the longer drive to check it out, despite her now-throbbing thumb and the related headache.

Things didn't start well when she got in the car, gave the thumb a quick suck to soothe it, and then noticed the steering wheel was missing. *Who breaks into a car and takes a steering wheel?* she fumed. *What is wrong with this country?*

She was looking around to see what else might have been taken when she noticed the missing steering wheel firmly fixed on the other side of the dashboard. Blast. She'd gotten in the wrong side of the car. Again. She got out and went around to the driver's side, pausing to take a few deep breaths to reset her mood and check that no one had witnessed her idiocy, before getting back in and setting off.

Despite a couple of angry honks and a near miss when she looked the wrong way for oncoming traffic at a roundabout, she eventually arrived on the outskirts of the city and decided to park on a quiet side street rather than facing the hassle of finding a space in the center of town.

Walking briskly to the market, she quickly filled a bag with fresh meat, fruit and vegetables, and even managed to find a stall with some interesting bread mix flavors that she could use in her top-of-the-line bread maker. It had been a wedding gift from one of Geoffrey's relatives and was yet to be freed from its box, but Vivien decided today would be the day.

On her way back to the car Vivien spotted the pharmacy where Hayley had mentioned she worked. She decided to stop and say hello. Unlike the American drugstore, which sold everything from medicines to lamps and ice cream, English pharmacies tended to stick to just the medicines and personal hygiene items. This one was a slightly larger version that also sold various candies and a few lunchtime nibbles, but Vivien headed toward the prescription counter at the back, where her eyes beheld the most stunning man she'd ever seen. Tall and lean, he was a dark-haired, blue-eyed cross between Tom Hiddleston and Tom Selleck and probably other great Toms she was suddenly too flustered to remember, all wrapped up in a bright white pharmacist's coat. It was as if a modern-day Mary Shelley had decided to take another crack at *Frankenstein*, but this time she wanted to ensure her creation was so gorgeous no one would want to take a flaming torch to him.

Vivien watched while the vision finished preparing a prescription. When he finally looked up she gave him her brightest smile, the one that showed her extensive American dental work to advantage. All she got in immediate response was the twitch of an eyebrow before his face assumed a polite expression and he walked toward her.

"Can I help you?" Wow. His voice was proper Peter O'Toole, she thought, unconsciously disrupting the whole Tom theme.

"Um, hi. My name's Vivien. I was wondering if Hayley Mason is available?"

"Ah, you must be her new neighbor, the American. She's spoken of you."

Vivien toyed with the idea of remaining silent. Maybe he would just keep talking in that marvelous voice. Heck, she'd listen to him reading the phone book. But courtesy did seem to require a response in this case.

"That would be me, I guess the accent betrays me yet again. I was in town and just thought I'd stop and say hello. Is she around?"

"Unfortunately she wasn't feeling well today, and she's gone home early. Something about dodgy lamb, I believe."

The eyebrow did its elegant dance again, and Vivien was momentarily lost imagining him in a tux and white scarf, à la Loki in *Avengers Assemble*. She mentally shook herself and tried another smile, hoping the increased wattage would eventually thaw this prime example of British reserve. But the Loki-like continued to silently regard her dispassionately.

"Uh, okay, thanks," Vivien stuttered. "I guess I'll catch her at home. Have a nice day, Mr...?"

"Mackay. Steven Mackay. As a friend of Hayley's, just call

me Steven. Please let her know I hope she's feeling better, and not to come in tomorrow if she's not. We can manage." He nodded at her and walked back to the shelves to fill another prescription.

Duly dismissed, Vivien meandered back to her car lost in daydreams she wouldn't be admitting to Geoffrey anytime soon. Fortunately, most of them involved Norse gods and magic staffs, so they were unlikely to intrude on reality as long as she managed to pay attention to the road.

After pulling into her driveway, she left the groceries in the car and went over to do a quick check on Hayley, who answered the door looking wan but still standing, if swaying a little. Vivien wisely decided a discussion of her boss's charms would be ill-received at the present time, so she simply made sure her friend had everything she needed and recrossed the road to retrieve her bags from the car.

Inserting her key in the front door she was surprised to find it unlocked. She cautiously opened the door to glance into the hall, but the house looked undisturbed. *Hmmm*, she pondered, *guess I must have left it unlocked this morning*. Good thing Geoffrey hadn't gotten home first, he was a bit OCD about locks, always checking them two or three times.

She shrugged and headed for the kitchen, where she set her bags on the counter and began to unpack their contents into the refrigerator. She looked around for Sydney, who was usually rubbing her ankles around this time in hopes of a kitty snack, but it appeared the cat was still snoozing the day away upstairs somewhere. For all that Sydney had made it clear he was unhappy with being hauled halfway around the world, he had wholeheartedly adopted the wide British windowsills as his bed of choice and spent most of the day moving from one to the other in order to catch whatever sun was available. He'd also decided he highly approved of radiators, as they not only meant warm windowsills but also hot water pipes under the floor, upon which snoozing was even more agreeable.

After she finished putting away the groceries Vivien decided she deserved a little down time, so she went into the living room to turn on the television, a somewhat largish flat-screen model that made watching Hollywood musicals a joyous event. It was a good time to catch random reruns of old American shows to ease the occasional homesickness. You could always find an old episode of *Everybody Loves Raymond* or *Frasier*, as the Brits seemed to find these series ironic enough to suit their national taste.

As she sat down on the sofa Vivien felt a slight breeze ruffle her hair. Curious, she glanced through the dining room to the conservatory. The glassed room was another bit of classic British architecture Vivien hadn't understood when they bought the house. I mean, if you want to look at the outdoors, just go outside! But after suffering through a few very wet weeks, she came to appreciate the protection such a room offered as well as the extra light it brought in.

Now, glancing down the length of the house, she could swear the curtains separating the dining room from the conservatory had moved, and she caught an unusually strong whiff of lavender, presumably from the plant just outside the back door. She must have left a window open or something.

Rising from the sofa, Vivien walked into the dining room and noticed with a shock that the conservatory door was wide open to the back garden. As she stared, slightly spooked, a gust of wind caused the door to swing shut, but then it bounced back open before it could close entirely. Looking at the bottom of the door frame, which was all she could see of the floor with the dining table blocking her view, Vivien saw a tennis shoe. Something in the back of her mind suggested this couldn't be good, and that tennis shoes were called trainers here, but at this point curiosity still had the upper hand.

Walking further into the dining room past the table, her eyes followed the shoe up the attached leg to a body that was now revealed lying face down on the conservatory floor. But it was the blood that finally pierced the fog filling her brain. The blood that was seeping out from under the body. It was so bright, so red. And it was still spreading, presumably out of some sort of chest wound she couldn't see.

For a moment, her brain froze, unable to take in the horror of the scene, but then Vivien accepted she had to act. Trying to remember all the best crime scene advice from her many years of reading detective fiction, she carefully avoided the blood pool to approach the body. The black clothing and blond hair had already led her to suspect who it was, but a glance at the face turned to one side confirmed the worst.

Sebastian. She gently lifted his outstretched hand off the floor and checked his wrist for a pulse. She thought she could feel a thready one, and this galvanized her.

Jumping up, she quickly stepped into the hall to grab the landline phone. Her mind froze for a moment when she started to dial 911, knowing it was wrong, and then she remembered it was 999 in England.

After a few seconds the call was answered, and Vivien took a deep breath before explaining the situation. Even so, her voice came haltingly, and she had to turn her back to the conservatory to force herself to concentrate. The calm voice on the other end of the line promised that an ambulance would be there shortly, along with the police. The woman advised her not to move Sebastian or administer CPR as the source of the bleeding was unknown and inaccessible, just to make sure he could breathe if possible.

Then came the longest fifteen minutes of Vivien's life as she returned to the conservatory to kneel next to the boy she'd so recently tried to befriend, her ears ringing with the shock as she carefully avoided the blood that had by this time stopped spreading.

Vivien gently opened Sebastian's mouth, kneeling with her face on the floor to see if she could spot any obstruction. She wasn't sure if she felt a slight breath against her fingers as she did so, or if desperation made her imagine it.

She fetched the mobile from her handbag and tried to ring Hayley, but there was no answer. She cursed herself for not getting Hayley's landline number, and yelling across the street for her would be fruitless, of course. She thought about careening through the neighborhood to seek help, but knew she couldn't leave Sebastian by himself. Wouldn't.

So she talked to him instead. She couldn't think of anything else to do. She stayed kneeling beside him and held his wrist, checking for a pulse that she now had trouble finding, and talked to him. About how sorry she was this had happened, how he needed to fight to survive. She promised she would take him to every comic book shop in a hundred-mile radius if only he stayed with her now.

When the ambulance came Hayley was close behind anyway, having seen the flashing lights and miraculously heard something of the high wail of the siren. She stopped in the front doorway and shouted to Vivien standing at the end of the hall, where the latter had moved to give the paramedics room to bring their equipment through.

"Honey, what's going on? Are you all right?"

Vivien turned a face full of sorrow toward her, then walked down the hall to clutch her neighbor in mute desperation for several moments before releasing her and walking toward the living room. Hayley followed, and for a moment they both watched the bobbing tops of the paramedics' heads as they tried to revive the boy with CPR.

"It's Sebastian," Vivien finally said, after touching Hayley's arm to get her attention. "I found him. I think he's been stabbed or shot or something. Oh God, what have I done?" Vivien choked back a sob but couldn't stop the tears that had started to run down her face.

"Oh sweetheart, I'm sure you haven't done anything. Come on now, let's sit down until we know what's going on."

Hayley sat Vivien down on the sofa while the paramedics did their work, then went to the kitchen to make her a cup of sugary tea to fight the shock. She clasped Vivien's hand when one of the paramedics came to tell her that Sebastian was dead and they were now waiting for the police to arrive.

Vivien nodded but remained silent, her mind replaying recent conversations with this young man who had seemed so troubled yet so alive, and she found herself utterly unable to comprehend his sudden and total absence.

13

"I'm a copper... as honest as you could expect... in a world where it's going out of style."

— Raymond Chandler, *The Big Sleep*

The police showed up fifteen minutes later, starting with two uniformed officers who stopped long enough to get Vivien's and Hayley's names and a brief outline of what had happened. After speaking to the paramedics one of them made a phone call while the other explained to Vivien and Hayley that the situation required further investigation and would they please remain as they were for a bit longer. A short time after that, one of the officers admitted two plainclothes detectives who, after a murmured discussion with their co-workers, flashed warrant cards for the two women before heading toward the conservatory. They were followed by three more officers carrying cases of equipment. As Vivien was still sitting in the living room dealing with her thoughts, Hayley liaised with the officers and paramedics, making sure everyone was offered drinks, which were politely refused. Somewhere in her mind Vivien registered this as her job, particularly as Hayley wasn't feeling well, but she found she couldn't function at the moment.

Eventually the two detectives came into the living room and stood in front of them. They were an odd pair. The short, black-haired man was dressed in a dark blue Italian suit without a wrinkle in sight, the sharp crease in his trousers leading down to well-buffed brogues, and his starched white shirt was accented by a thin black tie featuring electric blue zigzags. He exuded a calm bordering on boredom, but when he looked straight at Vivien she noted a burning intelligence in the dark brown eyes and suspected criminals relaxed around him at their peril.

His partner, on the other hand, was a throwback to the Norse Valkyries. Tall and striking, with long honey-blonde hair and a slim-but-muscular figure, this woman would have turned heads in the most jaundiced night club, even dressed in jeans and tennis shoes as she was now. (*Trainers*, Vivien absent-mindedly corrected herself.) The Valkyrie's intense green eyes took in the room at a glance before returning to the man next to her as she waited for him to begin.

"Mrs. Brandt?" he ventured, looking back and forth between the two women seated in front of him.

"Ms.," she said automatically, then realized it was a stupid thing to insist upon right now. "Sorry, I'm Vivien Brandt. Call me Vivien, please."

"As you wish," he responded, making a note in the small notebook in his hand. Vivien was surprised to see the police still carried notebooks. *There must be better technology for that now. They should all maybe have iPads?* she mused, before realizing her thoughts had strayed and the man was talking again.

"I'm Detective Inspector Fenton Torksey, and this is Detective Sergeant Marion Martin. We're from Doncaster CID. We understand you found the body?"

"Yes. His name is Sebastian. Sebastian Bonner. He lives a couple of doors down."

"And how did you know Mr. Bonner?"

"I didn't really. I just met his parents recently, and Sebastian sometimes came into the library where I work."

"Do you have any idea what he was doing in your house, in that case?"

Vivien thought she detected a touch of innuendo in his tone and glared at him. He looked placidly back at her as DS Martin, who had assumed the role of note-taker, glanced up with interest.

"Of course I do. I invited him to use the house and gave him a key!" Vivien heard the anger in her voice, but it was too late to change that and she wasn't sure she wanted to, anyway.

"Front and back door? Or did you leave the key in the back door?"

"No, that would have been silly. The back door key resides in a jar on the shelf next to the door. Sebastian must have found it and intended to go into the backyard. He was doing some work for me."

"And what exactly was this work, and why did he need a front door key to do it?" Torksey's own carefully bland tone failed to mollify Vivien's sudden irritation.

"It's a long story, officer, and I'm not sure I'm in any shape to tell it properly, but if you insist. Oh my God, Sydney!"

Vivien jumped off the sofa and rushed into the hallway and up the stairs, to the surprise of everyone in the vicinity. DS Martin quickly followed to find her anxiously checking behind chairs and under beds. Vivien finally located her Siamese crouched against the wall under the bed in the master bedroom. Sydney glared at his mistress, his eyes wide, and gave out a howl that must have reverberated through the entire house.

Watched by the detective sergeant, Vivien told her cat all was well and took a quick moment to cuddle him and confirm he wasn't injured in any way. She found that, in addition to calming Sydney, the action gave her a moment to ground herself. Once she was sure the cat was copacetic and had resumed his position under the bed, she and Martin made their way more slowly downstairs, where everyone else was as she'd left them except for the expectant looks on their faces. Martin subtly nodded to her boss to assure him all was well as Vivien breathlessly started to explain.

"Sorry. I just remembered I hadn't seen my cat since I returned. I wanted to make sure he was okay."

Pausing to inhale, Vivien lifted her chin and stared at Detective Inspector Torksey, daring him to think she was a crazy cat lady. She certainly wouldn't start by apologizing for anything to the police. Well, all right, she just had, but not from here on out. She was constantly frustrated with mysteries where the main witnesses were blithering women, and she was determined not to be one herself.

"I take it that ungodly noise indicates he is in a satisfactory condition?" said DI Torksey.

"Yes." Vivien was momentarily thrown by the humorous smirk on the detective's face. "Thank you for asking."

"All right. Glad that's settled. We will have to do a search of the house shortly, and now that Sergeant Martin knows where the cat is, we'll try not to disturb him. But before that,

Ms. Brandt, can you describe for me your actions of this afternoon?"

Vivien pushed down her feelings of violation at the thought of strangers going through her new home, knowing it had to be done and would only help to clear her of suspicion. Calm and control. This was the way to help find Sebastian's killer.

"I'll give it my best shot," she started with unintentional irony. "Immediately after lunch I drove to Doncaster to do a bit of shopping at the market. Mr. Steven Mackay in the local pharmacy can confirm I was there, as that was my last stop."

Hayley's eyebrows rose at the mention of her co-worker, but she remained silent as Vivien continued.

"I left there at about three, so I suppose I got home about thirty minutes after that, as I had to walk some way to the car from the market. After entering the house and putting away the groceries, I felt a breeze and went to check if I'd left any windows open in the conservatory. That's when I found Sebastian."

"And did you notice anything out of place, or anyone in the vicinity when you arrived?"

"No. Well, the door was unlocked, which I thought was odd, but it makes sense now that I know Sebastian was here. Oh, and I forgot, I went over to check on Hayley—Mrs. Mason—before I came in the door." She gestured to her companion.

The detective turned to Hayley and looked directly at her as he spoke. The paramedics had obviously informed him about Hayley's deafness.

"You were home this afternoon, Mrs. Mason? Did you see anyone enter or leave Ms. Brandt's house?"

Hayley shook her head. "Sorry, I wasn't feeling well, so I was in bed resting until Vivien came by. After that I made myself a cup of tea and when I went to the front room to drink it I saw the flashing lights of your cars and came to check on her."

One of the paramedics came into the room to inform Torksey that the police surgeon was on the way and they would be taking the body once she had documented the death, assuming the police had finished the photographs. Torksey nodded and turned back to the two women.

"Do either of you know how to contact next of kin?" he asked.

Hayley nodded. "I have his parents' contact information in my address book back at my house, but their house is just a short walk away if you want to check if they are home. Mr. and Mrs. Archibald Bonner."

Torksey paused, eyebrows raised. "The MP?"

Hayley nodded again.

"Wonderful," Torksey muttered under his breath. "A very important person. Just what we all needed today."

Vivien hesitated. "Can you tell us what happened to Sebastian? I mean, I saw the blood…"

Her voice petered out as the memory of it hit her afresh, and Torksey watched the emotions cross her face before answering.

"He's been shot, Ms. Brandt. Do you keep a gun in the house?"

"No, I don't."

The inspector nodded, then turned toward Hayley, again making sure he had her attention before speaking. "Please see Constable Wilson in the kitchen, he will need to take your fingerprints. Then DS Martin will go with you to your house for the address book. Once you have given her the information, I think you can stay there as you're not feeling well. We'll be around to follow up with you tomorrow. I hope you feel better soon."

The last comment surprised Vivien. It was the first evidence of a softer side of Torksey, although she considered he was still no Roderick Alleyn, the suave police detective created by New Zealand mystery writer Ngaio Marsh.

Hayley glanced at her for confirmation, and Vivien nodded to reassure her friend she'd be all right. Hayley hugged her quickly and headed to the kitchen with the statuesque sergeant.

Vivien turned back around to find Torksey regarding her thoughtfully.

"So you don't really know the victim, but you gave him a key to your house. Do you not consider that somewhat unusual behavior?" he queried.

"Not particularly. I liked him, and I felt sorry for him. He's a bit of an outcast, despite or maybe because of being the child of a local politician. He and his friend Lucius were being bullied in the library where I work and, I suspect, elsewhere. I've talked to him a couple of times, and I happen to know his life isn't…wasn't…the easiest, even taking into account the usual teen angst. I wanted to do something to help, so I offered them some work and a place to hang out after school. That's all there is to it."

"And you have no idea who might have murdered him? Or where his friend—Lucius, was it? —might be?" Torksey had resumed the look of cultivated boredom, but Vivien sensed he was braced for wild imaginings.

"I could probably come up with some ideas," she retorted, "but none of them would have the advantage of being supported by proof, so I'd rather not speculate to people who have handcuffs and the power to use them. Plus, I am a relative newcomer to the neighborhood, and the country, and therefore probably not the best source of gossip anyway. And no, I don't know where Lucius is."

The detective's brow furrowed as he scribbled in his notebook. *Ha!* she thought. He was expecting a busybody Miss Marple, or maybe Jessica Fletcher considering Vivien's nationality. Well, she wouldn't be annoying the police with any theories until she had something to back them up.

Which is when Vivien realized she would, in fact, be formulating theories and looking for something to back them up. She had to know who had taken that poor young man's life, so maybe there would be a bit of Miss Marpling after all. But without the knitting needles. Vivien really sucked at knitting.

14

"Family is a life jacket in the stormy sea of life."
— J. K. Rowling, *Harry Potter and the Prisoner of Azkaban*

Geoffrey arrived an hour later. He'd left work immediately after getting Vivien's short and carefully impassive call informing him of events but, Vivien having assured him she was fine and that he was not to incur the significant expense of a taxi when it probably wouldn't be any quicker, he agreed to wait for the next train home despite his concern. He was just in time to see the body being transported to the waiting mortuary van, which didn't help allay his worry.

Fortunately, DI Torksey had told the officer at the door to expect him (another bit of consideration that made Vivien rethink her image of the starchy inspector, ignoring his slight sigh when she explained her husband's last name wasn't Brandt), so he got in with minimal fuss and was soon enfolding his wife in a supportive embrace. Vivien had managed not to cry during the entirety of the police interview, but the effort was exhausting and she was grateful for her husband's soothing presence.

The inspector had just finished confirming Geoffrey's details and whereabouts at the crucial time when they heard the officer at the door announce a car had pulled into the Bonners' driveway.

The inspector and his sergeant left immediately to walk over there. Vivien knew from overheard conversations between the two officers that they'd found the house empty earlier. They hadn't been able to reach Rachel on the mobile number provided by Hayley, and Archie was apparently in a subcommittee meeting with instructions not to be disturbed. Messages had been left for both of them to call Sergeant Martin since this kind of news was better delivered live.

Torksey returned fairly quickly, presumably having left DS Martin to take any details and support whichever parent had come home. He signaled to his team to pack everything up and start loading it back into the van. While the police carried equipment outside, he came to talk to Vivien and Geoffrey.

"We're going to have to secure your house, I'm afraid, until we've processed things from today and are certain we have all the evidence we need. Do you have someplace you can stay for a couple of days?"

Vivien looked at her husband, who nodded. He was no doubt thinking of his mother's house, but Vivien thought she might ask Hayley and Will first. She wanted to keep an eye on the police's progress, and ensure they weren't harming her lovely home.

"Good," Torksey continued. "Please do not enter the house until you get the okay from us. Mr. Wooster, if you wouldn't mind us taking your prints before we leave, for elimination purposes. Constable Wilson awaits you in the kitchen."

Geoffrey nodded, turned to Vivien to give her another hug and a kiss on the forehead, and then he was gone.

"Which one was it?" Vivien asked the inspector.

He didn't pretend not to understand her rather vague question, which she appreciated. "Mrs. Bonner."

"How did she take it?"

"She's upset, as you might imagine. Do you know her as well as apparently you know her son?" he asked with some asperity.

"I didn't know either of them very well. But Rachel was very welcoming when we moved here, and I would like to return the favor if there's any way I can help."

Torksey took a moment to reply, his voice a little softer. "Well, this might not be the right time to disturb her, but eventually I'm sure she'll appreciate that."

Vivien looked up at him from her seat on the sofa. What with his height, it wasn't so very far, close enough that she thought she could glimpse the tiniest bit of pity in his eyes. Or maybe he'd just drunk too much coffee and needed the bathroom. *Toilet*, she mentally corrected.

"What do you mean?" she asked. "Did she say something about me?"

He cocked his head. "She's mostly still in shock. In my experience, it will take time for her to process what's happened, and she might have questions about your relationship with the boy. As may her husband, who I'm told is finally out of his meeting and on his way home."

"But I didn't *do* anything!" Vivien exclaimed, bringing Geoffrey back to her at a jog. "I was only trying to be nice. I felt sorry for the poor kid!"

"Pure as your motives might have been, Ms. Brandt,

the fact remains that he was shot in your house, and the circumstances have yet to be fully explained. You may not have killed him, but you provided the location and circumstances in which it happened, and his parents may feel some anger about that. I'm only telling you this so you can be prepared. If it happens."

"Really, Inspector!" Geoffrey protested. "I think my wife has dealt with enough today without being called an accessory to a murder!"

Torksey turned a bland face to Geoffrey. "We're not making any such accusation, Mr. Wooster, I just thought it best for you both to understand the situation. I've seen this kind of thing before, and somehow I think Ms. Brandt would rather be forewarned. I do apologize if I'm mistaken."

He turned toward Vivien. "We also need your fingerprints, of course, but before that we'll need to take samples to test for gunshot residue." Vivien's eyes widened but she kept silent as he continued. "It's standard procedure in cases like this. Gun crimes are quite rare in this country, so GSR tests aren't contaminated by…extracurricular gun activities. After that, Sergeant Martin will accompany you upstairs so you can pack a suitcase and retrieve your cat, and then we'll lock up after you've left. I'll let you know when we need you to come down and sign your statements." He finished with a curt little bow and left the room to check on his team's progress.

Vivien felt her temper rise, but part of her realized the man was attempting to shake her out of her shocked lethargy. She knew he was right, there would undoubtedly be fallout from Sebastian dying in their home.

Geoffrey sat next to her with his arm around her shoulders, and she turned to place her palm on his chest, part of her brain remembering how she'd woken up with her head there just that morning and had felt so safe.

"It's okay, Geoffrey. He's not wrong about being prepared. If I understand village life correctly, today's tragedy will be dissected far and wide, and people are bound to wonder what Seb was doing here." Vivien rose to head toward the kitchen so the police could fingerprint her. "We've got to talk to Rachel and Archie and decide what to tell everyone and what can be kept private."

Once they'd been fingerprinted and had samples taken (which involved tape being pressed to Vivien's fingers, presumably to gather particles of gunpowder), Geoffrey agreed to phone Hayley while Vivien began packing their case and getting a reluctant Sydney into his carrier. She was relieved when her husband reported they were welcome to stay in the Masons' guest room for as long as they needed.

Ten minutes later, as they crossed the street with luggage and cat in tow, they heard a door slam and saw Rachel Bonner quickly walking toward them. She stopped suddenly next to Vivien and resoundingly slapped her face before crumpling to her knees, her body wracked with sobs. Ignoring her throbbing cheek, Vivien put down the cat carrier and knelt next to the broken woman.

"Rachel, I'm so sorry. I can't imagine how you must feel, but I liked Sebastian and I don't know how this has happened."

Rachel looked up, her eyes wide in shocked disbelief. "You *liked* him?! You lured him over here to his death because you *liked* him?!"

Vivien took a moment to gather her thoughts before responding. "I know it must look odd, but I didn't lure him anywhere. I was only trying to help him out of a painful situation. Look, I'm happy to explain my part in this, but for now maybe it's best to get you home and wait for Archie before we get into all this."

She looked up at Geoffrey for confirmation, and he nodded and moved forward to help Rachel up. But Rachel waved off his hand before he could touch her, still glaring at Vivien.

"I don't know what happened, I don't know if I ever will, but I do know that everything was fine until you came here and started sticking your Yank nose into my family's business." She sneered at Vivien's raised eyebrows. "Yes, Archie told me about you offering Sebastian and his friend a place to be together. Now my son is dead, the police are in my house searching his room, and everything is shot to hell. So even if you didn't kill him, and I don't know that by any means, I still hold you responsible for his death and I will remember that for the rest of my days."

Rachel stood up and brushed a bit of dirt off the front of her immaculate suit. Holding her tear-streaked face high, she walked briskly back toward her home, her clenched fists uncannily reminding Vivien of her first sight of Sebastian. As Rachel reached the front door, where a startled police officer had emerged looking for her lost charge, they saw a taxi pull into the driveway. Archie got out and walked behind his wife through the door, his face visibly pale even from a distance, and together the bereaved parents closed themselves in to deal with their loss away from prying eyes.

Vivien looked back toward her own home, but there was no one watching from inside. Not now, at least.

"Well," she said, her mind finally free of shock and

all lethargy banished, "chalk one up to the inspector, he certainly called that correctly. And I don't think you're getting sponsored for a country club membership, my darling."

"That's all right," Geoffrey responded. "Their bartender makes lousy martinis, and the eighth hole on the golf course has molehills."

With that, they entered the Masons' house and were shown to the guest room, which was decorated in soothing shades of blue. It was here that Vivien finally got to curl up on the bed and have a good cry. Even Geoffrey, all English male that he was, might have shed a tear for a tragically lost life.

Sydney, who had quickly established himself on the windowsill above the radiator, was unmoved.

15

"Every man at the bottom of his heart believes that he is a born detective."

— John Buchan

The next couple of days found them both bleary-eyed with the lack of sleep. Whenever Vivien did manage to doze off, her dreams were full of violence and guilt. Dinners with the Masons were subdued affairs, although pleasant enough. Vivien felt she wasn't giving Will's excellent cooking the appreciation it deserved, but she found it hard to summon up the enthusiasm required, and Geoffrey uncharacteristically stuck to talking mostly about the weather.

Matters weren't helped when their mobiles started constantly ringing. After the first couple of interactions with reporters, Vivien and Geoffrey put them on silent and let all the calls go to messages, where one newspaper after another requested details about the murder. Vivien had cause to be grateful that her mobile number was so new it meant she'd given it to very few people, and Geoffrey informed his family and work colleagues where they were and how they could be reached in case of emergency.

Geoffrey offered to stay at home with her, but Vivien knew he was working on an important project, and she preferred to be alone anyway. Or at least, not to have him constantly hanging about with worry in his eyes. She sent him on his way, knowing that the press would no doubt also be trying to reach him at his workplace. She said a quick prayer for the poor receptionist fielding those calls.

With Hayley and Will also at work upon her insistence, Vivien spent much of her time watching English property shows. They provided her with an easy way to learn and remember the country's geography. ("Today we're looking to find Randolph and Bitsy a home in Wiltshire, known for its stone circles and house prices twenty percent above the national average!")

Hayley returned home from work in the early afternoon a couple of days after the murder looking almost completely recovered from her short illness, if still a little pale. Finding Vivien ensconced in front of the television, she held up a bottle of wine and a glass, her eyebrows raised in question. She looked relieved when Vivien nodded, and brought over two glasses of a chilled Chardonnay, handing one to her neighbor.

"How are you?" Hayley asked. "I've been wondering if I should be doing anything for you, not being *au fait* with manners for murders. Are you managing all right?"

"Yes, I've called the library and agreed to work tomorrow, figured it would be good to take a break from thinking about it. But of course we've got the lovely crime scene tape all over our front door and are having to burden the neighbors with our presence, so it's kind of hard to ignore."

Hayley snorted in an unladylike manner. "You're not a burden and your husband is an absolute delight. I'd take you in for the sake of his company even if you were Cruella de Vil."

"Gee, thanks. The fact is, I can't help feeling Sebastian deserves to be thought about right now. Poor kid. Have the police been in touch?"

"They followed up yesterday to confirm that I didn't see anything. I expect they're getting all the statements from neighbors and the results from the autopsy, so they'll have more questions after that. Did they tell you anything else the day of the murder? Other than the fact that Sebastian had been shot?"

"Not a thing," Vivien replied with a shrug. "But then, I wasn't in much shape to take it in anyway. And I suppose I'm a suspect depending on when Sebastian was attacked and if my alibi checks out. They're certainly not going to reveal details of their investigation to me. And I don't think they would even if I'm proven innocent."

"Hmmm," mused Hayley, "you're right, not to you. But there are always ways. And in this case the way is named Josh Marsden."

"And who's he when he's at home?" Vivien asked, quite proud to be trotting out this English idiom with such ease. Hayley's amused look made her suspect she wasn't being quite as clever as she imagined. Or maybe it was just the American accent that made it funny.

"He's my brother. Marsden is my maiden name. And he's just been taken on as a constable at the Bickford station. Torksey was either playing it cool the other day or he doesn't yet know I'm the sister of one of his newest co-workers. Josh was living in London, but he found it wasn't to his taste, so he's transferred up here to be closer to family; i.e., me."

"Well now, isn't that convenient. Will he share with us?"

"As you say, probably not until we're cleared of suspicion, and probably not with you anyway, but big sister has plenty of blackmail options, and besides he can refuse me nothing. Give me twenty-four hours and I'll test the waters, see what he's willing to tell us."

"Of course. In the meantime, what are your thoughts? Any devastating insights that could blow this case wide open?"

"Not particularly. You've had more exposure to the boy than I have lately, and from what you tell me, the other kids had it in for him and Lucius. Oh my goodness, has anyone seen Lucius? He must be so upset!" Hayley's eyes grew moist at the thought of the young man's pain. *She really is a lovely person*, thought Vivien.

"I told Detective Inspector Torksey about him when he interviewed me. But as for the other kids being nasty, I don't know. Much as I deal with kids and know how casually cruel they can be, would one of them really get hold of a gun and track Sebastian down and shoot him?"

"God yes," Hayley responded. "Absolute brutes, most of them. No sense of social responsibility. It's all about getting the latest iPhones and texting people standing right next to you."

"Ouch!" Vivien marveled. "Not a fan of the younger set, then?"

Hayley had the grace to look a bit abashed. "You try growing up deaf. Even now, the number of times I get slammed into by kids on bikes because they forget I can't hear them coming up behind me, it's enough to make you seriously fear for the future. But then, that's always what old people say, isn't it! And truthfully, I've met plenty of kids who are inspirational and polite, that just doesn't describe what I've experienced with some of the local ones. But to answer your question, yes, I do believe one or more of them could have done it. As I told you, prejudice runs deep in some of the smaller villages. It's why the far-right political parties do well out here."

"Well, even if that's so, his classmates certainly aren't the only possibility. Off the top of my head, Lucius's parents might not have been happy about his friendship with Sebastian, and there are probably other parents who might jump to conclusions about the boys' relationship. Archie might have enemies willing to seek revenge in such a vicious way, and the Bonners themselves can't have been happy about their son's behavior on all fronts, although Rachel was certainly convincing as the grieving parent. She seems to blame me for the loss of her son, and I can't help feeling she's partly right, no matter how illogical it might seem."

Hayley's protest was immediate and heartfelt. "Of course you're not to blame, no one in their right mind could have foreseen this happening. None of us can really understand what Rachel's going through, thank goodness, but she's tough, and she'll come to see that this isn't your fault. Particularly after the killer is caught. She just needs someone to blame right now to make any sense of it."

"I hope you're right. So you think this Torksey has the wherewithal to catch a killer?"

"He seems competent enough. It was nice of him to let me go home as soon as possible the other day. His sergeant's an interesting one. Didn't say much while we were at your house, but she asked some intelligent questions about the neighbors while getting me back to my sick bed. Hopefully I didn't point the finger at anyone while I was feverish! She also seems to admire fictional female detectives; she noticed my Sara Paretsky collection, and asked me if I liked others, like Patricia Cornwell."

"Ah, the Valkyrie likes the chick dicks, does she? That improves my opinion of her." Vivien noted Hayley's raised eyebrows and realized a translation was needed. "It means a female private eye. In America."

"Ah," her neighbor eventually responded, "maybe you two can have a natter about blue-nosed revolvers hidden in purses and the perils of a pursuit in heels as you 'pump her for information'. Why do Americanisms so often sound sexual?"

"Just lucky, I guess. I wonder what Inspector Torksey reads."

"Sergeant Martin said he's more of a film buff, likes the old black and white classics. I think she mentioned *Rebecca* as his favorite."

"Daphne du Maurier, eh? Seems a bit melodramatic for our inspector."

"She told me he's from Cornwall, du Maurier's home county."

Hayley was visibly wilting as she spoke so Vivien suggested a nap and then returned to her television shows, her mind full of people and their possible motives. Sebastian was so young and innocent to have been the center of this maelstrom. She would do everything in her power to see that he was taken care of, even after his death. Especially after his death. She owed it to him.

Catching movement out of the corner of her eye, she rose

to look out the front window and saw the police removing the crime scene tape from the front door.

16

"People are almost always better than their neighbours think they are."

— George Eliot, *Middlemarch*

Geoffrey confirmed when he arrived that evening that the police had phoned giving permission to move back into their house, so after dinner he and Vivien transferred their few possessions and one grumpy cat across the street, where they struggled to feel comfortable again. The police had left a note on the kitchen counter with the name and number of a recommended cleaning service for dealing with the fingerprint powder and any remaining stains, but neither of them had the strength to think about that at the moment so they just went to bed early, holding hands while they stared at the ceiling and waited for sleep to come.

Despite a restless night, Thursday morning Vivien was at the Bickford library with a solicitous Becky, who made endless cups of tea in an attempt to provide aid and comfort. They had a quiet day, which Becky told her was usual midweek, but then school was out and the kids began to wander in looking for computers, friends, and any whiff of excitement. Anything but books.

Vivien was surprised when Samantha shyly approached the desk. Vivien nodded hello and cocked a questioning eyebrow at the girl. Samantha smiled, and there followed a few moments of silence while the girl worked out what she wanted to say.

"We all heard about Sebastian. Plus, it was in the news," she finally ventured.

Vivien had been avoiding the news but gave Samantha another nod indicating she should go on.

"I was really sorry. He was a nice guy. Is it true he was killed in your house?"

Vivien's double nod here was affirmative, and she took a deep breath to maintain her composure as the memory of seeing Sebastian's body flitted unwanted through her mind. The pain must have shown on her face because Samantha continued in an even softer tone of voice.

"Well, I just wanted to say, I'm sorry about the way Justin acted last time. He's really not always that bad. Something about Sebastian just rubs…I mean, rubbed him up the wrong way, I guess."

Vivien tilted her head to the side just for the sake of variety, and because she didn't want to interrupt the flow. She knew adults rarely listen to teenagers, and she didn't want to be one of those adults. Listening was easier anyway as she still found it hard to talk about the murder.

Her attention was rewarded with yet more confidences.

"He has this image to preserve, like, sort of the Big Man on Campus. And sometimes he has to act like a total badass to make the others respect him."

Vivien decided words were needed at this point.

"So, you're saying your boyfriend wasn't really torturing poor Sebastian for possibly being gay?" she asked.

Samantha tried to look shocked, and almost succeeded. "Oh no! Justin isn't that prejudiced. I mean, his best friend isn't even from Bickford!"

"Ah, well then," Vivien nodded sagely, "he is obviously broad-minded indeed. Did Justin at any point explain to Sebastian about this need to put up a tough front?"

"Well, no," Samantha admitted, avoiding Vivien's eyes. "I'm sure he would have, but there was never the chance. And you never know who's watching, do you?"

Vivien shook her head from side to side in apparent sympathy. It felt good to use other neck muscles, the nodding was giving her a crick. "Of course. How hard it must be never to be able to let down your guard."

"Exactly!" Samantha exclaimed. "He's really much nicer than people give him credit for, because they don't know him like I do, don't see how he is when we're alone. He's really so sweet and thoughtful. Just last week, he helped me with my maths homework, and he didn't have to do that."

Samantha blushed and Vivien surmised she was thinking about what happened after the maths homework, which might have had something to do with Justin's sudden generosity. Ah well, young love, there was no fighting it, however blind and stupid.

"Have the police been round to see Justin about Sebastian?" Vivien asked.

"Yes, and they were very mean. The short man kept asking Justin where he was the day before yesterday, so I finally told him Justin was with me all afternoon."

"And was he?" Vivien prompted softly.

Samantha was suddenly all wide-eyed innocence. "Well, of *course* he was. It's not like I'd lie, is it?"

"Anyone might be tempted to lie to protect those they care about. But I've met DI Torksey, and I have a feeling he can sniff out a lie better than most, so I wouldn't advise it. If Justin doesn't know anything about the murder, it's best to make a clean breast of it before the inspector pays him more attention than he's worth."

Samantha's face had taken on a mutinous look. "I'm not sure you should be saying 'breast' in the library," she retorted before flouncing off in a huff.

Vivien's gaze followed the girl thoughtfully. She doubted Justin had anything to do with Sebastian's death. He was a bully, and most bullies were cowards at heart and never did much to back up their threats. Plus, there was the matter of where he could have gotten a gun, as such weapons weren't as free-flowing as they were in America. But the boy was obviously somewhere he wasn't supposed to be, or he wouldn't have prevaricated until Sam felt obliged to alibi him. Vivien wondered if it might be worth her while to save the inspector some time and find out where that might have been.

Young Thomas was next to approach the desk, his face alight with curiosity.

"Miss, did I hear you say that boy was gay? The one who died?" he queried breathlessly.

Vivien cringed internally at the awful excitement the boy displayed. "I don't know if he was gay or not, that's personal business and it has nothing to do with him dying." She hoped. "Are you worried about it, Thomas, about anything happening to you? Because we can find you someone to talk to about it if you are."

Thomas giggled. "Oh no, miss, I'm not worried about anything happening to me. I mean, I'm not gay or anything, right?"

"It doesn't matter if you are, Thomas. Lots of people are gay. The world is made up of all kinds of people with different likes, different beliefs, and different-colored skin. That's what makes it so interesting to listen to people and get to know them."

Thomas looked distinctly doubtful. "I don't think that's true, miss. Everyone I know likes who they're supposed to and goes to St Peter's up on the hill. And we're all the same color, except for Sam there whose dad is P…"

"Hold it right there!" Vivien frantically interrupted. "I want you to be very careful what you say next as I won't allow racial slurs in this library. Not only is it rude and intolerant, but I have to report such things to my management and I don't need the extra paperwork."

Thomas rolled his eyes. "Whatever. I'm just saying that Sam's dad isn't from around here."

"Which is why we all need to work hard to make him feel welcome. I hope someday you will get to travel the world and meet lots of interesting people, Thomas, who will do the same for you. Until then, why not enjoy learning about the world from people who have seen it? For instance, there's me. I'm from far away, and I might have different beliefs and ideas that you'd find interesting."

Thomas's mouth formed a perfect 'o' of surprise. "Miss, are you saying that you're a lesbo? And if you're not a Christian, does that mean you're a heathen, too?"

Vivien momentarily closed her eyes to stop herself saying something she'd regret. The boy was young and inexperienced. Here was her chance to open his mind.

"I may be, or I may not be, any of those things, Thomas. But like I said, none of that makes any difference to me being a good librarian, or a good person."

Thomas shook his head. "Bet me ma would have summin' to say 'bout that." He walked away, still mumbling, and Vivien decided on the spot never to pursue a career in child psychology.

17

"There is always a pleasure in unravelling a mystery, in catching at the gossamer clue which will guide to certainty."
— Elizabeth Gaskell, *Mary Barton*

The jungle drums were beating a steady rhythm as the African chief approached Vivien and Harrison Ford, who were both tied to posts. The chief was perfectly ready and willing to sacrifice them in order to mollify the angry gods causing a drought across the land. There didn't seem to be any way Vivien and her hunky lover were going to escape this time.

Vivien glanced desperately at Harrison, who treated her to his signature lip curl and suggested she answer the door.

"Whaaaa?" Vivien pried open sleep-encrusted eyes to find herself in her bedroom *sans* Harrison or—thankfully—African chief, but the drumming continued, now identifiable as someone knocking on the front door. Geoffrey had already gone to work, and since she didn't have a shift at the library that day, Vivien had hoped to enjoy a lazy morning. But the peremptory nature of the knock declared it was not to be.

Donning faux-fur-lined moccasins and a fuzzy bathrobe, she went downstairs and opened the door to find Hayley standing there. Her neighbor looked uncharacteristically mussed—in fact, her clothes almost matched—and she was obviously brimming with news.

"What?" Vivien spat out with all the linguistic charm of the recently roused.

"The gun. They've got a gun. Someone left an anonymous message at the police station to say the murder weapon would be found in the vicarage! Josh called and told me."

Vivien was having trouble getting her mind around this concept.

"The vicarage? The place where the vicar lives? Reverend Edwards?"

"Yes, yes, and yes!" Hayley practically yelled. "Inspector Torksey is over there interviewing Jonathan right now! Who would have thought he'd have anything to do with murdering Sebastian? I wonder if he's secretly homophobic. I mean, I know everyone's supposed to be tolerant these days, but it's always in the news how lots of religious leaders don't want to marry gay people…"

"Whoa, pull back on Silver there, Lone Ranger. Just because someone reports a gun in the vicarage, it's a long way from that to it being the murder weapon, and from there to that nice vicar being the murderer. Personally, if anonymous calls are involved, I think it's a sure sign that someone's taking the police down a handy little detour."

Hayley's enthusiasm dampened perceptibly, and Vivien suddenly remembered she had hostess duties, no matter how early it was. "Want to come in for a cup of something?"

Hayley smiled, perkiness restored. "Coffee would be nice."

She followed Vivien into the kitchen and continued to regale her with details once settled on the single kitchen stool as the latter started a pot of Colombian coffee.

"Josh says the call was left on the station's answering machine early this morning, and the voice is disguised so you can't tell if it's a man or a woman. But it said the police would find the murder weapon in Jonathan's office. Torksey was called immediately and went over to the vicarage where Jonathan allowed him to look around. They found it in one of the desk drawers."

"And what did Edwards say to that?"

"Josh doesn't know, he was sent to guard the front door at that point. But he says the gun looked pretty old."

"Well, I can't imagine Jonathan Edwards is involved. He's not a stupid man, if he knew the gun was in there, he would have asked them to get a search warrant, even if it made them suspicious. Just letting them walk in and find the gun you've used to murder someone is by far the worst option."

Hayley paused, head tilted. "Maybe he wanted to be caught? Maybe he's making some sort of statement with the murder?"

"Have you ever seen him with Sebastian? Has he ever said anything to make you think he disliked the boy for any reason?" Vivien asked.

Hayley thought for a moment and sighed. "No, I've never heard him say anything, and he's never been anything but friendly to Sebastian the few times I've seen them together. He really does seem to be a nice man, and I know he's worked closely with Rachel Bonner to improve the community with special events for the older residents as well as families with children."

Vivien smiled at her friend's disappointment. "What a pity. Well, we'll keep him on the list until we hear what the police do with him. He wouldn't be the first 'nice' man to commit murder when pushed too far, and there could be a motive we don't know about."

They were suddenly interrupted by a very firm knock on the front door. Vivien reflected it was her day to be visited by people with strong knuckles and made a knocking sign to alert Hayley before she walked through the hall and opened the door to reveal a young policeman in full uniform. Minus the gun, Vivien remembered. She felt comforted by the fact that, except for special forces, English police don't carry firearms. It felt ironically safer, she supposed. Not like at her cousin's wedding in Dallas when half the audience was packing as if Armageddon might interrupt the ceremony. Then again, the bride and groom were from different political parties, so it wasn't out of the question.

This particular policeman's features were fresh and handsome, and enough like Hayley's to immediately give away his identity. He ducked his head shyly as he greeted Vivien.

"Hello, Ms. Brandt. Hayley's told me a lot about you. I hope you don't mind me stopping by, but Hayley told me earlier she might be here and to try your house if no one was home at hers."

"Hey, Josh, come on in!" Hayley piped up from behind Vivien, having followed her from the kitchen. "Vivien, as you may have deduced, this is my younger brother. The one who used to break all my jewellery and try to read my diary."

Josh's face took on a distinctly pink color as they all trooped back to the kitchen. At Vivien's request he grabbed an extra chair from the dining room and started signing once they were settled. "Really, Hayley, Ms. Brandt doesn't want to know about all that now. And you're undermining my authority again. I've asked you not to be your usual flippant self toward me when I'm in uniform!"

Hayley sighed and threw her brother an apologetic look. "Well, now that I've spoiled your career, why don't you tell us what you found out. Are you on a break?"

"Yeah, I told them I had to pick something up from you and would meet them back at the station. You know I can't reveal everything about a working investigation, though, Hay. Have a heart."

"All right, what *can* you tell us, then?" Hayley went on relentlessly. "You know very well we'll keep it to ourselves."

Embarrassed again, Josh kept his face toward Hayley as he indicated Vivien with a quick left shift of the eyes. They were nice eyes, Vivien noted with detachment. He was going to be a good-looking man as he aged. Lucky for some local girl, no doubt. Or boy: it never paid to assume. She had a fleeting thought about introducing him to her stepdaughter someday, before returning to the present to address his unspoken concern.

"Call me Vivien please, Josh. And yes, I promise nothing you tell us gets repeated. I don't know enough people yet to be the town gossip." She smiled with what she thought was motherly reassurance, but Josh looked thoughtful for a moment before continuing.

"It's not certain yet, but I did overhear William, one of the older guys, say that the gun found was a Webley Mark IV. Evidently, it's an old army issue, used up until the late 1970s. Will says it might even be worth something. You know, aside from being evidence and all."

"Did anyone know who it belonged to? Did Reverend Edwards say he owned it?" Vivien queried.

"Well, no, he says he has no idea where it came from, but..." Josh tailed off and looked at Hayley, whose wrinkled brow indicated deep thought. She surfaced and looked toward Vivien.

"What my brother is too cautious to say is that everyone will think of Colonel Jay. He was still fighting in the 1970s, Rhodesian Bush War, I believe, and may very well have owned such a gun, although technically I suppose he should have given it back when he left the service."

She paused. "It does put a different perspective on things. If it is the colonel's gun, Reverend Edwards never would have used it to kill someone and left it in his own office. He spends quite a bit of time with the colonel, and they've always been friendly, I don't think he'd want to frame the man for murder."

"Hmmm," mused Vivien. "It sounds like it might be time to pay the colonel that visit he offered me. You free, Hayley?"

Josh groaned. "You can't go now. The police are headed over there, and if you show up it will be obvious I've told you things. Come on, ladies, don't do this to me!"

Vivien relented. "You're right, Josh. We'll pay our respects on Sunday, if that works for you, Hayley?" Hayley nodded, still clearly distracted by whatever thoughts the news of the gun had triggered.

"Come on, Josh," said his sister. "I'd better go get you something so you don't walk into the station empty-handed and put the lie to your kind deed. What do you want to borrow?" Hayley got off her chair and Josh walked backwards in front of her out the door, obviously accustomed to the requirements of conversation with his sister and signing as he went.

"I could use a nice tablecloth. I'm having Angela over to dinner in the flat tonight, and she'd be impressed if I laid a nice table. What about wineglasses too?"

They left the house chattering happily to each other and Vivien took advantage of the ensuing peace to pour herself a cup of coffee before settling down on the sofa in front of an episode of *Gilmore Girls*. She just loved those girls. They made living in a small town seem such fun, even though things rarely happened there. *If only*, Vivien thought.

18

"The light music of whisky falling into glasses made an agreeable interlude."

— James Joyce, *Dubliners*

The next morning was one of those that made you think all the rumors about English weather were no more than malicious gossip put about by the French. Certainly, there was a cloud or two in the sky, and the temperatures weren't balmy by any means, but the air was crisp and fresh and the sun shone with a cool, mellow beam that was as understated as an English compliment.

It was also the anniversary of her first meeting Geoffrey, so Vivien amused herself thinking of things they could do to mark the occasion. She was even more excited when Geoffrey asked if his lovely wife wanted to go tour a stately home to celebrate, this time without the tumble down the stairs.

His lovely wife most certainly did, so they set out for a local English Heritage property which promised Chippendale furnishings combined with wonderful gardens, satisfying both Vivien's love of interior design and

Geoffrey's fondness for greenery. Since Geoffrey and Vivien already had two complete households to try and combine after they got married, instead of home appliances they'd asked for contributions to life memberships of the National Trust and English Heritage as wedding gifts, and their family and friends had come through in spades. Now they could visit any of the many properties in either scheme for free and they greatly enjoyed walking around grand houses pretending they were members of the idle rich for a few hours.

Despite all the lavish English historical dramas Vivien had watched growing up in America, she tried to keep in mind while touring crystal-laden drawing rooms and marble-panelled halls that this had been the domain of the .001 percent, not the vast majority. If war and taxation hadn't intervened, the upper crust would probably still be whacking croquet balls on the lawn before tucking into some Battenberg cake in a fully kitted folly. The cake, of course, having been carried out by numerous servants who felt themselves lucky to have a half-day off on Sundays so they could walk ten miles to visit their ailing mothers.

These were the remnants, however beautifully evocative, of an unfairly privileged few, and she always ensured she gave the servants their due by taking an interest in what happened below stairs as well, even though it was seldom as prettily decorated.

Mind you, Vivien mused, America was just as bad or worse, as she'd discovered when she went round the Rhode Island mansions of the Vanderbilts and their ilk, who forbade President Roosevelt's name to be uttered in their hallowed homes after he raised their taxes to ninety percent following

World War II. "That man" was evidently as close as anyone was allowed to come when referring to the former president, and any slips of the tongue would have echoed off the thirty-foot-high gilded ceilings and caused instant dismissal.

But no matter what necessitated the sale of these places, Vivien loved that you could now roam around them and imagine donning a Worth gown to dine with the duke and duchess, at least until you were brought back to earth by the cramped coldness of the servants' quarters.

She slightly preferred National Trust properties because they restored the houses to their previous grandeur. English Heritage tended to simply preserve the homes in the state they got them, and their generally run-down appearance made it harder to visualize the lifestyle in its heyday.

For Geoffrey, it was his chance to enthusiastically point out all the members of the nobility who had married Americans for their wealth, their tendency to install modern heating in drafty castles, and because they had a way with the servants. All of which suggested to Vivien that she'd be the one dealing with plumbers and electricians when things went wrong in their own house.

Today they were visiting Brodsworth House, which had two distinct advantages: it was local, and they'd been there before, so Vivien had already explored it looking for hidden passages. Geoffrey had been somewhat taken aback the first time he went through a stately home with his beloved, watching her run her fingers over cracks in the wall or bumps in the bookcases, looking for triggers to pop open concealed doors. More often than not, they received stern looks and reprimands from watchful guides, but eventually Geoffrey learned to shrug and utter the words "She's American", earning him a sympathetic nod as he steered his recalcitrant wife into the next room.

They went through the house without incident, and afterward Vivien and Geoffrey wandered through the gardens hand in hand. Vivien gazed over the still-blooming collection of bright flowers and immaculately trimmed hedges and breathed a sigh of satisfaction. This was exactly what she'd needed, and Geoffrey sensed her change in mood.

"Feeling better?" he asked with just the right amount of light concern. He truly was proving to be an excellent spouse so far, but it reminded Vivien that today's enjoyment was merely a break from recent horrors.

"Better than the day I found that poor boy dead in the conservatory, you mean?"

Geoffrey sighed. "You and your American forthrightness. I never would have put it that way, but yes, I suppose I do."

"Except for the fact that I knew him, had talked to him, it all seems a bit unreal. I never imagined myself some sort of Jessica Fletcher running around discovering dead bodies."

Geoffrey's eyebrows rose. "I should hope not. I used to wonder why anyone would agree to meet that woman anywhere, even for coffee, considering how many people dropped dead in her vicinity. But seriously, how are you handling it? Any nightmares? Feelings of depression? You will tell me if you need to talk, or if you want professional help? There's nothing wrong with getting some counseling to help you deal with a traumatic event. You'll tell me, right?"

Vivien's eyes widened. "Now who's being naive? In California we have counseling for breakfast, it's the perfect way to start the day. It's your country that gets squidgy about mental health issues, resorting instead to a dose of 'stiff upper lip.'"

"Low blow!" Geoffrey replied in mock protest. "And unfair. We all talk to our dogs and horses while fox hunting, especially after a stirrup cup of sherry has loosened our tongues, and it does us a world of good!"

Vivien laughed, but then became serious as she addressed his previous question. "I keep going over how poor Sebastian was bullied from all sides, I suspect at home as well as at school. I feel horrible that I wasn't there for him when he needed me."

"When he was murdered, you mean? I'm personally just as glad you weren't. And I know it won't make a bit of difference me saying it, but I do wish you'd be careful about how closely you get involved in this situation. There's still a murderer out there, and it's just possible they know who you are."

"Likely, I'd say, someone must have gotten fairly close to Sebastian to kill him, so he probably knew and trusted whoever it was. Or at least, wasn't as afraid as he should have been. But please don't think I'm not listening to you, I understand you're concerned, and I promise to be careful."

She paused, deciding to lighten the mood. "Wait, are you sure this isn't just jealousy? Are you worried about me establishing a crime-fighting relationship with the devastatingly debonair Inspector Torksey?"

Geoffrey placed a splayed hand on his chest, silently mouthing "*Moi?*" before answering. "A poor substitute for a husband I'd be this early in our marriage if I wanted to wee in a circle around you every time something male approached. No, my dear, I trust you implicitly, and you are proving a good and faithful wife. So far. Although I suspect you have indeed impressed the good inspector."

Coming around a corner they found themselves in the extensive pet cemetery. Surrounded by trees, it was a peaceful, quiet spot with small, rounded tombstones featuring names such as Coup, Dash, and Nell, canine members of the Thellusson family, who had built the house. There were even grave markers for a couple of parrots.

"Wow, these folks loved their dogs. Maybe that's where I went wrong," Vivien moaned. "I should have gotten a dog. A dog wouldn't have deserted me in favor of the newest flavor of the month."

Geoffrey laughed. "Sydney hasn't deserted you, my darling. He and I are simply exploring a little male bonding. I'm sure if worse came to worst, he would be there to protect his beloved mistress with all the feline fury he could muster."

"Hmpf," was Vivien's response. "That theory may be tested based on my first month here." She paused to sniff a bloom on a nearby rosebush. "This wasn't how I thought moving to England would go. I had such dreams. But now it's all death and secrets and familiar words with strange pronunciations. My new exercise video keeps telling me to switch to my al*ter*nate leg, for heaven's sake. Throws me off every time."

Geoffrey turned and took her in his arms, smoothing her hair with his hand. "I know it's hard, but this will pass, and it's nothing to do with you, my love." He pulled back to look her in the eye. "There's still a lifetime together for us to fulfil those dreams."

Vivien gave him a weary smile. "Sebastian thought that, too."

Geoffrey sighed. "All right, then, let's *carpe diem*, darling, and live every minute to the fullest. If there are no guarantees, then let's just be incredibly glad we found each other and enjoy the hell out of what we have."

Vivien's smile was more genuine this time, so after she nodded her agreement they took themselves off for an overpriced full-blown English tea in a café that was once probably used to house some rich owner's very spoiled horses. They even managed to avoid thoughts of death and despair until they arrived home and spotted Hayley and Will across the street listening intently to Hayley's brother Josh, who was dressed in his police uniform. Despite the cheerfulness of Hayley's purple-striped leggings and daisy-enhanced pink sweater, the expressions on both their faces revealed that whatever Josh was telling them, it wasn't making them at all happy.

19

"Looks like we've got another mystery on our hands."
— Fred Jones, *Scooby-Doo*

"They've just taken Colonel Jay down to the station and dumped him in a cell!" Hayley exclaimed from her position on Vivien's new wine-colored sofa, where she and Will had come over and plopped themselves after Josh left. As Hayley rested the side of her slightly tearful face on one of the cushions, Vivien felt a fleeting moment of regret that she hadn't ordered the protective upholstery treatment. She quickly dismissed the thought as shallow and selfish and donned a concerned look, adding a supportive head shake for good measure. Will sat next to his wife, his hand stroking her arm. Geoffrey was emanating manly concern from across the room. Sydney had fled to less emotional climes.

"Did they actually arrest him? And charge him with the murder?" Geoffrey asked.

"Josh says it's on suspicion of murder. What with it being his gun and him not being able to provide an alibi, they've just jumped ahead to accusing him of murdering his grandson."

Vivien shook her head. "I don't fully understand how it works here, but surely that's not the same as arresting him for the murder? Isn't it more like a chance to keep him for questioning under caution? They can't seriously have any proof that Colonel Jay murdered the boy. I know I'm a relative stranger, but I saw nothing to indicate he was anything but fond of the child."

"They simply have to have reasonable cause for suspicion," said Will. "They can detain him for up to seventy-two hours for questioning before they have to decide if they want to charge him for the crime."

Geoffrey took a practical tack. "Has he called a solicitor or gotten any legal advice, Hayley?"

"No. That's the odd thing. Josh says he hasn't said anything. He won't say anything. He's just sitting there staring at the wall, and he won't respond to any of the police's questions. Josh says you can see he's closed down. Maybe it's something he learned in the army, but I don't think it's going to help in this case. I'm so worried for him. He's not young anymore, and this can't be doing his heart any good."

"Well, keeping quiet won't do any harm either, I suppose," Geoffrey soothed. "And I'm sure the police will make sure he's comfortable enough. But I wonder why he won't say anything if he didn't do it? And don't give me that look, Vivien, there's been many a stranger murderer than Colonel Jay, and we don't know the circumstances. Sebastian's death could have been an accident of some sort, or Jay could have been protecting himself or someone else. He could still be protecting someone with his silence." He turned back to Hayley. "You say his daughter has an alibi?"

"Yes. I suppose that's the first thing everyone will think,

that he's protecting her, but Josh says her alibi is solid. She has a receipt and a witness to prove she was at a petrol station at the time of the murder. Besides, if it's hard to believe the colonel killed his grandson, how much more heinous to think of a mother killing her own child!"

"I say again, stranger things…" Geoffrey mumbled before being silenced by another look from Vivien. It was Will who came to the rescue with a suggestion for action.

"I have a solicitor friend who is quite well known for his experience in criminal trials. I'm sure he would be willing to help if the Bonners haven't retained somebody already for Colonel Jay. Geoffrey, why don't you and I go check with Archie and Rachel and offer any assistance that might be needed."

Geoffrey nodded and the two men stood up, casting worried glances at Hayley before leaving the room. After she heard the front door close, Vivien carefully watched her tear-streaked friend, waiting until Hayley looked up before she spoke. She was a bit surprised at the depth of emotion Hayley was obviously feeling, but reminded herself there was a lot about the village and its people that she didn't yet understand.

"Torksey and his people aren't villains, Hayley. They'll take care of Colonel Jay. And I'm sure he's been in worse places than in a warm jail cell."

Hayley nodded and took a deep breath, mastering her emotions enough to offer a wan smile. "I know. It's just all this trauma, and bad things happening to the nicest people. I've been trying to stay stoic, but it all reminds me…" She petered off as another sob came bursting forth.

Vivien waited patiently for her friend to continue, which

she eventually did. "I don't often talk about it, but my little sister was killed in a hit-and-run when we were children. They never found the driver, and I blamed myself because I'd run ahead to try to keep her from following me when it happened."

Vivien leaned over to put an arm around her. "But you were only a child, you can't blame yourself for that."

Hayley nodded. "I know. I'm better now, thanks to quite a bit of counseling and the support of my family. But when people die violently, especially young people, it tends to trigger bad memories for me, and they've been building since Sebastian's death." She paused, staring down at her hands clenching her knees. "I'm sorry, I know it must have been awful for you to find him, and now to have to listen to me moaning…" The tears restarted, with another of Vivien's new cushions taking the brunt of the shower.

Vivien stayed silent, knowing there was nothing useful to be said immediately, especially since Hayley was busy crying and wouldn't have been able to read her lips. When Hayley finally looked up, Vivien resumed the conversation with a softer, more sympathetic tone, somehow knowing it would be conveyed despite Hayley's deafness. "Of course you're upset by all this. Anyone would be. But know that I'm always here to listen."

She paused and considered how best to help her friend recover, deciding to approach it from another, more positive, angle. "Did your sister's death have anything to do with Josh's decision to go into law enforcement?"

Hayley nodded. "He was barely more than a baby at the time, but I think so. Fortunately, he's good at it, and I know he takes pride in that. He'll make sure Colonel Jay is comfortable, but he too must be wondering if he's guarding a man who has killed a child, just as our Maisie was killed."

"Well, I suppose the best thing to do is to establish Colonel Jay's guilt or innocence as quickly as possible, so everyone can stop wondering. Are you up for a bit of reconnaissance at the church tomorrow? Reverend Edwards told me at the Bonners' party that Colonel Jay quite often attends on Sundays along with many of the other people from the retirement homes, although he implied it was more to partake in the gossip after the service than to listen to the sermon. Maybe we can learn something about his state of mind from some of his contemporaries."

After a final sniff, Hayley straightened up and took on a more determined look. "You're right, Vivien. All hands on deck. Any port in a storm. Now is the time for all good women to come to the aid of the party. Etcetera, etcetera, etcetera." She intoned this last platitude in her best Yul Brynner *King and I* voice, which told Vivien she was starting to recover her sense of humor.

"Is a puzzlement," Vivien quipped back using a quote from the same film, and the two friends smiled at each other.

They heard the front door open again as Geoffrey and Will returned from their errand. The two men entered the living room sporting an identical set of knitted brows.

"What happened? You look a bit confounded," said Vivien.

After a quick glance at Will, Geoffrey responded. "We have been informed in no uncertain terms that the Bonners take care of their own, and our advice is not required."

"By whom?"

"Well, rather nicely by Archie, then more firmly by the lady of the house."

Hayley spoke up. "I suppose you can't blame them for circling the wagons, as Vivien would say. First their son is murdered, and now Rachel's father is accused. Aside from the domestic tragedy of it all, Archie's no doubt being bombarded by advice from his fellow ministers and spin doctors about how to handle it, as well as being hounded by the press. They'll want to turn to people they know and trust to keep this business as private as they can."

"Indeed," Vivien agreed in a tone that indicated a 'but' was coming. "But you have to wonder how far they'll go to defend the father accused of killing their son. It's the mother of all conflicts of interest."

20

"The family—that dear octopus from whose tentacles we never quite escape, nor, in our inmost hearts, ever quite wish to."

— Dodie Smith, *Dear Octopus*

After the Masons had left, Vivien gazed glumly at the beautiful sunset through her kitchen window and felt utterly exhausted. Damn the British weather for not matching her mood, she thought. Any other day, grey skies and rain would have been a given.

After some careful introspection she decided her ennui had two causes. First, there was the fact that there was little she could do to advance her informal investigation into Sebastian's death except talk to people and hope something resembling a clue was dropped into the conversation. It left the awful possibility that the case might be closed after the police's arrest of Colonel Jay.

And second, she was dreading the weekly online chat with her family back home.

She knew her mother and father regularly braved the

technological wilderness to surf the Internet for news of England now that they had a daughter living there (or "the Interweb", as her father called it, his voice full of pride at his own trendiness). They'd also taken to watching the American PBS channel's broadcast of the BBC news, constantly surprising Vivien by asking her about British events she wasn't even aware of. This meant Vivien would have to tell them about Sebastian's death and her part in finding him before they ran across any references to it themselves. The fact that they hadn't been in touch yet undoubtedly meant they'd so far missed this particular news tidbit, but she couldn't rely on them remaining ignorant forever, and there would be hell to pay if they discovered she'd kept such a thing from them.

She still had some time before the eight-hour difference made it acceptable to call, so Vivien closed the drapes to block out the annoying sunlight, popped in a DVD of *The Monkees* TV series, then grabbed a blanket and curled up on the sofa to cheer herself up watching the whacky capers of those madcap musicians. After a few minutes she was joined by Sydney, who was licking his whiskers in appreciation of a tasty snack surreptitiously provided by Geoffrey. Her husband also wandered in a moment later and settled on the other side of her to enjoy listening to 'Last Train to Clarksville'.

Vivien was awakened sometime later by a tinny ringing indicating she had a call coming in on her iPad. The TV was turned off and she was stretched out on the sofa, the blanket tucked around her. The lack of light coming through the drapes told her she must have been asleep for over an hour.

Reaching over to pick up the iPad off the teakwood coffee

table, she opened the cover and touched a green check mark to accept the call from her parents. Showtime.

"Hello, honey!" her mother chirped. Her parents' faces were squished together to fit within the camera range of her father's laptop. Even in their seventies they radiated the healthy glow that was the result of a life lived largely outdoors. "How are you? You look sleepy. Did you go to bed early? Is everything all right?"

Vivien moved her lips into a tremulous smile, hoping to transmit reassurance.

"Everything is fine, Mom, Dad."

An electronic blurp told them all that Vivien's younger sister had joined the call a moment before her face appeared. While Vivien had her father's red hair and height, Melanie was more tall and willowy like her mother, and they also shared the same dark hair and eyes.

"Hey y'all, what's happening? Vivien, you look plumb worn out!" Since Melanie had moved to Texas with her husband and three children, she'd taken to talking like she was in a John Wayne film. Vivien suspected she played it up especially for these family chats.

"Melanie, Charlotte, leave the poor girl alone, why don't you?" her father admonished fondly before returning his gaze to his eldest. "But seriously, Viv, is there something on your mind? You do seem a bit pale." Her father was the only one allowed to call her by the shortened version of her name, and Vivien suddenly felt a wave of love envelop her from across the ocean.

"As a matter of fact, there is something you all should know about."

Her mother screeched. "I knew it! You're pregnant!" She

turned to slap her husband on the shoulder. "I told you, Ted, she just needed to get settled with the right man!"

"Mom. Mom!" Vivien interrupted. "I am not pregnant. I am not going to be pregnant. I'm forty-eight, for heaven's sake. Plus, you already have three utterly spoiled grandchildren"—a protesting yelp from Melanie could be heard at this juncture—"and I will be delighted to renew your acquaintance with your step-granddaughter when you next visit. But I'm afraid that's going to be the extent of the reproduction in this family."

Her mother settled back in her chair with a sigh as Vivien continued. "This is something else, and it's not nearly as delightful. I'm afraid there's been a murder in the village here."

Her announcement was followed by a shocked silence as Vivien watched various emotions ranging from concern to fear flit across her parents' faces. Melanie just looked curious and was the first to respond.

"What's happened, Sis? And I assume it doesn't involve Geoffrey, or you'd have let us know earlier."

"No, Geoffrey is fine. But it has affected us both as I'm afraid I was the one to find the body, which was in our conservatory. It was a young neighbor, someone I'd met through my library job. I hired him and a friend to do some work for me, and I came home from the market on Wednesday to find he'd been shot."

"Oh dear Lord in Heaven, Vivien," her mother exclaimed. "What the heck is going on in that village of yours? I thought you didn't have guns over there, that it was all so much safer than here. Do you know who did it? Have the police arrested anyone?" Charlotte turned to her husband. "We never should have let her move there, Ted, she's too far away, I told you this would happen!"

Ted put an arm around his wife and gently squeezed her quiet while still talking to the screen. "Pretty sure you didn't tell me someone would get shot in Vivien's conservatory, hon, and I'm also pretty sure Vivien's not twelve anymore and would have rightly protested any attempt to stop her marrying her handsome Brit and moving to the country of her dreams. Now Vivien, why don't you tell us what's happening with this case, and if there's anything we can do to help you through what must be a very troubling time, eh?"

Vivien gave her father a small, grateful smile and proceeded to tell her family about Sebastian and the subsequent arrest of his grandfather for murder.

"But honestly, folks," she continued, "I really don't think Colonel Jay did it. I mean, I only met him the once, but I didn't see any indication he would murder anyone, much less the grandson he told me he adores."

"Well, I suppose you can't always tell just by looking into their eyes. Do the police have any other suspects?" her father wanted to know.

"If they do, they're not telling me, but it had to be someone who knew where the colonel kept his gun and where Sebastian was that afternoon. And had a motive to kill him. Most of the people close to him have alibis, but it's hard to imagine a stranger finding the gun and then randomly killing someone in a private home on the other side of the village."

Screams were suddenly heard somewhere in the background of Melanie's San Antonio home, and after spitting out some finely chosen swear words Melanie walked away from her computer to deal with the situation. They could hear her yelling, "Doug, what in the name of all that is holy is going on out there?"

Charlotte sighed. "I don't know where that girl got such a mouth on her. It's certainly not from my side of the family."

Ted shot his daughter a look that clearly stated, "Yeah, right", as her mother continued. "Vivien, you aren't thinking of interfering in this investigation, are you? I know you love to read all those murder mysteries, but this isn't some game, someone evil was in your house and killed that boy, and *ohmigod*, you've changed the locks, right?"

"The killer didn't have a key to the house, Mom, the victim did, and the police have it now. And no, I've no intention of trying to beat the police to a solution, do not worry." There was really no reason for her family to know she was throwing around theories with a neighbor, that was something they wouldn't be able to discover in any news broadcasts or internet forums. She hoped.

Melanie came back to rejoin the conversation just as Geoffrey approached and bent over behind his wife to wave to his in-laws. "Hello Charlotte, Ted, Melanie. Hope you're all well. And please don't worry about your daughter, I'm watching her like a hawk, I've put a monitor on her ankle so I know where she is at all times! And may I say, Charlotte, your new haircut is stunning, the perfect complement to your own natural beauty." He flashed a winning smile and Vivien saw her mother preen. Vivien was constantly amazed at what her husband got away with thanks to his English accent and dashing looks, but her father's laughter indicated he wasn't fooled by this blatant attempt to curry favor.

Geoffrey, his mission accomplished, waved goodbye and receded back into his man room to do manly things. After a few more expressions of concern from her mother and assurances from Vivien that she would be very careful of absolutely everything, the remainder of the conversation centered around Melanie's unruly brood followed by a discussion about who was experiencing hotter weather, something Vivien could take no part in and which only made her homesick for autumn barbeques and sipping a cool lemonade on the back deck.

As they started on their goodbyes, Charlotte looked at her daughter's somber face and Vivien could see the concern writ large in her mother's eyes.

"Are you sure you're okay, honey? This isn't getting you down? Because you can always come home for a visit."

For just one moment Vivien felt the almost irresistible pull of swimming pools, sunshine, and bounteous Mexican food, but she pushed it deep down inside before answering her mother.

"I'm good, Mom. I miss all of you very much, and the language and cultural differences are proving more troublesome than I thought they'd be. I ordered lemonade in a restaurant last Sunday and got Sprite again. I keep forgetting about that one. But I've met some lovely people who definitely aren't murderers, and Geoffrey and I are delighted to be living in the same country at last. Even Sydney has made himself at home and loves his new toasty conservatory. This is all just a blip, I promise. Everything will turn out fine."

"Well, all right, but you will call us if anything else happens? You know we're here any time you just need to talk. Tell Geoffrey to take good care of you or he'll have to answer to me, and I won't be sidetracked by his compliments. You're our baby and we love you. And Melanie too, of course." This last bit was followed by another snort from Vivien's sister.

"Take care of yourself, Viv honey," her father added.

Vivien looked at her parents and her sister and thought how lucky she was to belong to this family. She gave them her best smile.

"Try not to worry, please. Like I said, I'm sure this is a one-off situation and will be resolved in no time."

Melanie ended the call with her usual style. "Let's hope so, Sis. Now it's time to put out the fire and round up the dogs. Keep your saddle oiled!"

Vivien sat in silence for a moment after they'd all hung up. She had a distinct feeling that she'd just lied to her family. But then again, maybe she and Hayley would discover something at church tomorrow that would shine some light on the case. Heaven knows, there was no better place to wish for a miracle.

She made her way up to bed more hopeful than she'd been hours before and managed to sleep through the night for the first time since finding Sebastian's body.

21

"No, that is the great fallacy: The wisdom of old men.
They do not grow wise. They grow careful."
— Ernest Hemingway, *A Farewell to Arms*

To say Sunday dawned was optimistic, Vivien thought. It was rainy and overcast, once again jarring with her mood, which today was sunny and bright. She cheerfully reminded herself this was the weather that kept England's gardens green and beautiful, and donned a warmish tartan skirt, olive-green sweater set, and low-heeled knee-high boots in preparation for attending the local Church of England service with Hayley.

One of the many things Vivien appreciated about her new country was its fairly private attitude toward religion, compared to the noisy evangelism of the American version. Of course, if you lived in a country where historically your religion could have gotten you killed, keeping quiet about it seemed a sensible course of action. And she'd been stunned to discover that, even in this day and age, Tony Blair had felt he couldn't be Catholic and Prime Minister simultaneously, although Boris Johnson had later given it a go and the country had somehow survived.

Vivien also loved the peace and tranquility of the many old churches, despite hoping a hefty amount of gossip went on behind the scenes (if the *Father Brown* television series was to be trusted). She grabbed her umbrella and headed over to pick up Hayley, who met her at the door with her coat already on. Seeing her neighbor's gloomy glance at the sky, Hayley wisely avoided the traditional introductory chit-chat about the weather, and they began their short walk to the church in companionable silence.

As they approached St James the Lesser, Vivien couldn't help admiring the architecture. The looming steeple and gargoyled gutters had a haunting air, appropriate for the surrounding cemetery and the many tombs she knew were lodged around the walls inside. She'd been told by a parishioner during her first walk round it that George Washington's ancestors had lived in the area and attended services. The woman's tone seemed to suggest the American Revolution was a most ungrateful response from a very naughty descendant.

Entering, Vivien inhaled deeply to appreciate the slightly moldy smell present in such buildings, and Reverend Edwards smiled in their direction as they took their seats in a pew halfway down. Looking forward over a sea of grey hair, Vivien was reminded most churchgoers these days were elderly and attendance was waning. She sometimes wondered if this was because of the prevalence of religion in British schools, giving children something to rebel against. Maybe America had gotten it right with the separation of church and state.

But whatever the reason, today Vivien was pleased to note the church was at least fairly well populated. She could see Archie Bonner near the front, his head bowed and hands clasped, although Rachel was conspicuously missing from his side. Vivien supposed grief took people in different ways and everyone found solace where they could. Today, at least, Rachel was not looking for it here, but her heart went out to Sebastian's father, whose beautiful dark blue Italian suit couldn't hide the despair apparent in his bent back and hunched shoulders.

There was a particularly large gathering of elderly people a couple of rows in front of Vivien and Hayley. They muttered to each other as a group, making it likely they were the contingent from the retirement community, and Colonel Jay's contemporaries. Although many of them wore clothes well past their best, it was a generation that believed in dressing up to show respect, so woolen suits and tweed skirts were predominant. Vivien was glad she hadn't given in to her desire to be comfortable in pants. Or trousers, as they were called here; she mustn't forget 'pants' was used to describe underwear. And, oddly, as a swear word. Like she didn't have enough language pitfalls to worry about just around food and drink (chips? biscuits?) without also having to deal with fashion *faux pas* (or was it *faux pas*es?). Glancing sideways she confirmed Hayley had likewise dressed in a plaid skirt and collared blouse, so there would be no scandalized looks when they approached the retirees after the service. Well, not to do with their clothes, anyway.

As they listened to the readings and the sermon (today's topic was the Good Samaritan, as if Vivien needed to be reminded of her duty when finding someone injured), she noted that Edwards was careful to keep his face angled where Hayley could easily read his lips, which made Vivien like him even more. His sermon was interesting and full of historical insight about the various issues in play at the time the story was written. The village was certainly lucky in their vicar.

When the final hymn was sung, the blessing given, and the notices read, Vivien nudged Hayley and they began to edge their way forward to get nearer their quarry. Pretending to consult a hymnal, they loitered in the aisle near the older folks, and Vivien realized it was their lucky day as she overheard some of them talking about Colonel Jay. One of the men was telling the group that the colonel had been released the day before due to lack of evidence, as it was determined too many people had access to the murder weapon. This welcome news put the group in good humor, and they started reminiscing about the colonel's more outrageous antics.

"Do you remember that time he decided he needed a pot-bellied pig to keep him company?" said one plump-yet-wizened lady in a grey cloche festooned with pink roses.

"Oh yes," her companion snickered, a tall, thin woman with sharp blue eyes behind half-moon spectacles. "That pig went everywhere with him. One night I went to visit the colonel and it was sitting in the wingback chair opposite him in front of the fire. He'd even put something in a teacup for it, for all the world like it was his wife. He can be a bit eccentric."

Vivien thought that was an understatement, and idly wondered what else the man and his pig might have done together. Shopping? Showers? Watching *Babe: Pig in the City*?

"Mind you," said the first woman, "I never thought he was all that kind to his actual wife. He did tend to order poor Jessie about. And he fairly ignored little Rachel after her mother died, even though she was only nine at the time. A pig may have been amusing company for Jay, but it was certainly no proper parent for a child."

The other ladies nodded in solemn agreement as the whole group got up and started to wander toward the church hall, a modern wooden building located behind the church and accessible via a short path through a lawned area, where tea and cookies (*biscuits*, her mind automatically translated) were served following the service. They chattered as they went, some shuffling forward and others either hanging back to help or striding to the front. Vivien and Hayley brought up the rear, regulating their pace to stay close to the group as they entered the church hall where a dozen small tables and accompanying chairs were set up. Vivien took a moment to quietly mouth the news of the colonel's release to Hayley, who hadn't been able to see the faces of the speakers, and she could tell from her friend's expression that Josh would be getting a lecture about not keeping her up to date.

The walls were painted a pale pastel green inside and featured colorful pictures of Jesus doing shepherdy things for his flock, some of whom were actually sheep. There was the ubiquitous set of shelves containing second-hand books for sale in the back corner, and an open hatch on another wall gave onto the kitchen, where cups were being efficiently topped up with tea and coffee before being pushed through for serving.

The retirees split into groupings without discussion, their habits long set, and Vivien quickly looked around and spotted a table in the middle that no one had reached yet. She hurried over to claim it, purposely ignoring the annoyed stares of its usual inhabitants who arrived to find their seats taken and shuffled away mumbling grumpily. Vivien sat her handbag on the chair next to her, and two more of the people following veered off to sit elsewhere as Hayley caught up and moved the handbag to sit down. It was a good table for eavesdropping, you could hear and see everyone around.

They were both surprised when young Samantha emerged from the kitchen to grudgingly ask what they wanted to drink.

"Tea would be lovely, Sam, thank you. I didn't know you attended this church?" said Vivien.

Sam mumbled something about her mother making her help out once a month, then looked expectantly at Hayley, who also ordered tea, and the girl sauntered off to get it. Hayley and Vivien settled in to listen to the surrounding conversations as surreptitiously as they could, Vivien with ears and Hayley with eyes.

"Hard to believe Jay was locked up for this," said one of the older men, who looked very much like Hume Cronyn in *Cocoon*. (Or, come to think of it, Hume Cronyn in anything.) "Not possible he could have done the thing, of course."

"I don't know, Harold," said the plump lady. "It was his gun, after all. And you know poor Sebastian had tendencies toward an alternative lifestyle, as I believe it's called. Many's the time I've heard you and the colonel tell derogatory stories about 'sissy soldiers' and how they brought shame to the uniform."

"Aw, come now, Maude," Harold protested. "Everyone knew about that gun and where he kept it. He loved waving it around to impress us. And the other stuff is just talk. Even if we made fun of nancy boys back when we were soldiers, that kind of thing is all over the television and the news now, what with them being able to marry and everything. Jay never would have held that against his own grandson."

"Maybe so, maybe not. Prejudices are seldom rational. I tend to agree with you, but who knows what really goes on inside another person's head?"

This proclamation was answered by a series of grunts as the group fell into silent contemplation of the mysteries of humankind. Or they might have been mentally ranking the various biscuits, thought Vivien, it was hard to tell. At this point Sam came back with the tea and caught Vivien and Hayley quietly concentrating.

"What are you listening for?" she asked loudly, smiling as her victims practically jumped out of their seats.

Vivien's protests were all the more vociferous for being tinged by guilt.

"Listening? We're not listening to anything. And it's not exactly tactful to accuse Hayley of such a thing, young lady."

Sam's smile quickly faded as she plonked the cups on the table, sloshing tea over the edges.

"Whatever. Like anything you all say could be interesting anyway." She stalked back to the kitchen, and Vivien felt suitably chastised for taking her embarrassment out on the girl.

The inhabitants of the other tables were gazing curiously at them now. With eyes cast firmly toward the floor, the two would-be sleuths finished their tea and gathered their belongings to beat a hasty retreat.

"Well that was a waste of time," Vivien complained as they walked back home.

"I don't know," said Hayley. "We learned even more people knew about the gun and that Seb's, um, preferences were acknowledged in the wider village."

"I tend to agree with Harold, though. Homosexuality isn't the 'sin' it was once portrayed as, and if the elderly contingent has grown tolerant, is it likely anyone younger would have been that mortally offended by it? As something to bully someone with, maybe, but not to murder over. No, I think the cause must be elsewhere, and if we can uncover other motives, we'll be that much closer to finding Seb's killer."

Hayley looked at Vivien curiously. "Weren't you the one who said the other kids were threatening Sebastian and Lucius in the library?"

"Yes, but kids don't particularly care what the sin is, they just want to have an excuse for their bad behavior, which is undoubtedly the case with Justin and his posse. If it wasn't being gay, it would have been religion, or weight, or something else. Children can be brutal little beasts."

"And so speaks the purposely childless," Hayley laughed. "I know I've been harsh about these kids, but I still hope to enjoy my own pitter-patter of little feet someday, and will be depending on you to act as the firm-but-kind babysitter, à la Julie Andrews. Of course," she smiled wickedly, "my child will be perfectly obedient and charming to his or her elders. It's all in the parenting. Now, let's go roust our husbands from their sofas and have some lunch!"

22

"A good local pub has much in common with a church, except that a pub is warmer, and there's more conversation."

— William Blake

After an uneventful day subbing for a sick employee at one of the branch libraries, including exciting tasks such as cleaning the books, Vivien fed a very vocal Sydney and then collapsed on her living room sofa, closed her eyes, and put off thinking about what to have for dinner. Which was just as well because Geoffrey's arrival twenty minutes later came with a proposition.

"How about going to the Donkey for the weekly pub quiz?"

The local pub was actually called the Three-Legged Mare, which had made Vivien gloomily imagine a horse that had lost a leg in some farming-related accident. In fact, Geoffrey informed her, it was a term for a gallows that could hang three people at once, which strangely didn't make her feel any better about it. Whether it was because the villagers shared her distaste or they just liked catchier names, they unanimously called it the Wonky Donkey instead.

Vivien opened one eye. "They have a weekly quiz on a Monday night? Are they sadists?"

"Nonsense. It's just a way of extending the social joys of the weekend. Although I must warn you, I've heard some of them take winning quite seriously."

"And why would we want to leave our nice quiet house and subject ourselves to trivia-maddened neighbors?"

"Because they also serve large sandwiches at the break and the prizes include bottles of alcohol as well as cash."

Vivien sat up sharply. "Well why didn't you say so? No cooking plus Bacchanalian revelry. A winning combination. I'll go up and change. Can we go early and get an *amuse bouche* beforehand, so I don't feel the need to attack the poor sandwich carrier when the time comes?"

Geoffrey paused to form that mental picture and decide his answer. "Yes, I suppose. But there's no need to dress up, best to wear your trainers in case that attacking thing proves necessary and you have to give chase."

They wandered over to the pub well ahead of the nine o'clock quiz start only to find the tables already full of people. Fortunately, Will and Hayley were there and Hayley waved them over while Will went in search of extra chairs. Vivien nodded her way through the crowd, acknowledging several now-familiar faces.

The pub had the usual sturdy oak chairs and hideously swirly carpet she'd come to expect in such establishments. (It was almost as appalling as the pink shag carpet she'd seen in the bathroom of one of the houses they'd viewed when looking to buy, and which now featured prominently in her decorating nightmares.)

Vivien knew from experience the wine wouldn't be up to

her Californian standards, so she asked Geoffrey for a pint of lager and he made his way to the bar.

Hayley waited until they were all seated with their drinks to avoid having to repeat herself.

"So, evidently they released Colonel Jay because they didn't have enough evidence that he'd used the gun to be able to hold him. Although he's been given the usual advice about not leaving the area, blah blah blah, according to my brother. But I'm just relieved the poor man doesn't have to sit in a jail cell anymore." Hayley paused to take a sip of her wine as Vivien nodded in agreement.

Will, after emitting a sigh that told everyone he'd already heard all of this, took advantage of the pause to change the topic, signing the conversation for his wife. "I didn't realize you two were quiz fans!" he said to Geoffrey and Vivien. "Do join our team, we can use Vivien's knowledge of American politics and sporting teams."

"I'll do my best with the former," Vivien assured them, "but outside of baseball I'm afraid I'm not going to be of much use on sports. Well, not unless the unlikely subject of beach volleyball comes up. My first husband spent most of our money betting on that, so winners and losers on the sand courts came to have very personal consequences, including contributing to our divorce."

"You divorced him because he bet on beach volleyball?" asked Will.

"Only because he bet badly. If he'd made a fortune on it love might have survived." Vivien winked to make sure they understood she was being sarcastic, not shallow. "In truth, the betting was merely a last straw on that particular camel's back. Charlie also had an aversion to showing up on time for anything. Oh, and there was his tendency to make me feel like I was crazy." Vivien stopped and sipped her drink, aware she was once again sharing more than was proper by English standards.

"At least you've traded up," Hayley said, earning a grateful smile from Geoffrey. She passed a piece of paper covered in blurry black-and-white photos over to them. "See if you can identify any of our missing celebrities."

Geoffrey scanned the page. "You've done well to get that many of them, these aren't the clearest pictures. I think you'll find number ten is Joan Jett."

"Wow, our quizmaster is really reaching back in time for these now. I'd never have got that. Go ahead and fill it in," said Will, passing over a pencil.

Vivien glanced at the photos as her husband wrote in his answer. "Geoffrey is a fervent fan of girl bands from the 80s. Don't get him going on Bananarama, you'll hear the lecture that almost ruined our romance before it began. Number three is a very young Barack Obama, I believe."

"See!" Hayley crowed. "I knew you two would be an asset to the neighborhood!"

Vivien laughed. "I'll be happy if I can help win that bottle of rum the quizmaster is waving around as a prize."

Eventually eight out of ten photographs were identified and Vivien felt free to check out the neighboring tables. Neither the Ramakrishnans nor the Fredericks were there, which she supposed made sense as one couple owned a late-night market and the other had to guard people's felines. Obviously no one would expect the Bonners to be there after their personal tragedy, assuming they ever did consider it politically seemly to take part in drunken quiz revelry.

She did note the presence of the Reverend Edwards, and some of the elderly faces at his table were familiar from her earlier visit to the church. There were a couple of barflies seated appropriately on stools next to the bar, and some tables containing younger couples. There was also a large table of singles, already packed with empty bottles and glasses, and from which the occasional shriek of laughter cut across the general chatter. Hayley's brother Josh was one of them, although not, Vivien hoped, doing the shrieking. She wondered if one of the other women at the table was his girlfriend Angela, and if so how their dinner went.

As it crept toward nine o'clock, Vivien was pleased to observe there were no children present. She couldn't help judging parents who took kids out late on a school night, assuming it was either because of a lack of planning or simply because they didn't care if their children fell asleep in school the next day. Yes, all right, she didn't have children so maybe she didn't understand all the issues. But she'd been a child and bedtime had been strictly enforced, so that remained her model.

She was, on the other hand, charmed to see a couple of dogs lying spread out under tables. Dogs didn't have to go to school, and they added a homely feel to the proceedings. They could probably also guide their inebriated owners home if necessary.

The pub manager—a burly, balding man sporting a sizeable beer gut over which a stretched T-shirt proclaimed "Hal's Beer Removal Service"—took his place at the front of the room and turned on a portable microphone to announce the start of the quiz. Disappointingly, the first section was on sport, and it was all cricket and rugby and football. Vivien once again reminded herself the last was soccer, and then wondered if it mattered, since she didn't know the answers anyway.

Having nothing to contribute, she relaxed and listened to the other three arguing over team managers and Golden Boot awards. She noted how Will signed all the questions for Hayley, and ensured his wife knew when someone was talking to her. Vivien made a mental note to ask Hayley for help learning British Sign Language. As she was growing quite fond of her neighbors it seemed well worth investing the time to be able to communicate better and help out when Will wasn't around.

Looking around the pub, she noticed a man sitting by himself at the opposite end of the bar from all the activity. He looked to be in his fifties, certainly not old enough to justify his slump over the pint of beer on the bar, which he clutched with one hand as if it were his only friend. His slightly red nose suggested there might be some truth in that, and his five o'clock shadow did not bestow a George Clooney sexiness, but he was well dressed and Vivien could see he might be attractive in other circumstances.

She nudged Hayley's arm to get her attention and surreptitiously pointed out the man. "Who is that?" she whispered before remembering she could have just mouthed it silently.

Hayley looked over and then back. "That's Clive Foster, he was vicar before Jonathan. But he was—I don't know what it's called, excommunicated or maybe just fired—a couple of years ago, which is when Jonathan was assigned to the parish. I don't know why he lost his job, but instead of moving away Foster bought an old cottage on the outskirts of town and set up house there with, rumor says, a parrot."

"What an odd thing to do," said Vivien. "You'd think he'd want to live somewhere else, where his history isn't so well known and he could make a fresh start. With the parrot, of course."

"Well, like I said, I don't think most people know what really happened, and he was here for quite a few years before that, so maybe it feels like home to him. I would guess the church gave him some sort of pension or compensation to keep him quiet, so maybe he doesn't have to work." Hayley scowled. "None of us will probably ever trust church governance again after all the scandals that have come out."

"Not sure I trusted them before that," Vivien responded. "To my mind, at least in America, there's a difference between faith and religion and it's a rare church where there isn't a power struggle at the top, whether it's managing the budget, the hymn books, or the flower rota. And contrary to your standard cozy crime novel, competition is definitely not limited to the spinster women of the parish. I once witnessed a screaming match between two elderly gentlemen over an inconsistency in the takings from a bake sale."

"Yes, it's much the same here. But I think Clive probably did something worse than nicking a bob or two from the offering plate."

"Hmmm. I do believe it's time for another round of drinks." Vivien gathered the empty glasses and headed for the space next to the defrocked vicar. After ordering another round from the bartender, she turned to Foster and held out her hand.

"Hi, I'm Vivien. I just moved here."

Foster looked suspiciously at her extended hand before lifting his own and giving it a short shake. His hand was a bit sweaty, and Vivien did her best to surreptitiously wipe hers on a trouser leg while distracting him with a smile. "You're not a quizzer?" she asked.

"Not really into group activities," came the reply, in something approaching a low growl. "What do you want?"

"Want?" Vivien widened her eyes in her best innocent look. "I don't want anything. I just thought I'd introduce myself since you were on your own. I hear you used to be the vicar here."

Foster squinted at her. "Uh huh. That all you heard, then?"

"Pretty much. Unless you mean that you were fired, although no one seems to know why."

Foster let out a choked exclamation somewhere between a laugh and yelp. "So I guess it's true that Americans have no verbal filter. I suppose you think it's charming, this in-your-face honesty."

"I think it saves time, whether it invokes admiration or anger. But really I was hoping, considering your in-depth knowledge of the village, if you might be willing to help me get a handle on the situation around Sebastian Bonner's death. You know about that?"

"Yes," he sighed, turning back to the bar and sipping his drink before giving her a sideways look. "I heard he was found at your house. You do the finding?"

Vivien nodded and Foster gave a grunt that could have meant anything from simple acknowledgement to boundless empathy.

"That's rough. Death isn't ever pretty, but it's worse when it's so wrongly done, and to someone so young."

"You have any insight into who might have done the

doing?" Not how she'd intended that sentence to come out, but it would do. "You must know people around here pretty well, considering your career."

"Past career," Foster corrected. "And it isn't like any of the kids come to church once they're past the age of ten, so I mostly only knew the older residents."

"What about the Bonners? Did you know them?"

"Not much in my official capacity. You'd have to talk to the new man about that. They only arrived about a year before I was…let go. But Sebastian and his friend Lucius went hiking out near my house, so we'd occasionally get to saying hello and talking a bit. Had them both in for coffee one time. He seemed like a nice kid. Real shame what happened to him. Almost makes you wonder if there's a God."

Foster shifted uncomfortably in his seat, as if conscious that he'd talked too much, and pointed a finger at Vivien to change the subject.

"So what, you think you're going to play amateur detective, then? Like one of those little old ladies from the TV mysteries?"

"Hardly." Vivien gave him her most winning smile. "I don't knit, for one thing. But I do feel sort of connected to it, what with it happening in my house and all. And I too liked Sebastian. The real question is, who didn't?"

"Can't help you there, I find it hard to believe anyone could have that big a grudge against a teenager, outside of the parents, of course." He chortled at his own wit. "But before you start to share your theories, as you seem set to do, I believe your friends require your assistance back at your table." He pointed his chin over her shoulder. "And I require the bartender's. So what say we return to our proper places?"

Foster signaled to the bartender and Vivien had no choice but to take the hint. She returned to the table where she supplied answers on US history, American muscle cars, and David Lynch films. The post-quiz sandwiches were gratefully scarfed, which almost made up for the fact that they came in second place to the table of youngsters. Vivien was naturally suspicious that the twenty-somethings were consulting Google under the table, but she managed to rein in her competitive spirit before she alienated everyone in town by yelling an unprovable "*J'accuse!*"

Glancing over at the bar on the way out, she noted the ex-vicar was still planted firmly on his stool, looking like he was settling in for the night as the bartender handed him another pint.

23

"How we behave toward cats here below determines our status in heaven."
— Robert Heinlein, *To Sail Beyond the Sunset*

Vivien was up early the next morning to meet a gardening service. She'd discovered that England's "green and pleasant land", while beautiful when viewed outside a stately home, required serious effort when it came to your own backyard (or back garden, as it was called here). Her own was choked with what she thought might be some version of knotweed as well as the ever-present ivy. Both seemed to grow with supernatural speed, and Vivien quickly realized she'd need help to get it all tamed.

Unfortunately, she wasn't prepared for the shortage of gardening contractors in the UK. Hayley told her it was due to the lack of young people wanting to apprentice in professions such as gardening and bricklaying. These days they all wanted to be social media gurus instead. But through constant phoning and following up, Vivien had managed to secure a promise from a local firm to come out and estimate what was needed. As long as she made them tea.

Once she'd done this and translated the various "Hey ups" into a plan to get a quote for the work, she was told it was clematis choking off her other plants rather than knotweed, which was a relief until she realized she didn't really know what clematis was. She negotiated a date for the work and then bid her future gardeners good day before setting off in time for her appointment at the local cattery. She'd found owners Beth and James to be charming, and the award they won was comforting, but she would have been remiss if she didn't do her own surveying to ensure Sydney received only the very best care when she and Geoffrey took their next holiday.

It was a mere ten-minute walk down the high street to the gates of the cattery. She rang the bell and after a couple of minutes a smiling Beth Frederick approached and opened them to let her in. Beth was more practically dressed than at the party in matching green cotton trousers and a sweatshirt with vibrant daisies painted on it. Her greying hair was pulled back in a loose bun at the nape of her neck, exposing another pair of cat earrings, and her bright white tennis shoes (*trainers!*) matched the flowers on her shirt. Though the outfit was smart casual, Vivien was encouraged to see a few cat hairs attached to her top. She didn't want a cattery owner who eschewed cat cuddling.

"Hello, it's lovely to see you again," Beth murmured in a voice meant to soothe the savage feline breast, and possibly the feline's owner as well. "James said you wanted to have a look around and check booking dates?"

Vivien nodded. "I'm sure your facilities are wonderful, but Sydney and I have come through a lot together, and he'd never forgive me if I didn't scope out his holiday digs beforehand."

"Of course. Our little darlings are ever so demanding, aren't they? Come with me and I'll give you the tour."

Vivien followed her hostess through a side door and down a paved pathway that led into a sizeable back garden much neater than Vivien's own. A series of large cages ranged around two sides of the space. Well, they were technically cages, but as she followed Beth through a netted door into the protected walkway that led past them, Vivien noted that each space had an indoor and outdoor section, with staggered shelves where cats could perch to be on top of their world. There was also a slight space between each cage, presumably to keep little paws from swiping at each other.

Beth entered one of the cages, and beckoned Vivien to follow. It was easily seven feet high from smooth, painted concrete floor to wire-fenced roof, and there was a window and a door in the wood partition between the inside and outside space, with a cat flap that could be propped open or shut. Everything smelled clean and looked bright. Vivien, used to the small cages in a back room at her local veterinarian's, was stunned by the luxurious quarters on offer. This was obviously a country that knew how to treat cats as the gods they believed they were.

"Your Sydney will have his own chalet, of course, and as you can see through the window, there is a heat lamp and a fleece-lined bed to ensure he will be toasty warm during the cooler nights. We just need to know what kind of food he likes, which is included in the price of the chalet, and we encourage you to bring his favorite toys and something that smells of you for him to sleep on."

"Wow," said Vivien. "This is all very impressive. In fact,

I'm thinking I'll stay here with Sydney and Geoffrey can go away by himself!"

Beth smiled. "James and I both love cats, and therefore love what we do. I like to think it shows. Shall we go inside for a cup of tea and discuss Sydney's needs and your holiday schedule?"

Vivien followed Beth into the house through a small kitchen and into the lounge. It was immediately clear who ruled this particular roost. Not only were three cats draped over the most comfortable cushions, but a variety of cat toys littered the carpet. Vivien seated herself on the edge of an unoccupied chair that was mostly free of cat hair as Beth gathered the tea things from the adjacent kitchen.

"How many cats do you have yourself?" Vivien enquired loudly.

"At the moment, just these three," Beth responded as she returned to set out teacups. "We sometimes end up taking in cats of past clients who, for whatever reason, can't care for them anymore, but we try to keep it to a maximum of four at any one time. Even devoting your entire life to cats doesn't leave time enough to give more than four cats the attention they consider their due, and we have to ensure our boarders receive premium care as well."

She returned to the kitchen and soon brought out a steeping teapot, kept warm by a quilted cat-patterned cozy, and poured the tea into the cups. Vivien noted the cattery owner was a milk-in-second person but wasn't prejudiced enough to care, a benefit of not having such things ingrained by family tradition. Geoffrey would have been appalled.

"I didn't see you at the quiz last night. Is it not your thing?" said Vivien.

"No." Beth handed her a cup and pushed the plate of cookies (*biscuits!*) toward her before continuing. "We're not big quizzers and we don't like leaving the cattery unattended in the evenings, so we tend to make sure at least one of us is always here. The only reason we were both able to come to the Bonners' the other evening is because my son agreed to catsit. I think there was something he wanted to watch on Netflix and we promised to bring back some of Rachel's excellent nibbles for him as well as buying him a takeaway." She smiled at the memory of her son and his appetite.

"Well, I think the food certainly lived up to its reputation. Do you know the Bonners well?" Vivien asked casually, sipping her tea. Nope, she couldn't tell any difference having the milk in second rather than first, no matter what Geoffrey said.

"Not very. There aren't any pets in their family, as you probably guessed from the expanse of white carpeting in their house, and our children are older than Sebastian… was. Aside from the occasional political event or community gathering we don't see much of each other. But it's still nice to know your MP spends time in the neighborhood, and Archie is usually willing to listen when we have a complaint."

Beth paused to add sugar to her cup. "We used to have trouble with kids climbing over the back wall of the cattery, the one that borders the park, and he worked to add lighting to the pathways so they would be more visible, as well as ensuring the police do regular patrols. We cemented glass shards into the top of the wall and added a couple of cameras, which has eliminated that particular problem. But as I've already mentioned, we make sure to be home in the evenings and overnight to keep an eye on things anyway."

"That's very comforting. I'm sure Sydney will be very happy here. Well, as happy as he can be anywhere that isn't home. Cats are never shy about letting you know when they're displeased, are they?"

"It's what I like about them," Beth replied. "I love dogs too, but they are so dependent on you for their happiness, whereas cats just go about the business of letting us worship them."

"Speaking of worship," said Vivien, "I met your previous vicar, Clive Foster, at the quiz the other night. He seemed a bit…unsociable for a vicar."

Beth's eyes narrowed slightly and she paused before answering.

"Clive was a very good vicar, actually. James and I both thought it was a shame he gave up the parish. But these things happen and, as they say, the Lord works in mysterious ways."

"Do you know why he left the church? It seems odd that he left the job but still stays in the area."

Beth sighed as she topped up their cups with more tea. "There were plenty of rumors at the time, but that happens in a small village like this. Clive himself has never said a word so I've never asked, although I've had cause to wonder since."

The cattery owner was still for a moment, lost in whatever thoughts the conversation had spurred, but before Vivien had a chance to follow up on this interesting comment the woman resolutely shook her shoulders and continued.

"It's hard enough to keep things private around here without passing on gossip, so I try to encourage our clients to restrict discussions to our furry families. Not that clients don't tell me things anyway, whether I want to know them or not. And our security cameras sometimes catch things we'd rather not see." Her mouth twisted in a moue of distaste.

"Like what?" Vivien asked quickly, innocent look firmly in place.

Beth looked up, her face purposefully bland. "Let's just say I was aware Sebastian was a troubled soul. He tended to wander the park when upset." She gazed into the distance, struck by a memory. "I've often wondered if I should have gone to him that night a couple of years ago, he was so very sad…"

Returning to the present and noting Vivien's look of interest, her hostess suddenly straightened up and tucked a stray lock of hair behind her ear. "But as I said, I try not to encourage the spreading of gossip. Now, shall we write down some details about how we can make your little darling's time here more pleasurable?" She set her cup down and rose to get pen and paper.

That's told me, Vivien chuckled to herself, then wondered if there was another way to narrow down Beth's chatty clientele. If Beth herself wouldn't reveal anything, maybe Vivien could go right to the source!

"I hope you don't mind me asking, but do you take care of other cats in the neighborhood? I've been thinking about letting Sydney outside, but I'd like to get a feel for how many other cats he might run across."

"Oh yes, of course we do." Beth took a moment to reflect. "There's a ginger cat about halfway down your street who comes here, that's Oscar. Oh, and you've met the Ramakrishnans, they have a lovely fluffy thing called Kali. Your neighbor has a black cat, Jezebel, but she's been lodged with friends while her owner is away for an extended period of time."

"You know our neighbor? I've been wondering if anyone actually lives there."

Beth's smile had a hint of mystery to it. "I'm not sure where she went or when she's coming back, but I'm sure she'll come and introduce herself when she returns. She's a very... interesting woman."

Vivien waited a few seconds, but it seemed there was no more information forthcoming on that topic, and at least she had some names to follow up with. She decided it wasn't worth exacerbating Sydney's future caretaker further, so the two women spent the rest of the visit discussing his very particular needs and desires, which were many.

24

"Time goes by so fast and the friends you have sometimes leave, but it doesn't mean you stop loving them."
— Heather Wolf, *Kipnuk the Talking Dog*

Walking home from the cattery, Vivien was passing the park when she heard the pine tree next to her hiss. Knowing from her reading that there were few poisonous snakes in England, she cautiously peeked behind the trunk to find Lucius standing on the other side. He beckoned her further into the copse until they were surrounded by the scent of fresh pine. The boy seemed calm as he stopped and turned to face her, but Vivien could see his eyes were red-rimmed from crying. He stood silent for several moments, obviously struggling to figure out how to say what he wanted, so Vivien decided to help him out.

"I'm so sorry about Sebastian, Lucius. This past week must have been dreadful for you."

Lucius shook his head slowly and found his voice. "It's been the worst week of my life. And it's all my fault!" he cried.

"What do you mean? How could any of this have been your fault?"

Lucius hiccupped back a sob before continuing. "I was late. My teacher held me back after school to compliment me on an essay I'd written. If I'd been there on time, I could have stopped Sebastian from being killed."

"Oh Lucius. You must know that's not true. In fact, you could have easily been hurt as well."

"Maybe I should have been!" he protested, tears forming in his eyes. "I should have been there for Sebastian!"

Vivien reached out and took the boy's limp hand in both of hers, waiting until she had his full attention before she spoke.

"There's no one to blame for this other than the person who did it. I can see you're aching in so many ways right now, but don't give Sebastian's killer the satisfaction of ruining your life too."

"I can't help it," the boy responded as he broke down again. "And I do wish I'd been there, even if I'd been killed. At least I wouldn't be left behind, feeling this way. I miss him so much!" This declaration was followed by a stream of Spanish that Vivien's fifth-grade lessons failed to help her translate. The boy spoke such perfect English thanks to his British mother that Vivien had forgotten he lived in Spain for years.

She took a chance and stepped forward to hug the poor kid, at which point he collapsed into her embrace, crying on her shoulder. She let him go on for a bit, then gave him an extra squeeze before releasing him to arm's length. She gently placed a finger under his chin to get him to look up at her.

"Have you talked to the police and told them everything you know about that day?" she asked.

He nodded. "They came to see me at home. My father wasn't best pleased, and now I have to come straight home from school every day until the killer is caught, and probably longer. Mama was nicer about me being with Sebastian, but I can tell she's worried too."

"Well, it's nice to have parents who care about your wellbeing. You're on your way home now, then? Would you like me to walk with you?" Lucius nodded again and they fell into an easy saunter side by side. Vivien pondered how to ask her next question without hurting him further.

"Did Sebastian ever tell you about anyone threatening him?" she finally asked.

"Not beyond the stuff you've already seen in the library. We had some trouble at school, but there were usually enough teachers around that no one got physical. And we searched out safe places to go after school, like we hoped your house would be."

"Yes, I'm so sorry that didn't turn out to be the case. I hope you know I would never have done anything to put Sebastian in danger. I have no idea why someone was in our house that afternoon, other than Sebastian."

"I know," Lucius responded. "And don't worry, you were so nice to us, I'm certain you had nothing to do with it. As I told the police."

Hmmm, Vivien mused. *The innocence of youth. I could have been doing all sorts of things in there for all they knew*, and she could just imagine how Inspector Torksey had received Lucius's assurances. Still, in this case at least, he was right about her lack of involvement, and it wasn't the time for a lecture on misplaced trust. She tried another tack.

"I met Mr. Foster the other day. He says he sometimes saw you and Sebastian going for walks in the woods. Was that one of the places you went?"

"Sure. None of the kids around here are into nature, so we usually had the woods to ourselves. Mr. Foster was nice, he even gave us tea and biscuits a couple of times. Seb knew him better than I did, and kind of hinted that Mr. Foster was sympathetic to our particular situation."

"What, you mean he's gay?" Vivien unconsciously blurted, then instantly regretted being so blunt. But Lucius seemed to take it in stride.

"I don't know for sure, it's just the impression I got from Seb. Seb was really good at keeping secrets, he knew all kinds of things about people, though most times he wouldn't even tell me about them."

They had reached Lucius's home, a small, terraced house which looked immaculately kept. Giving the boy another supportive one-armed squeeze around the shoulders, they said goodbye and Vivien stood on the pavement watching as Lucius let himself in. She couldn't help wondering if one of Sebastian's secrets had gotten him killed, and she fervently hoped he had told someone something or his murder might never be solved.

25

"A woman especially, if she should have the misfortune of knowing anything, should conceal it as well as she can."
— Jane Austen, *Northanger Abbey*

Once home, Vivien changed into a lavender pantsuit (*trousersuit?*) hoping to channel the professional style of Hillary Clinton. Hayley had convinced her to attend a meeting of the local Women's Institute, or WI as it was commonly known, in the hope of hearing something useful.

Vivien was trying not to let preconceived notions about women in gloves, bake sales and educational lectures dim her anticipation, although she supposed she was counting on there being some decent gossip. She wondered if that was a bit sexist, but comforted herself with the thought that men almost certainly gossiped when they got together, they probably just called it something different, like "shooting the breeze". She'd have to ask Geoffrey later.

And who knew, maybe it would be one of those exciting WI chapters where they created a nude calendar every year.

Not that she'd be angling for a spot as Miss June, her desire to be part of the community had its limits.

No, Vivien imagined this was a one-off meeting for her, a chance to meet people and pick up on the mood of the village, maybe chat to a suspect or two. All in a day's work.

After adding some tasteful gold earrings, she donned comfortable flats and headed across the street as Hayley came out of the front door of her own house. Her neighbor's outfit was a masterpiece even by Hayley standards, consisting of yellow-and-black-striped bell bottom trousers topped by a hip-length acidic lime green silk shirt with cut-out shoulders. Hot-pink hoops in her ears completed the swinging sixties look and made Vivien feel slightly frumpy.

"You ready for this?" Hayley chirped as they fell into step next to each other and headed toward the main street of town. The meeting was taking place in the church hall, which seemed to be the *de facto* gathering place for anything happening in the village.

"I suppose so, though I'm entirely uncertain what to expect." Vivien suddenly tripped on a crack in the pavement but recovered quickly. Ensuring Hayley could read her lips while they were both walking forward was a learned skill, and she obviously had more learning to do.

"I forgot to ask, have you been baptized?" Hayley asked.

"What? Why?" Vivien spluttered.

"It's still part of the WI rules, members have to be baptized. Although I'm pretty sure no one checks anymore. But just in case, if you're asked, be prepared to run if you're not baptized." Hayley grinned at Vivien's discomfiture.

"Well, fortunately I have been, but you're not helping me

view tonight with unadulterated joy. Do you know what the lecture is going to be about?"

"No, I forgot to ask, but from the couple that I've attended that's not really the purpose of the meeting, it's more about all the village women getting together to talk about goings on without their menfolk or children around. I think you'll find that's one of the greatest English traditions, that an organization with a reputation as staid as the WI is really just an excuse to get out of the house and have a good old natter and some snacks. That's why I thought it might be advisable for us to attend."

"Who's in charge, then?"

"Usually it's your old buddy Rachel Bonner, although I don't know if she'll be there tonight, what with losing Sebastian last week and all."

Vivien stopped dead, causing Hayley to look round in surprise.

"I don't know why I didn't think of that," Vivien said. "Of course she'd be in charge. And I'm certainly not her favorite person at the moment. Maybe this isn't such a good idea."

Hayley looped her arm through Vivien's and pulled her on. "It will be fine. Even if she's there, Rachel would never air her dirty laundry in public, and will most likely ignore you."

"Oh great, and me without an anorak to ward off the frosty air." Vivien smiled ruefully.

They entered the hall to find over two dozen women chatting in small groups, some of them munching on fairy cakes. On one side of the room a long table was covered in a pristine white cloth, on top of which a selection of cakes and vegetable crudités and dips was attractively arranged. Small china plates, napkins, and stainless-steel cutlery were positioned at one end. On another table, canned sodas, bottles of red and white wine, and tea and coffee urns were surrounded by the appropriate cups and glassware.

As she followed Hayley to the drinks table, Vivien surreptitiously looked around to suss out who was there. Quite a few of the elderly ladies from the church were in attendance, but she also saw Susan Ramakrishnan and Beth Frederick representing the younger set, having obviously given their respective spouses responsibility for the businesses. And yes, there was Rachel, looking superficially cool and calm in a classic skirt suit that perfectly matched the pastel green of the walls. She was chatting to a man in a kilt who Vivien assumed had something to do with tonight's lecture as he was the lone male in attendance. Rachel spotted Vivien looking at her, but the latter couldn't read her expression from that distance. After a moment, Rachel returned her attention to the kilted man, finished their conversation with a smile and turned to walk toward the wooden lectern at the front of the room. She stationed herself behind it and tapped the microphone to get everyone's attention. Moving closer, Vivien could see lines of stress on the woman's face in the strong light attached to the lectern, and she wondered what had driven Rachel to attend the meeting. Was it a lack of feeling, or the need for a distraction from her misery? Whatever the cause, Rachel's voice was clear, calm, and controlled.

"If you'd all like to take your seats, ladies, Mr. McGregor is ready to begin tonight's talk, to which I know we've all been so looking forward."

Hayley handed Vivien a cup of tea as they glanced toward the guest lecturer, and Vivien was surprised to see him open a large black case stowed against the wall and remove a set of bagpipes from it. He carried them over and set them down next to the lectern, shaking hands with Rachel and taking his place behind the microphone as all the women obediently settled themselves in chairs. Vivien and Hayley followed and sat in the last row, suddenly interested to see where tonight's entertainment would take them.

"Thank ya furrr invitin' me to yurr wee meetin', ladies," McGregor said in an exaggerated Scottish accent that garnered laughs from the women. He continued in a more normal tone that still carried the musical lilt of the Highlands, although Vivien was disappointed to note he bore little resemblance to Jamie Fraser from *Outlander*. McGregor was a bear of a man, with strands of grey lacing his full beard and woven amidst the carrot-colored hair escaping from under his traditional Scottish beret. Black Watch pattern, if she wasn't mistaken.

McGregor got right to it. "I'm here tonight to tell you about the origins of some of our finest Scottish myths and legends, and we'll finish up with a lesson in playing the Piob Mhor, which means 'big pipe' in Gaelic. I call this presentation 'Pipe doon, Nessie!'"

McGregor went on to give an entertaining talk that easily held his audience's attention followed by the promised lesson, but it was the sight of elderly women with beautifully coiffed hair and puffed-out cheeks trying to get a sound out of the pipes that Vivien knew she would remember most. Never one to resist a challenge, she had a go herself and managed to get a slight squeak out of them, for which she received approving nods from McGregor and a couple of the ladies. Rachel didn't deign to try, instead spending her time ensuring everyone had refreshments and carefully ignoring Vivien, as Hayley had predicted. Vivien wondered again at the reasons why the woman felt she needed to be there so soon after her son's death. Maybe it was as simple as an overzealous sense of duty. Regardless, her self-control was impressive, as well as her ability to be where Vivien was not.

Vivien did her best to help avoid confrontation by working her way around the room learning about a range of subjects from the inadequacies of the local school to the much-anticipated visit of a revered psychic. It was obvious from people's questions that she and Geoffrey had been the topic of village conversations.

"So this is your second marriage?" inquired a blue-haired matron who couldn't hide her avid curiosity. "Has your first husband gone to his maker, then?"

"Only his bookmaker," Vivien assured her before smiling politely and moving on.

She grinned at the sight of Hayley hemmed in by a group of older women who could be heard hypothesizing about what was under Mr. McGregor's kilt (if anything). Unless there was good reason, Hayley felt it was rude to lip read from a distance, an invasion of people's privacy. But she admitted that this sometimes resulted in her being trapped in awkward conversations where a hearing person would have steered clear. Proving the point, Vivien did this now, choosing instead to chat to Susan Ramakrishnan, co-owner of the Mill Shop.

"Are you settling in all right?" Susan asked.

"Pretty well," Vivien replied, "although I'm afraid I haven't had occasion to visit your shop yet."

"Well, it's the type of shop that you rarely need until you find yourself short of an ingredient in the middle of a recipe. Although I hear you're decorating your house, and I have a decent collection of candles and other knickknacks that you might want to take a look at. I make the candles myself."

"Thanks, I will definitely do that. That sounds like fun, making candles. Where did you learn it?" Vivien asked.

"Here, actually. It was one of the WI talks a couple of years ago, and from that I researched more on the internet and found I liked the creativity of it." Susan stopped to sip a glass of white wine and Vivien was again struck by the woman's beauty.

"It sounds like this is an inspiring group, then. How long have you been coming?"

"Oh, years now, ever since Rachel started it. She's an amazing organiser, takes a real interest in local businesses and ensures we all work together for the good of the village."

Vivien nodded. "I wasn't sure she'd be here tonight, what with the tragedy of her son's death and all."

Susan shook her head sadly. "Such a horrible thing to happen, and then to have their misery compounded by Colonel Jay's arrest. But I think Rachel is one of those who has to do things. It's not for her to sit and mourn alone in the house, and she takes her village responsibilities very seriously. I often wonder if she wouldn't have made a better MP than her husband, charming as he is. But I guess that's part of the job, to be charming, and he's got that in spades."

"Do you think Colonel Jay did it, actually killed his grandson?"

Susan sighed. "Honestly, I try not to think about it at all. I've got two girls to raise and a shop to run, plus my father to take care of. I just don't have time to be speculating about a murder I know nothing about, so I have to trust the police will do their job. But speaking of my daughters, they've given you a positive review."

"I like them, too," smiled Vivien. "They come into the library quite often, and it's always a pleasure to see them."

"Yes, well, I suppose if Samantha must hang out with that Justin boy, at least I'm glad it's in a public place where her sister can play chaperone. And it's hard to object to a library. I don't suppose they actually touch any books while they're there?"

"Nicole does. She's one of my best readers."

Susan nodded. "Nicole's very bright. I have great hopes for her." She took a couple of steps sideways to place her empty glass on the table before turning back to Vivien. "I know we don't know each other well, but I just want to say how sorry I am for what you've already had to go through here. Emotions are running high since Sebastian's death, but ordinarily this is a nice, peaceful place to live, and I hope you stay long enough to experience that."

"Oh, don't worry," Vivien assured her. "I have no plans to leave anytime soon."

Susan took her leave and Hayley and Vivien followed not long after. The two friends were silent on the walk home, which Vivien found was a relief after an evening filled with the sounds of amateur bagpipe players and multiple conversations happening at once. Hayley, frowning, was no doubt still recovering from the raunchy speculations of the elderly ladies of Nether Chatby.

26

"Never be afraid to raise your voice for honesty and truth and compassion against injustice and lying and greed. If people all over the world...would do this, it would change the earth."
— William Faulkner in a speech to the 1951 graduating class of University High School

On Wednesday, Vivien was scheduled to work at the Bickford library again. It was Halloween and she was ready with treats to hand out to any costumed children who came through that afternoon. The morning was spent processing and shelving new books, as well as discussing interesting residents with Becky, when Reverend Edwards made an appearance. Placing his books on the desk, he gave Vivien a tiny, listless smile.

"No fines this time, I promise."

The poor man had dark circles under his eyes and was unusually pale, so Vivien decided humor wasn't the order of the day.

"I never doubted you," she assured him. "How are you

holding up? It's not every day a murder weapon appears on your premises, I assume?"

Edwards flushed slightly, and Vivien cursed her too-quick tongue for making him uncomfortable.

"Thank goodness, no," he replied. "What an absolute mess. I'm horribly embarrassed to admit that for a short time I was worried I'd be implicated in the murder of that poor young man. But the police were smart enough to realize I wouldn't have left the gun there like that, and anyway I was in a meeting with my bishop far from the rectory when Sebastian was killed, which seems to be the gold standard in alibis."

"Do you have any idea who could have left it there?"

The man shifted nervously from foot to foot. "No. I have grave doubts about it being Colonel Jay either. I've always found him to be a decent person, even if he does stretch the truth on occasion. And I know he loved his grandson very much, both from talking to the colonel and seeing them together."

"So who else could it have been?" Vivien felt a bit cruel pressing the point but knew this was a rare chance to try to get some facts. She thought she detected a slight pause before the vicar answered her.

"I simply can't imagine who would have done this. I feel so predictable saying this, but I can't help hoping it's some stranger who found the gun and did the killing before dumping it. My brain knows it's not likely, but on the other hand it's so hard to believe someone you know would do this. I think I remember your Abraham Lincoln saying that if you only look for the evil in people, you will find it. So I try not to look."

Vivien smiled. "Actually, that quote was attributed to Lincoln in the Disney film *Pollyanna*, but the director later admitted he'd made it up, after the marketing department printed it on souvenirs for selling in Disneyland. I don't imagine Walt was too pleased."

She flushed slightly when the vicar gazed at her with raised eyebrows.

"Sorry, you pick up lots of trivia in a lifetime as a librarian, it's sometimes hard not to trot things out like a party trick. By the way, I met your predecessor the other evening. Clive Foster?"

Edwards nodded a couple of times. "Poor man. I've seen him hanging around the village. But before you ask, I have no idea why he was removed from his position. We're not encouraged to pry into the personal lives of our fellow clergy. I just hope he's able to move on and find another purpose. I can't imagine what I'd do in his situation."

Vivien noted the look of worry that flitted briefly across the vicar's face before he turned to leave, lifting a hand in farewell. Something was bothering him, but it was unlikely she would be his confidant with so many other possibilities among his acquaintance. She hoped he found someone to help him.

It was soon time for the influx of the after-school crowd, including a few of the smaller children who came to claim their treats in full Halloween regalia. The older kids watched with carefully bored expressions, too cool to come in costume but mildly jealous of those receiving candy (*sweets*, she corrected). Vivien had just gotten the first six lucky teens settled on the available computers and the rest signed up to follow when she heard a loud thwack on one of the windows that lined the side of the room. It was repeated a few seconds later, and then again. Vivien approached the windows and opened the blinds to see a white soccer ball (*football!*) thrown straight at her face by a boy who couldn't have been more than six years old. He caught the ball and grinned at her, before throwing it again, this time so hard that the reverberations sounded throughout the library.

Vivien glanced over at Becky with a questioning look and received a warning shake of the head in response. She grinned at her worried co-worker and headed outside, determined to deal with this latest disruption. As she approached, the child steadfastly ignored her, so Vivien put on a burst of speed and grabbed the ball on its rebound off the window. Turning to him, she put the ball on the ground and set her foot on it. Then waited.

Junior let out a howl of protest. "Give me back my ball!"

"Nope. Not until you promise me you're not going to throw it at the windows or the walls of the library. You might break something, and plus it's very annoying. What's your name?"

"You can't tell me what to do!" the perpetrator announced. "I'm gonna tell my grandpa you took my ball."

"Why, does he like to hear about the minutiae of your day? Is his life that dull?"

There was silence while the child tried to work out the meaning of this response and organise his comeback. He finally gave up and turned to face a two-story stuccoed terraced house across the street. "GRANDPA!" he bellowed at a volume worthy of a rock concert, then turned back to Vivien with a look of smug satisfaction on his face.

After a minute, an upstairs window in the house was slid up and a bald man with a scraggly grey beard and scruffy eyebrows poked his head out to yell, "For Christ's sake, Denny, what the hell is wrong with you?" Lung capacity obviously ran in the family.

"This mingin' slag took my ball!" Vivien made a mental note to check on the meaning of "mingin" with Geoffrey later on. She was pretty sure she knew what slag meant.

Grandpa glared in her direction. Even from this distance, Vivien could see the food stains on his greyish undershirt. "What the hell do you think you're doing, woman?"

Vivien gazed calmly back as she reached over to pick up the ball and straighten back up. "I'm preventing your grandson from breaking a window, which will result in an anti-social behaviour order for him, and a sizeable repair bill for you."

"Well, they'd have to find me first, and no Scottish bitch takes my grandson's property away."

"Wow, so much to work with there," Vivien mumbled before raising her voice to respond. "First off, I'm happy for you to call the police if you want to discuss the matter. Or if you prefer, I will call for you so they can come and talk to the many people who witnessed this child's attempt to damage council property. Second, if I sound Scottish to you then you really need to get out more. Although I will proudly lay claim to the latter term."

Vivien turned to Denny and spoke loud enough for his grandfather to hear. "I will keep your ball behind the desk for the next hour until the library closes, at which time you may come to claim it. In the meantime, there are several books on football inside this building you are so determined to destroy, and I wouldn't be at all surprised if some of them were of interest to you."

Vivien turned and walked into the library, leaving

stunned silence in her wake. Inside, Becky's eyes were wide, but she too remained silent as they got back to work. A glance outside showed the window of the house opposite was now closed and young Denny was nowhere in sight.

Samantha and Nicole had joined the crowd standing around waiting for computers, and they sidled up to the desk where Vivien was working.

"Denny's a total pain, but his grandad is really mean. You need to watch out," Samantha warned her. Nicole nodded in agreement.

"A bully is a bully everywhere," Vivien told them. "They're only as powerful as you let them be."

Nicole bit her lower lip, her eyebrows scrunched together. "Fred Turnbull has pretty powerful fists. He's beat up lots of people."

"Really? And do you know any of these people?" Vivien asked.

The girls looked at each other and shook their heads.

"Then I suspect Mr. Turnbull's power lies in his stories. Never take a person like that at his word, ladies. Lies and puffery are a bully's stock in trade. Expose them, and they are revealed as the weak, ugly little insects they truly are. Although that's not fair to insects, which on the whole are quite beautiful and useful."

The girls continued to shake their heads mournfully as they rejoined their friends. Becky's raised eyebrows suggested she too was unconvinced, and Vivien was glad to avoid further conversation by turning to help a customer who had just come up to the desk, only to find it was Clive Foster. He, at least, was smiling, although she sensed a bit of mockery in there somewhere.

"Picking your battles, are you, Ms. Brandt?" he asked, his eyes dancing with humor.

"They seem to be picking me, Clive. And it's Vivien, please." She took the books he handed her and efficiently checked them in, putting them on the shelf to be transferred back to their home library. "Can I help you find anything today?"

"No, I know my way around a library, thank you. But I do have to echo the young ladies' warning. Turnbull is a nasty piece of work, and he's a pro at spreading vicious rumors and disinformation. Your reputation may suffer, if not your face."

"Do you speak from personal experience, then?" Vivien responded.

Foster just looked at her, his smile tinged with sadness. "Turnbull wasn't needed to ruin me. I did that all on my own. And that's already more than you need to know about it."

Vivien was tired of all this prevarication.

"What of the police? Is it everything they need to know? It's come to my attention that Seb harbored secrets, and some of them might be yours. Are you so sure that his death is nothing to do with you?"

This was a bit of fishing on her part, but as Foster turned and quickly left the library, his face thunderous, she wondered if he did indeed have something important to hide. She realized she would have to be considerably more subtle if she wanted to find out what it was. And that was never easy for her.

27

"The grocery store is the great equalizer where mankind comes to grips with the facts of life like toilet tissue."
— Joseph Goldberg

Vivien managed to sleep in a bit the next day, then spent a satisfying morning unpacking the few remaining boxes stored in the garage. The house was starting to look really good, with pops of color in the Turkish-style carpets echoed on the Indian pillow coverings flanking the new sofa. She loved that mementos from her travels and gifts from friends could be seen scattered around the shelves and cabinets in the house. There was the Japanese puzzle box from her childhood friend Klara, and next to it another gift, a hand-painted Egyptian wooden box topped with a cat sphinx. One of her favorites was the wooden mermaid that she'd picked up in Marie Laveau's House of Voodoo in New Orleans during a work conference, which was said to bring a house luck. Travel certainly had added spice to her life, and she was grateful to have had the opportunity. There was nothing more likely to open the mind and encourage tolerance than seeing how other people lived, which was why she had trouble understanding those who didn't care for it.

The thought of spice made Vivien long for homemade chilli (it was weird to have to spell it with two 'l's now) so she decided to surprise Geoffrey with some for dinner. Although there was no lack of great Indian food in England (thank you, Empire), her taste buds occasionally craved the remembered pleasure of peppers and chilli powder. She could even make some guacamole using the precious store of cilantro she'd bought in a cooking class in New Mexico. (Coriander, the only option she could find in her new country, did *not* taste the same, no matter how many people tried to tell her it did.)

Going through her kitchen cupboards, Vivien realized she was lacking a couple of ingredients, so she decided to walk over to the shop to see if she could pick them up there. Having learned about the vagaries of English weather over the years, she tossed a long beige sweater (*jumper!*) over her workout wear and stashed a folding umbrella in her purse (*handbag!*) before setting out. As she passed the pub, she glanced in and saw Clive Foster on his usual barstool, but she didn't stop. She needed to come up with a plan of action before she approached him again.

The shop was quiet as it was too early for the rush of students buying junk food for their lunch. Kartik was reading behind the counter and looked up as she entered, returning her smile of greeting before going back to his newspaper. Vivien cruised the two aisles, finding most of what she needed before approaching the till.

"Hello, Kartik, it's lovely to see you again."

"And you, Vivien. Did you find everything you wanted?"

"Mostly, thanks. I couldn't find any powdered cumin, though. Did I miss it somewhere?"

"No, I'm afraid there's not much call for it here in the village. But I'd be happy to loan you some from our personal stores. My mother wouldn't speak to me if I didn't keep cumin in my kitchen."

Vivien smiled and nodded. "That would be great, if you don't mind. I'm hoping to cook homemade chilli for dinner tonight. I don't need much, just a couple of teaspoons."

Kartik rose from his chair and headed toward the back of the shop, calling out to her that he'd be back in a moment. She heard him climb the stairs to the upper floor. How weird it would be, she thought, to live above your place of work, although of course many people did just that since the pandemic. For herself, she needed space and time between work and home to reset her attitude. Still, it was probably handy when you worked late hours not to have to travel far at the end of the day.

While she waited, Vivien decided to take a more detailed look around the shop. She soon found the bits of home décor Susan had mentioned, including brightly colored plant pots and candles in soothing scents of lavender, wintergreen, and sandalwood. She picked up a lavender candle and added it to her items on the counter.

Kartik returned with a small jar containing more than enough cumin for her needs. "Free of charge for a new customer," he told her as he started to ring up her other items.

"Thank you, that's very kind. These candles are lovely," Vivien noted as Kartik got to it.

"Yes, long-lasting as well. Susan actually makes them herself, it's a hobby of hers."

"Yes, she mentioned that to me when I saw her at the WI meeting. She must be a great help to you." Vivien looked at him thoughtfully. "Did I hear that you weren't born here, Kartik? That you were once a rank outsider like myself?"

"Well, not exactly," he replied. My parents moved to Doncaster when I was a teenager, so I was able to make friends before I left school and also at university in London. I've now been here more than twenty-five years, but yes, it still sometimes feels like a foreign country."

"Well, at least coming here allowed you to meet and wed your lovely Susan. Your daughters are often in the library when I'm working. They certainly are wonderful girls, you must be very proud."

"Indeed. Although raising two headstrong girls is a challenge anywhere, I think." The sparkle in his eyes said he wouldn't have it any other way. "But as long as my daughters can grow up to be intelligent, caring, confident people, it doesn't matter to me where we live."

Vivien warmed to him immediately and decided to risk a more personal question, hoping to learn from a fellow immigrant's experience.

"Forgive me for asking, but do you face prejudice in a small village like this? Are you able to follow your own traditions in raising your family?"

She got a snort in response.

"People assume that India is still a place of ancient traditions and forced marriages, but most of the very traditional Asians you meet here are ones whose grandparents came over more than fifty years ago, bringing the older ways with them. They weren't around to see the more modern India that exists today. Plus, faster flights and the internet make it much easier to keep in touch with family and events back home now."

"So you don't miss anything from your other country?"

Kartik smiled. "Arranged marriages are still very popular back home, although with much more autonomy, and they have their advantages. I know I would like to be able to recommend who Samantha and Nicole date and eventually marry," he laughed. "But I am happy there is more freedom and choice for women now, even if there are still some outdated views on things like homosexuality."

He finished bagging Vivien's items and looked directly at her to emphasize his next point. "Of course, you can find intolerance and prejudice everywhere, even America and Britain."

Vivien returned his straightforward gaze. "I have no doubt. I've seen the flag of St George proudly displayed by people drunkenly shouting anti-immigrant chants during sporting events. And I'm no doe-eyed disciple of American exceptionalism. But tell me, what made you decide to settle in Nether Chatby?"

"Susan's father lives near here and this shop was for sale, of course, which was the driving factor. I admit, some members of Susan's family were less than welcoming, but on the whole they've come to accept me. It seemed as good a place as any to raise a family, and overall the people here are nice and the community is fairly close. When you have a local shop, you get to know everyone pretty well, whether you want to or not."

Kartik had filed the receipt from her purchases but seemed in no hurry to return to his paper. Vivien imagined it probably got a bit lonely during the day, making the occasional conversation welcome.

"Then let me ask you," Vivien hazarded, "who do you think could have killed poor Sebastian?"

Kartik lowered his head and shook it slowly. "I don't know. There are people in the village that I don't particularly like, but I simply can't imagine any of them doing something like that. Colonel Jay is a randy old man and Susan complains about the way he leers at our girls, but there's no way he'd harm any of them, much less his grandson. Of course, I suppose no one wants to think their neighbors might be murderers, that you might have sold sugar to someone who was contemplating killing another human being." He looked up again. "I'm afraid I can't help you there. The village has its share of small-minded bullies but none, I would have thought, with that much anger or resolve. I have to hope it was either something very personal to the boy or that it was a random act of violence by a stranger."

"Surely a stranger in town would have been noted?" Vivien queried.

Kartik shrugged. "Maybe, maybe not, I get enough strangers through here to make it fairly unremarkable. But I must favor that possibility, otherwise I'd be looking suspiciously at all my regular customers!"

He pushed Vivien's groceries toward her, which she took as a hint that it was time to leave. She thanked him again for the cumin and stepped out onto the pavement. Down at the other end of the village high street she could see an ambulance parked outside the terraced retirement houses, lights flashing but without any obvious activity around it. As she made her way home she prayed it indicated the natural death of a very old person. There had already been too much unnatural death in the village for her liking.

But when Hayley once again appeared at her door that evening, her face a picture of despair, Vivien knew her prayers were not going to be answered this time.

28

"Any coincidence, said Miss Marple to herself, is always worth noticing. You can throw it away later if it is only a coincidence."

— Agatha Christie, *Nemesis*

Vivien showed her friend into the lounge where she and Geoffrey had been cozied up on the sofa catching up on the news. At her nod, Geoffrey turned off the television as Hayley settled facing them in one of the wingback chairs. Then they waited while their neighbor tried to compose herself enough to speak.

"I'm sorry to disturb you," she began, "but I thought you'd want to know as soon as possible. There's no good way to say it, Colonel Jay is dead. Josh says it looks like suicide."

Hayley stopped as tears threatened to emerge and Vivien nudged Geoffrey, who correctly interpreted this as an order to get their guest a glass of water and rose to obey.

"Oh honey, I'm so sorry," Vivien sympathised. "I know I only met him once, but I was quite charmed by him. I have no doubt he'll be much missed. Did Josh say if there was a note or anything explaining why he did this? I mean, he'd just been released, why now?"

Hayley shook her head. "Josh said there wasn't anything to explain it, they just found him sitting in his chair with a tipped whisky glass on the floor next to it. They're testing the remains of the whisky, but the symptoms seem to indicate poison."

"But why do the police think it's suicide?"

"I suppose they think it was done out of guilt from killing Sebastian. He refused to raise a defense when he was arrested, and his neighbors said he's been keeping mostly to himself since he was released. They've been taking turns checking on him, and today the lady next door found him dead."

Hayley paused as she took in the ramifications of Vivien's question. "Why would it be anything else but suicide?"

"I don't know. Maybe I read too many murder mysteries, but it just seems odd to have two deaths in the same family so close together, without there being a connection. Other than the colonel having killed his grandson, which I still can't believe is true."

Hayley cocked her head, tears momentarily stalled. "Maybe the connection is just that the death of his grandson pushed Colonel Jay into depression, and he didn't make it out?"

Vivien paused. "Maybe—and please don't be offended, I know I'm new here—but as you said, he just didn't seem the sort of man who would do that. He'd dealt with random death before, and no doubt lost people close to him during wartime. And while he was obviously fond of Sebastian, it seems more likely he'd want revenge or at least justice than to just give up on life. What if, instead, he knew something he shouldn't have? Maybe something about Sebastian's murder that meant he had to be silenced? Although that seems unlikely too, as the man usually did more talking than listening."

Vivien realized she was speculating without considering her friend's feelings as she saw tears trailing down Hayley's face. Once again, she regretted her habit of speaking before thinking as she attempted to soften her comments.

"But who knows? As I said, I certainly didn't know him as well as all of you did. We'll just have to wait and see what the police say. Is there anything I can do to help in the meantime?"

Geoffrey returned with the glass of water and Hayley smiled tremulously as she accepted it and took a couple of sips before setting it on the table next to her chair. She turned back to Vivien as Geoffrey resumed his seat next to his wife.

"Not at the moment, but of course there will be another funeral and probably some sort of memorial at the retirement home. I'm sure there will be opportunities to volunteer. Right now, we're all just reeling from the fact that there's been another death. The Bonners must be devastated, but I don't imagine they'll want any company for a while yet."

"And probably not my company ever," Vivien wryly added. Hayley shot her a look of commiseration.

"They'll get over it all someday, and realize it wasn't any fault of yours. But it's hard to think straight at times like this."

It is indeed, mused Vivien as Geoffrey walked their neighbor back home. And there seemed to be plenty of fault to go around. But someone wasn't bearing their fair share, and that was the person who had committed at least one murder, and maybe two.

29

"When you have no basis for an argument, abuse the plaintiff."

— Cicero

Vivien had already fallen into the habit of doing most of the regular housework on Fridays, ensuring the weekend would be clear so she could relax with her husband. She was putting the first miniscule load of laundry into their tiny washer-dryer combo (while internally bemoaning the loss of her full-size energy-gobbling American utilities) when there was a knock on the door. She looked through the peephole to see a very serious-looking Detective Inspector Torksey and Detective Sergeant Martin and tried to match their expressions as she opened the door.

"Inspector, how nice to see you again." Her nod included Sergeant Martin in the greeting. "Is there something more you needed from me regarding Sebastian's death?"

Torksey looked down and performed a little embarrassed shuffle. "Actually, Ms. Brandt, we're here on a different matter. We've received a complaint about you that we are duty bound to investigate."

"A complaint?" Vivien's wide eyes conveyed her disbelief. "I wouldn't have thought I'd been here long enough to have inspired complaints. Even for me." Then she remembered the incident from the library. "Wait, it isn't by any chance Grandpa Fred complaining, is it?"

"Grandpa Fred?" Torksey looked nonplussed. "Fred Turnbull is your grandfather?"

"No, sorry, it's just that's the way I was introduced to him, while trying in vain to discipline his grandson. Why don't you both come and have a cup of tea while you ask your questions." Vivien turned toward the living room and the two detectives followed, settling themselves on her plush new sofa which fortunately showed no signs of having been recently cried upon.

"Give me a moment, I'll be right back," she assured them.

DS Martin spoke up. "You're not going to try to sneak out via the bathroom window are you, like in one of your hardboiled American gumshoe novels?" She smiled, enjoying her joke.

"I'm way past being able to fit through a bathroom window and would at any rate use the quite serviceable back door. But no, I'll just go get us a pot of tea, if that suits everyone?"

They both nodded, so Vivien headed into the kitchen, turned on the kettle, and gathered the tea things, putting some biscuits on a plate. She could hear the detectives talking quietly to each other and wondered how they felt about pursuing nuisance calls when they obviously had more important work to do. As she re-entered the living room, they sat up straighter and thanked her for the tea as she poured. She noted Torksey taking a chocolate Bourbon even as Martin snagged a custard cream. They were obviously as diverse in their biscuit choices as in their looks and personalities. She imagined it made for a good working relationship and probably better crime-solving.

"Now, what's the nature of this complaint from Mr. Turnbull?"

Torksey took a deep breath before answering. "He claims you are guilty of child abuse and theft, Ms. Brandt. Do you recall the incident outside the Bickford library on Wednesday? Can you give me your version of what happened?"

"Of course. Young Dennis, who I gather is the grandson of the aforesaid Mr. Turnbull, was kicking a ball against the windows of the library. In addition to the noise, there was a threat of breakage. After multiple warnings, I removed the ball from Denny's possession and told him I would store it behind the desk until we closed, at which point he could retrieve it. He bellowed for his grandfather—the child's lungs are almost as impressive as his grasp of profanity—who threatened me from the upper story window of his abode. I explained the situation, and he then called me a Scottish female dog. I think that about covers it."

Martin paused in her note-taking. "Why did he call you Scottish?"

Vivien took a moment to raise her eyebrows at the sergeant's lack of curiosity about the latter term before she answered. "You would have to ask Mr. Turnbull that, although I expect as it was couched in other less-than-flattering terms, he believed it to be an insult." Vivien gazed back at the pair with equanimity and saw Torksey's shoulders slump. He took another biscuit.

"Do you have any witnesses to this incident, Ms. Brandt?" he asked.

"I'm sure my co-worker, Rebecca McColl, will testify on my behalf. She was watching from inside the library, but she assures me Mr. Turnbull's voice carried through the window. She does have a Scottish surname, though, so she might not be impartial."

A snort escaped DS Martin, who quickly tried to cover it by sipping her tea. Torksey wasn't fooled and threw her a look of disapproval, which Martin received with a grin, before he turned back to Vivien.

"Thank you for that, Ms. Brandt, we'll speak to Mrs. McColl, who I believe is of Irish descent, and get back to you with the result of our investigation in a few days." He brushed his hands together in preparation for getting up to leave, but Vivien wasn't through with them yet.

"Obviously I'm no expert in British police procedure, but this seems a low-level thing for a detective inspector to be spending time on. Particularly when there's a second mysterious death to investigate."

Torksey settled back onto the sofa with a look of annoyance. "You're right, ordinarily it wouldn't be me here, but as Turnbull has a history with the Bonner family, it came out during our investigation. I've been asked to be more hands-on as this involves a local politician, to ensure everything is done by the book. So, until the investigation is concluded, if you can avoid Mr. Turnbull and his family as much as possible, it would be appreciated."

"A history with the family?" Vivien ventured, but she could see by the inspector's stony face she'd get no more detail on that. "I'll do what I can, Inspector, as long as it doesn't prevent me from doing my job. I can't keep his family from entering the library. But while you're here, can you tell me anything about how Sebastian's murder case is proceeding? Or am I still a suspect?"

Torksey considered her for a moment. "Your GSR test came back negative, and someone saw you returning from town at the time you stated." He paused. "I'd say you're not out of the woods yet, but you're not at the top of my list. Currently. But this is an ongoing investigation, so there isn't a lot I can reveal to you."

Vivien leaned forward, her forearms on her thighs and her hands clasped together in a subconscious pleading gesture. "I know you're limited in what you can share, but as the person who found him, you can see how I might experience more than a passing interest." She looked straight into Torksey's eyes and thought she spotted a flicker of sympathy. Holding his gaze, she leaned back again, her hands falling palms up on the sofa. "For instance, have you found any link to Colonel Jay's death?"

Torksey blinked before relaxing in turn. "I understand your involvement makes it personal for you, Ms. Brandt, but let me assure you we see no reason to think you are in danger from the perpetrator unless you make yourself a target. And though I can't reveal details, I can tell you we are still pursuing multiple leads."

Vivien was silent as she tried to figure out how best to ask a final question. "Inspector, I expect you've had the results from the autopsy by now. Can you tell me, is there... anything...I could have done for Sebastian?"

Torksey's face softened slightly, but his voice remained firm. "There was nothing you could have done. The bullet ricocheted off his scapula, causing internal damage before lodging in his heart. It's surprising he lived as long as he did, if he was in fact still alive when you found him." He stared steadily at her to reinforce his words. "As for the colonel, tests are being run on the scene, but so far it does look like suicide, and without a note we can't be sure of the reason. Have you thought of anything else that might help us?"

Vivien tilted her head back to stare at the ceiling as she considered her response, then straightened to address the inspector. "He won't thank me for telling you, but I have it on good authority that Clive Foster was a friend to Sebastian and might have known some of his secrets. It may be worth interviewing him?"

"We would love to, but so far he hasn't responded to any of our messages, and we haven't been able to find him at home. However, we'll continue our efforts."

"I hear he spends quite a bit of time at the Wonky Donkey, if that's any help."

"Thank you for the information, we'll check there." This time Torksey's rise was swift and definitive, surprising even Sergeant Martin who nevertheless quickly followed, though she smiled and grabbed a last custard cream with a goodbye salute.

After they left, Vivien returned to her seat, munching on the remaining Bourbon biscuit. It hadn't escaped her notice that the inspector's information meant she must have just missed running into Sebastian's murderer. No matter what the inspector said, if she'd been a little quicker getting home, she might have been able to stop it happening. Or, she acknowledged ruefully, been killed herself, as she'd told poor Lucius. Still, she needed to do something to make up for not being there for Sebastian. Since the police hadn't told her what leads they were pursuing, she couldn't be accused of intentionally getting in their way, and she felt that discussions with multiple people were in order. She'd catch up with Hayley and find out if Josh had any more information. But before that, she might see if she could corner Justin at the library tomorrow and suss out where he'd actually been the day Sebastian was killed.

Until then, time and laundry waited for no woman.

30

"Although he had been found attractive enough by women, he knew he had little to offer beyond his own conformity. But this stranger, who had sought his advice, seemed to regard him as a normal human being."
— Anita Brookner, *Strangers*

Vivien waited anxiously for Justin to come into the library on Saturday. She knew from experience that teenagers were not early risers, but this didn't make her any less impatient. Her mood rubbed off on Becky, making them both so grumpy that even their usually soothing tea break failed to calm the nerves. On the plus side, Denny was absent as well, so Vivien didn't have to worry about giving him a wide berth.

In apology for her bad mood, Vivien spent some time processing interlibrary loan requests and then calling patrons to tell them their books had arrived. She disliked doing the latter job because she found it hard to decipher Yorkshire accents over the phone, but she knew it wasn't fair to push it on Becky because of that. Practice makes perfect, she consoled herself, but it was frustrating to have to constantly ask people to repeat themselves. One poor boy had to ask her for the key to the toilet four times before she understood what he wanted, by which time the kid was practically jumping up and down in agony.

Her good behaviour was rewarded when Justin and Samantha walked in just as she finished the phone calls. Samantha was wearing jeans with decorative colored sparkles on the back, appropriately forming a peacock on each of the pockets.

"I love your pants, Sam," Vivien said in greeting, and then could have bitten her tongue off. She'd gone and forgotten the most important of cultural differences.

"What?!" the girl screeched, twisting around to try and glimpse her backside. "You can't see my pants!"

"Sorry! I forgot you call them trousers here. I meant your trousers. We call them pants in America," she apologized, slightly red-faced. Justin laughed, enjoying her discomfort, before walking ahead to the bank of computers.

"Oh." Samantha took a moment to gather herself together and resume her cool girl attitude. "That's stupid. What do you call pants, then?"

"Underpants. Or underwear. Because you wear them under your pants."

Samantha seemed mollified by this explanation and wandered over to join her boyfriend, probably to listen to the latest top ten hit or watch videos of cats playing a piano. Even with the ubiquity of cell phones, the kids liked sharing their online experiences on the larger screens. It was obviously much too early in the weekend to think of doing homework. Vivien tried to hear what they were saying, but they were too far away, and for the next couple of hours until closing time she was kept busy by a regular stream of children wanting computers and even—would wonders never cease—a couple of people requesting books. But she kept an eye on the two teenagers in the hopes she could talk to them privately at some point.

Her chance came when Vivien found them sharing a Coke outside the library as she was leaving.

"Hey, you two," she started in what she hoped was a breezy, devil-may-care tone, "I was just about to head over to the chippy to grab some, um, chips. Would you like anything? I'm buying if you want to come with me."

Vivien could see the obvious thought cross their faces, that it would be embarrassing to be caught hanging out with an adult, but after a few seconds their hunger plus the delight of getting someone else to pay for snacks won out. Vivien muttered a silent apology to whoever was home cooking the meal she was about to ruin.

"Um, oka-a-ay," Samantha replied after receiving a confirming nod from Justin. "But we don't have much time, we can't be talking to you all afternoon," she qualified.

"Of course not," Vivien replied, as if she too had better things to do. "But I know you probably hear quite a bit about what happens around here, and obviously I'm clueless as an outsider. I'd appreciate getting your view on things." She hoped that would appeal to their egos. Every teenager wanted to be the one who knew what was going on.

Justin shrugged. "We don't promise nuthin', but buy the chips and we'll see. I want gravy on mine."

Chips (and more drinks) duly purchased, the trio grabbed a picnic table outside the shop and Vivien wasted no time.

"Have the police talked to you both yet?" she asked. Two confirming nods. "And were you able to help them at all?"

"They didn't so much want help, they just wanted to try to blame us, as usual," complained Samantha.

"Why would they want to do that?" Vivien asked with her best innocent look. Her two companions looked at each other and Justin shrugged again, this time as permission for Samantha to continue. Vivien made a mental note to introduce Samantha to the tenets of Power Chickdom, particularly the part about not needing male approval for everything you do. But this was not the time as she didn't want to stop the flow. Samantha went on, her eyes shifting side to side, looking anywhere but at Vivien.

"Well, they might have found out that we weren't entirely truthful the first time we talked to them." She paused, and Vivien merely raised her eyebrows in a questioning way, encouraging her to continue.

"I told them Justin and I were together, but then my sister went and narked on me, told them I was at home on the phone." Samantha pursed her lips in universal disapproval of annoying sisters everywhere.

Vivien remembered how she'd doubted Samantha's truthfulness at the time and had to stop herself looking smug.

"Ah, that's right. I remember you saying you two were together. I presume the police followed up for the revised story, then?" The two teens exchanged a quick glance and applied themselves to their chips.

Vivien tried again. "Surely you didn't have anything to do with Sebastian's death, so why make something up? Or did you have something to do with it? Did you decide the world could do without one more gay person?"

Her bluntness finally pierced Justin's shell of nonchalance. "I wouldn't kill someone because of that! My auntie goes on about it, she's a regular homo hater, but personally I don't really care who Sebastian hangs out with, and I certainly wouldn't go around shooting people over it!"

Vivien paused before saying quietly, "No, you'd just bully them about it so you could look cool in front of your friends."

Her comment was received with narrowed eyes and a mulish silence, except for more chip munching, but Vivien hoped the point was taken. She continued.

"Okay, folks, we've all been young once, believe it or not, I get the whole peer pressure thing so I won't go on about it. I just hope you'll be more understanding the next time you meet someone who is different. But I still would really like to know why you lied to the police. It can't have been anything like as bad as murder, can it?"

She looked expectantly at them as they shifted uncomfortably for a few seconds before Justin gave another of his trademark shrugs followed by a throat-clearing grunt.

"I was at my grandmother's house. Sometimes I help her out in the garden. She's, like, really old, so she can't do a lot of stuff, so I help her plant things."

"I'm guessing the police talked to your grandmother and now everything is hunky dory?" Vivien queried.

Another shrug. "Yeah." *He must have very strong shoulders with all the exercise they get*, mused Vivien, as the two teenagers quickly finished their chips and ambled off without so much as a thank you or even a goodbye.

She marvelled once again at teen priorities, where the embarrassment of planting flowers for your grandmother outweighed the dangers of lying to the police. But at least now she could cross these two off her list of suspects. If only she had a list of suspects. Vivien made a mental note to create a list of suspects.

31

"I have looked upon all that the universe has to hold of horror, and even the skies of spring and the flowers of summer must ever afterward be poison to me."
— H. P. Lovecraft, *The Call of Cthulhu*

After a relaxing evening watching the latest Marvel superhero installment with her beloved (Vivien had made Geoffrey promise to purchase a subscription to Disney+ as part of the wedding vows) and a night highlighted by its own conjugal marvels, Vivien enjoyed a lazy Sunday morning lie-in and once again woke to the sound of sizzling.

Donning a very fuzzy, warm bathrobe, she wandered down to the kitchen where Geoffrey was cooking up a storm. There were sausages (vegetarian), eggs (scrambled), and slices of fried bread (probably fattening and unhealthy, but who cared?). Plates were warming in the oven and apple juice was poured. Vivien felt immensely satisfied with her life and especially with her obvious good taste in husbands; so much so that she gave him a big hug from behind and dropped a kiss on the back of his neck.

"Well, I guess someone slept well and is ready to face the day!" Geoffrey smiled as he gave the bread a last flip. He turned off the burner, turned in her arms, and proceeded to turn her on with a passionate kiss. But before Vivien faced the cruel choice between bed and breakfast, her husband gave her a final squeeze and stepped away to take the warmed plates out of the oven and fill them with food. Breakfast it was, then.

Vivien dutifully followed him to the dining room table where everything else was laid out and took a seat, breathing in the magnificent aroma that always accompanied food cooked by someone else. She fleetingly wondered if another hug would get him to clean up after the meal as well, and then decided she was being greedy. After all, she wasn't a prostitute willing to sell her favors for…well…favors. Besides, she calculated, if she was going to trade sex for things, she'd better have a think about what she really wanted before Geoffrey grew weary of her charms. Not that she planned to let that happen!

"What are your plans for today?" Geoffrey asked as they munched contentedly, naively unaware of his wife's carnal calculations.

"I promised Hayley I'd stop over this afternoon for a cuppa, but other than that, nothing planned."

"And will that cuppa include a discussion of village doings, and speculation about who has been doing the doings?"

"Our interests are varied and far-ranging, I'll have you know, and may comprise everything from nail varnish to the socioeconomic effects of Brexit on the special relationship," Vivien replied in her haughtiest tone.

"Undoubtedly, but do your simpleton spouse a favor and try not to get too obviously involved in this murder. There is still a killer out there somewhere, and I'd rather he or she doesn't feel threatened by my new wife's searing intelligence and dogged determination."

Vivien sighed. "I do know that, my love, and I'm not going to go around taunting potential suspects with leading questions. And if I do find out anything by chance, I will immediately tell you and the police everything, not just call up and whisper, 'I know how it was done, meet me in the churchyard at midnight', before being strangled by an eavesdropping murderer. God, I hate when that happens, you can see it coming a mile away."

Geoffrey squinted at her. "Sometimes I'm really not sure if you recognize the difference between real-life crime and all those books and TV shows you ravenously consume. Let's be clear: vampires, werewolves, and extrasensory detectives are not part of real life, right?"

Vivien gave him a look of wide-eyed innocence. "Of course not, darling." She followed it with a mischievous smile. "Although to be fair, I do hear the village has a coven."

Her husband shook his head in defeat and gathered the dishes to load them into the dishwasher while Vivien congratulated herself once again on her superior spousal selection. Then he left to pick up his nephew for an afternoon of Leeds United football.

After showering and donning leggings and a baggy sweater (*jumper!*), Vivien strolled across the street to knock on Hayley's door. The two of them were soon ensconced at the breakfast bar with cappuccinos courtesy of her neighbor's new Nespresso machine. Hayley's outfit this morning included a hot orange jumper with a sparkly unicorn on it and neon green tie-dyed sweats. Her slippers were a muted grey but had elephant heads on them.

Will was lying on the sofa in the lounge consumed with the morning papers, so the two women were free to converse without fear of being overheard.

"Have you heard anything more from Josh about Colonel Jay's death?" Vivien asked.

"Only that they've identified the poison as methyl salicylate. I looked it up, it's basically wintergreen oil, and pretty readily available. It's even used in candles."

"Where did they find it?" Vivien asked. At Hayley's look of confusion, she clarified. "Was it in the glass of whisky? Or in the decanter? Or neither?"

"Ah, I see what you mean. I think Josh said it was in both. Why?"

Because if you're going to poison yourself, why would you put it in the decanter. Why not just in the glass you're going to use to do the deed?"

Hayley thought for a moment. "Maybe he planned to drink the whole decanter to be sure the job was truly done? Or maybe it was just easier to mix it in the decanter by shaking it up?"

Vivien sipped her coffee, idly wishing she could get those lovely, flavored creamers she enjoyed in America. "Maybe. But it just seems like a less direct method to me. Whereas if someone wanted to poison him, but not be there at the time, they would obviously leave it in the decanter knowing he would drink it eventually. I think it does open that possibility."

"But what if someone else drank it? That seems an awfully dangerous thing to do. And it always comes back to why anyone would want to kill Colonel Jay anyway, doesn't it?" Hayley responded.

"True, but by the same token, why would he commit suicide? There's definitely something going on here that we don't know about. Someone has information about something that is getting people killed. Speaking of which, I realized a couple of days ago that I've been failing Detecting 101. I haven't even written out a list of suspects for Sebastian's murder. Do you have paper and pen?"

Hayley got up and walked to the other end of the kitchen to rummage through a drawer before returning with a small pad of lined paper and a pen, which she handed to Vivien. "Where do you want to start?"

"Well, let's include eliminations. We know both parents have alibis, Missus from the petrol station and Mister was in a government meeting." Vivien wrote down their names followed by their alibis.

"Good," Hayley noted. "I really don't want to be thinking about what kind of parent would kill their own child. It's a horrible notion."

"And yet it happens quite often if the news is to be believed. There are some messed-up people in this world. Now, I found out yesterday that young Justin has an alibi, as does his girlfriend Samantha, not that I think the latter is capable of murder, but we'll note it nevertheless." She did some more writing.

"You've been busy!" Hayley exclaimed. "How did you find all that out?"

"From the horse's mouth, in fact. The boy was so embarrassed about doing something noble, in this case involving his grandmother and some flower planting, that he made himself look guilty. He'll probably have to work up a couple more ASBOs just to reinvigorate his street cred if that news gets out."

Hayley laughed. "You really are getting an education working at that library, aren't you? It took me months to figure out what an antisocial behavior order was, but Josh tells me the kids often brag about how many they've got, so I'm not sure they're terribly effective as a deterrent."

Vivien nodded. "I gather from Becky that we're lucky to work where we are, as some of the branches in the more downtrodden areas have to call the police on a regular basis. She says there's one branch library next to a pharmacy where the kids have to constantly walk past junkies shooting up on the doorstep to get to the books. That can't be setting a good example for our impressionable youth."

Hayley nodded. "Josh also told me he lectured some kids recently for wreaking havoc in one of the libraries and told them to go outside and find something better to do. So they went out and set fire to a derelict building."

"Jeez Louise, never a dull moment for our constabulary. And yet, at least kids don't have easy access to guns. In America there aren't many city libraries without armed guards these days. I do not miss that part of my home country." Vivien sighed, causing Hayley to refill their cups and add some cheeriness to her tone.

"So, who's next on the list?"

"Hmmm. Well, we have to add Colonel Jay, of course. Even though the police couldn't prove he'd used the gun recently, it could still have been him, and if he did commit suicide, that does make him suspicious. No one can think of a decent reason why he would do such a thing, otherwise. And now can't interview him to find out."

Vivien once again couldn't shake the feeling that suicide wasn't a method the brusque and military Colonel Jay would have chosen. He'd seemed to have such a healthy ego.

"Good enough, he's on the list," said Hayley. "Who else?"

"What about Clive Foster? He's a particularly murky figure in the background of all this and was evidently friendly with both boys. He's very evasive about some past event that got him defrocked. Could Sebastian have found out what it was and threatened him? And are Church of England vicars 'defrocked', anyway?"

Hayley took a moment before replying, choosing to ignore the last question. "Since he was already 'defrocked' long before this happened and is already pretty much a pariah in the village, what is there to threaten him with? And didn't you say Sebastian and Lucius were friendly with him? They didn't seem to have a lot of friends, would they be threatening one of the few they did have?"

"I guess it depends on how bad the thing was. I haven't heard that Foster was arrested or anything, which I suppose points to something immoral rather than criminal. It still might be something he doesn't want everyone to know."

"A sexual peccadillo, maybe?"

"Lucius says Sebastian implied he was gay, but in a way that made him sympathetic to the boys' plight, so at least it wasn't a penchant for underage boys. Unless, of course, he had made a pass at Sebastian and that's what the boy held over him. But you're right, we don't have enough information to decide either way. I mentioned him to the police, who were already trying to find him, so maybe Josh can tell us more once they interview him. If it doesn't get your brother in trouble with the PTB, of course."

Both women nodded at this reference from the Buffyverse to the Powers That Be, higher beings who oversaw people's fates. They were conscious that if Josh seemed too curious about the case he might be reprimanded, and they would lose their inside source. Plus, he was such a sweetheart, not to mention part of the family.

Hayley smoothly took up the topic of her brother, and Vivien conceded to herself that there'd been enough talk of murder and suspects for now. She was happy to hear that his date with Angela had gone well, the wineglasses proving impressive as expected. *Ah, to be young and in love*, thought Vivien. And then reminded herself that she was in fact in love and not *terribly* old. The next hour was spent in pleasant conversation, but with no mention of nail varnish or Brexit.

32

"Let us read and let us dance; these two amusements will never do any harm to the world."

— Voltaire

Later that evening, Vivien and Geoffrey sat watching the *Strictly Come Dancing* results show, or *Dancing with the Stars* as Vivien knew it in America. It was Bonfire Night, the odd celebration of the anniversary of Guy Fawkes's attempt to blow up the Houses of Parliament, and fireworks could be heard enthusiastically exploding outside. Much as Vivien appreciated the warmth of the giant bonfires that were also built on this night, she'd been to such celebrations on previous visits and decided she preferred a quiet night at home with her new husband. Even if it involved watching a clumsy politician attempt to do the foxtrot.

It never ceased to boggle Vivien's mind that her logical, cultured, deeply intelligent husband, who claimed to hate reality shows, was a fan of a dancing competition involving minor celebrities. She figured it had to be because his family watched it and he liked to have something to discuss with them. It wasn't like he could talk about his research. Nor could he, for that matter, share with his mother many of the other things that bonded him with Vivien. So dancing it was.

On the whole, Vivien didn't mind since it meant he didn't have any right to complain when she indulged in her own guilty pleasure, *Say Yes to the Dress*. She was discovering the second time around just how much a successful marriage was made up of a series of compromises and the balance of favors.

To keep that balance, Vivien waited to claim her husband's attention until there was a segment reviewing the couple's weekly 'journey'. The segments were so fake and boring that Vivien figured no one could possibly be interested in them.

"What do you know about methyl salicylate?" she asked.

Geoffrey answered while keeping an eye on the television. "It's the chief ingredient in wintergreen oil, similar to aspirin, and is used in products such as muscle ache creams and also to flavor foods in small doses."

"Could it kill someone?"

Unsurprisingly, Geoffrey turned to give his wife his full attention at this point, forsaking the start of a painfully awkward rhumba performed by an actor from *Hollyoaks*.

"Now why do I think you have a specific reason for asking? It had better not be research into how to knock me off and get your hands on my millions."

"Wait…you have millions? How did I not know this?" Vivien put on her best 'shocked' face, but Geoffrey was not to be distracted.

"All right, my darling, start talking. What's going on in that overactive brain of yours?"

"Okay, but I'm still going to want to know about those millions eventually." She readjusted her position on the sofa so she was directly facing her husband, causing Sydney to look up hopefully from his position on the coffee table and then settle back down when it became apparent no one was getting up to feed him. "I'm asking because it turns out that's what Colonel Jay died from. Methyl salicylate, ingested in his whisky. So how much would have to be in there to kill him?"

Geoffrey's brow furrowed. "Not much, if it was pure wintergreen oil. Less than ten milliliters. About a teaspoon in a glass of whisky would do it. But it would have a very strong mint taste. It's unlikely he would consume it by accident, so that does lend credence to the suicide theory."

"Except that it was in the whisky decanter, not his glass. If you wanted to be sure it would do the job, wouldn't you just add it to the glass?"

"Possibly. Although maybe the taste could be diluted somewhat if you mixed it in a larger quantity of whisky, but then so would the potency. Heavily peaty whisky would hide it better. Do you know what kind of whisky he drank?"

Vivien thought back to her talk with the colonel in the library at the Bonners' party. He'd been drinking whisky then. "Something very smoky. I can remember smelling it while I talked to him and thinking how strong it was."

"Well, that would help disguise the taste of the oil. But I think it still would have tasted slightly odd to him."

"Is it easy to get this oil?"

"Well, you could boil it from macerated leaves of the wintergreen plant, but it's much easier to purchase it on Amazon, where it's readily available. How did you find out what killed him?"

"Oh, Josh told Hayley." Vivien's mind was furiously running through ways to find out who had purchased wintergreen oil. There was something niggling at her memory, but she couldn't quite grasp it.

"You're trying to come up with a way to find out who purchased wintergreen oil, aren't you?" Geoffrey asked.

Blast, he knew her too well! He took her hand and looked her in the eyes, concern overriding even his desire to predict Craig Revel Horwood's score on the rhumba.

"If the police know about the oil, then they will already be doing that, utilizing resources that are much superior to—and less dangerous than—yours. Promise me you won't go around snooping through the neighbors' medicine cabinets looking for it, or asking to borrow some?"

Vivien sighed. "You're right, it would be stupid to do that when, as you say, the police can do it more effectively. I just feel so useless. In any of the many murder mysteries I read, the amateur sleuth would have found the key to the whole shebang by now. Hercule Poirot would be gathering the suspects in the dining room. Chief Inspector Alleyn would be setting the trap that forces a confession. Eve Dallas would be grilling the murderer with Roark in attendance. And the Honourable Phryne Fisher would be doing all of the above while dressed in the height of fashion and seducing multiple men. But I haven't a clue."

Geoffrey shook his head in sympathy. "It's that real life versus fiction thing again, my darling. I know you can't stop thinking about these murders, so all I will advise is to keep your eyes and ears open, report anything you discover to the police as you've promised, and try not to seduce any men along the way."

He was surprised to see his wife's eyes fill with tears. When he moved closer to hug her, she waved him away and then covered her mouth with both hands, working hard not to cry. She wasn't entirely successful.

"I'm so sorry, Geoff!" she whimpered. "I really wanted to present a new and improved me to your lovely country. This was my chance NOT to be loud or pushy or nosy. But it's all gone wrong and people are dead, and I can't help thinking it's at least partly my fault!" Vivien bent over, her head in her hands.

Geoffrey ignored her previous protest and moved nearer, gently putting an arm around her shoulders and kissing the top of her head. Vivien looked up at him, her cheeks wet, and grimaced.

"I must seem so silly to you. You've been through so much, with Kathryn's death and raising Sara on your own. I hate that I've brought more death and despair into your life!"

She watched Geoffrey's eyes glaze over for a minute, as they often did when his first wife was mentioned. Then he refocused and looked down at her, stroking her hair.

"I want you to listen to me. None of this is your fault. You have been trying to help people since you got here. I know it must be hard adapting to a different culture, we English can be a stubborn, taciturn folk who get more emotional with our dogs than our families. But you are a confident, beautiful, and intelligent woman, and that will always win out with those who matter. I love you exactly as you are, barring your tendency to misplace your keys, and others will too. Just give it time." He gently squeezed her for emphasis, and Vivien put her head on his shoulder and gave a last sniff and a tremulous smile.

"As for Kathryn," he continued, his voice rumbling in his chest against Vivien's cheek, "I will always love her, and it's true I was miserable for years after her death, which can't have been great for Sara, either. But it was you who brought joy and hope back into my life and made me see that I could look back on the time she and I shared with gratitude. You have been a breath of fresh air. My whole family has noticed I am a happier man, and knows they have you to thank for that. So on any rational scales, your good deeds are far and away tipping them in your favor." He smiled and kissed her gently on the lips, and Vivien felt the warmth spread through her that happened every time he was near. Drying her eyes, she sat up straight and put a hand on his cheek.

"Thank you, darling. I guess this has all been more stressful than I realized. Please bear with me while I work out how to be American and British at the same time."

"Forever, my love. And now let's relax and watch the tall young woman who claims to be an 'influencer' attempt to save her place in the competition by jiving in a very skimpy costume."

Ah, thought Vivien. Maybe it wasn't just familial influence that made him watch, then. She intertwined her fingers with his and they vicariously danced the night away.

33

"Don't cry because it's over, smile because it happened."
— Dr. Seuss

As if Mondays weren't difficult enough, this particular one included Sebastian's funeral. The Bonner family was having a private ceremony at the graveside in the morning, then hosting a reception at a nearby restaurant in the afternoon. Hayley had to work but promised to be back in time to drive herself and Vivien to the reception. Vivien wasn't sure how welcome she would be, but she decided to go in honor of the friendship she had started with the boy, and which she was sure would have blossomed if tragedy hadn't intervened. She also wanted to be there to support Lucius if he needed it.

There was quite a crush in the room set aside for the reception. The restaurant staff had tables set up in all four corners and filled them with a combination of sweets and crudités, with little bowls containing various dips. Drinks were served at the bar near the front of the restaurant, both to leave more space in the function room and, Vivien suspected, to give the bartender a chance to judge if someone was staggeringly drunk as they approached, so they could be cut off if necessary.

The whole village seemed to be there, and Vivien raised her glass of Chardonnay in greeting when she caught Reverend Edwards' eye. He nodded in return and gave her the slightest of smiles. James Frederick and Susan Ramakrishnan were both in attendance, their spouses undoubtedly holding down the fort at their respective businesses, and Vivien noted that Samantha and Nicole were talking quietly to a very somber Lucius on the other side of the room. The girls had probably been dragged there by their mother, but Vivien appreciated that they were keeping the boy occupied with something other than his own mournful thoughts.

Outside the open French doors at the back of the room, Vivien spotted Inspector Torksey talking to his Viking sergeant on the patio, both keeping a wary eye on the crowd. For their sake she was glad it was a warmish day. She wondered if police ever really caught offenders at the victim's funeral, then figured there must be some proven advantage to attending or they wouldn't waste precious resources.

Many of the others were unknown to her and to Hayley as well, and the two women surmised they were probably extended family or else business or social acquaintances of the parents. Sebastian had undoubtedly been an intelligent and sensitive child, but also very much a loner, and the lack of school-aged friends at his funeral reflected this.

Vivien did, however, spot the senior citizen crowd to their left, and nudged Hayley to get her attention and subtly point in their direction, raising her eyebrows in a questioning manner. Hayley nodded and they headed over.

"Hey folks, how are y'all doing today?" Vivien asked. One of the other things she had learned over the years of her visits to the UK was that lots of people expected all Americans to say "y'all". Fortunately, conversations with Melanie and her family meant Vivien was able to make it sound fairly authentic. In this case, the response to her friendly greeting was mixed, some of the elderly people smiling slightly and nodding, while others frowned in disapproval. One particularly grumpy gentleman spoke for the frowners.

"It's a funeral, how do you think we're all doing?" he growled.

"Oh, I'm so sorry," Vivien replied. "Were you close to Sebastian?"

There was the sound of a giggle quickly suppressed and the speaker frowned even more alarmingly. "That's neither here nor there, young lady. All we ask is a modicum of respect for the departed."

"Yes, of course," said a chastised Vivien. "I was fond of Sebastian myself, and his death is a loss to us all. As of course was Colonel Jay's, who I know was a friend to many of you."

Hayley had been watching the chatter in the back of the group and whispered to Vivien that they were talking about Vivien's part in Sebastian's death. Unfortunately, Hayley's whisper was loud enough for the grumpy man in front of her to overhear and she saw him make the connection.

"Ah, you're the one who found him in your house, eh? Or did you? How do we know you aren't the one who killed him, then?"

This was too much for the surrounding seniors, who gasped in horror at such an outrageous breach of etiquette. The plump woman, who Vivien remembered from the church service was called Maude, came forward to pinch grumpy man's arm, causing him to yelp in pain. But Maude wasn't through yet.

"That's enough out of you, Jerry Turnbull, this lady has been cleared by the police and that's all you need to know. Plus, she's taken your disreputable brother down a peg or two and tried to make your horrid nephew behave. She gets points for courage, if not intelligence."

Grumpy man suddenly became grinning man. "Flippin' 'eck, you're the one who narked Fred, are ya? Well, why didn't you say so! Anyone who annoys that wanker is a friend of mine, and he's been beefin' about the 'Scottish bitch' for days! Jay used to make him crazy too, it's one of the reasons Jay and I became mates!" Jerry raised his pint glass to Vivien before his expression became more serious.

"Now Jay, that's one that's got my goat, young lady. There's just no way Jay would be taking his own life, that I know for sure, and anyone who says otherwise will have me to deal with." Jerry punctuated this declaration with a long gulp of lager.

"Why do you say that, Mr. Turnbull?" Vivien gently asked her new bestie. Nicole Ramakrishnan came up and tucked her arm into Jerry's at that moment, informing 'Grandad' that her mother wanted to go soon. He sent her back with a promise to join them in a couple of minutes. Vivien marvelled that this quiet young girl was a distant cousin to the terror that was Denny. An example of environment winning out over genes, no doubt. Although she could see Jerry's high cheekbones and strong chin clearly translated into the beauty of his daughter and granddaughters.

Jerry finished his lager and continued where he'd left off.

"Simple. I served in the same war he did. We didn't know each other then, but we were in some of the same battles, and we saw 'orrible things, even talked about it after. Lotta soldiers, their minds couldn't deal with it, but Jay came out level-headed and stronger. He loved life even more after having seen it end for so many, so I *know* he couldn't have done what they're saying."

Before Vivien could pursue this insight, Archibald Bonner came over and gave Jerry a gentle pat on the back.

"Is everything all right over here? We heard raised voices," Archie said, glancing nervously at Hayley and Vivien.

Hayley stepped up and put her hand on his arm. "It's fine, Archie, and I just want to say how very sorry we are about everything you've been through these past weeks. I can't imagine what it's like, but of course if there's anything we can do, please let us know." The group all nodded in agreement.

"We appreciate that and thank you all for coming." His eyes cut to Vivien. "Ms. Brandt, may I have a word in private, if it's convenient?"

Vivien glanced toward Hayley as she replied, ensuring her friend could understand. "Of course, let's find a quieter spot."

The two of them moved to an empty corner just outside the doorway into the room, with Vivien positioning herself so Hayley could see her and catch her attention if she needed to leave.

"What can I do for you, Mr. Bonner?"

"I'm really sorry to have to tell you this, but Rachel is a bit upset to see you here. I've tried to convince her none of this is your fault, but as you might imagine she's not in a great place emotionally right now, so she's looking for people to blame." He gave a shrug of resignation. "Please don't think she's usually like this. She's not, she's a wonderful wife and mother. But he was our only child, and she's just having a lot of trouble dealing with his death, not to mention her father passing away so shortly afterward."

Vivien was instantly contrite. "I'm so sorry, Archie, I certainly didn't mean to cause any problems, I really just wanted to pay my respects to Sebastian, and I echo Hayley's sentiments. We'll leave, but please know my heart aches for the loss of your son, and I so dearly wish things could have been different. He was a wonderful young man."

"Thank you, he certainly was." Archie nodded, tears in his eyes, before turning away to rejoin his wife. Vivien's gaze followed him and she caught Rachel glaring at her with undisguised hatred, something she hadn't previously glimpsed, even at the WI meeting. Obviously, Rachel's feelings were intensifying and that was unsettling, but she trusted Archie's explanation about his wife's emotional state. Her grief seemed to be burning her up inside, and Vivien determined to steer clear until the woman had time to come to terms with her losses. If that ever happened.

She was reminded again that this was not the way she'd intended to ingratiate herself to her new country. She beckoned to Hayley, who walked over to her, and Vivien explained why she needed to leave. Hayley decided to go as well, so the two of them waved goodbye to the others and headed toward the door.

On the way out they passed Susan Ramakrishnan smoking a cigarette and Vivien stopped to tell the woman how much she liked the scented candle she'd bought at their shop. Susan paled, then nodded and quickly turned and walked away.

Vivien frowned. Here was another person who apparently didn't want to talk to her, despite their amiable chat days earlier. As if sensing her friend's dismay, Hayley gave Vivien's shoulders a quick squeeze as they left the church, reminding Vivien that she had made *some* friends since moving here. Including, evidently, Jerry Turnbull.

34

"Yes, it was dangerous, but we are not put into this world, Mr. Burton, to avoid danger when an important fellow creature's life is at stake."
— Agatha Christie, *The Moving Finger*

Vivien had a full day of work at the library on Tuesday and the morning passed quickly. The branch's regular librarian had decided to extend her leave of absence, providing Vivien with fairly regular work, so Vivien asked and was given permission to start a toddlers story hour. Today was the first one scheduled. She and Becky had designed posters and put them up in the surgery and around the village, and the response was gratifying, with over a dozen parents bringing their young children to the library.

Even here there were cultural differences to note. England's children didn't go on a lion hunt in the famous song, they went on a bear hunt. And Becky taught her a song about the grand old Duke of York that Vivien found distinctly odd considering the current one's escapades. But this and other songs went over swimmingly, as did her reading of a

Maurice Sendak book, *The Queen Only Wanted to Dance.* Parents and toddlers left in a cloud of happy conversation after sixty minutes.

The afternoon was uneventful, and since it was the library's late closing day, the neighborhood was quiet and already dark when Vivien locked the outside door at eight o'clock. As things had been so peaceful, she'd let Becky go home a bit early to catch her favorite television show.

Vivien turned from the door and started to put the library keys into her purse before looking up to find Fred Turnbull standing ten feet from her, wearing the same dirty undershirt and blocking access to her car. She took a deep breath.

"Is there something I can do for you, Mr. Turnbull?" she asked.

The man growled, which did not bode well. "You can keep your gob shut to start with, ya mingin' slag. I heard you were hanging round with my brother and his tosser friends yesterday, talking me down, and I've a mind to shut you up myself, since those stupid coppers won't do their job. Should have known better than to talk to that poncey inspector." Turnbull spat out the last few words. "He's just as useless as that posh MP with his nancy boy son. No one wants to hear from real people who do the real work anymore. But dammit, they're gonna!"

Vivien could see the man's fists compulsively opening and closing. She kept her hand on the keys, poking one out between her fingers in case worse came to worst and she needed a weapon. Peering at him closely in the fading light, she suddenly suspected he might have been the man arguing with Archie Bonner, the one who had stepped out in front of their car when they were on their way back from lunch that

Sunday. If so, she pondered, it would mean he was familiar with the neighborhood, and could have seen Sebastian enter her house on that fateful day.

But conjecture was for the future, once she was safely home. Now, she kept her voice calm to try to defuse the situation.

"I've got no quarrel with you, sir. My only concern is making this library a safe and entertaining space for the people of this community. Nor did I say anything derogatory about you at the funeral."

"Lying whore!" exclaimed Turnbull. "My missus heard about you all making fun of me, and she told me. You *will* be sorry."

Vivien was not happy to hear some poor woman was chained to this man whose chief accomplishment seemed to be his vast knowledge of offensive synonyms for sex workers. But now was not the time to marvel at vocabulary. She made one more attempt at appeasement.

"I'm not saying your name didn't come up, but I assure you I said nothing to your detriment. Now you may believe me or not, but either way I need to get home, my husband is expecting me."

Vivien took a couple of steps toward her car, but Turnbull didn't budge. Instead, he reached behind his back and pulled what looked like a lead pipe out of his waistband. Vivien's heart caught in her throat as she realized things were about to get very ugly indeed. If she retreated back into the library, he could easily follow her and she'd end up as a real-life Clue (Cluedo?) character. She glanced past Turnbull, but the street behind him was empty except for her car. And though he was older, the man seemed fit enough to overpower her, even without the weapon. She mentally cursed her decision to wear kitten heels that morning. She probably couldn't outrun him, but apparently she was going to have to try. She braced herself and looked around for the easiest escape route.

Just as she was about to take off, she heard a voice from behind her. "Uncle Fred, leave her alone. She ain't done owt."

Vivien slowly turned her head to see Justin and a couple of his friends appear from around the corner of the library building. Turnbull stared at them momentarily, but then his bloodshot eyes returned to Vivien, who looked steadily back at him and held her breath.

"She needs a lesson in respect. 'Sides, I heard she's a damned Scottish lesbo heretic," Turnbull snapped, letting more spittle fly.

Oh for heaven's sake, thought Vivien. *Not the Scottish thing again.* She couldn't help but be impressed by the speed of the village grapevine. Young Thomas obviously had connections.

She looked back toward Justin, who nodded to her almost imperceptibly before addressing his 'uncle', which Vivien hoped was just a courtesy title for an older man in this case. She didn't want to think about how close it would make the relationship between Justin and Samantha if it was factual. Surely there were laws about inbreeding, even in a country ruled by royals who were sometimes overly fond of their cousins?

"Yeah, sure," Justin agreed. "She can be a pain in the arse, but trust me, beatin' 'er up isn't going to make that go away. It'll just bring the police back here. You know they're waitin' on you to do something so they can arrest you again. Let me explain to her how things are, and you go back and let Aunt Flora get you some of her seed cake. Has she baked any today?"

"Aye," growled Turnbull, lowering his arm after a very long minute of consideration. He spat in Vivien's direction, his aim thankfully a foot short of Vivien's shoes. "Just make sure missus here doesn't mix with me or mine unless she wants a hole in her head." He gave her one last withering glance and turned on his heel to cross the street to his home. Vivien waited until he was in the front door before she turned to face Justin. She remembered now, his friends' names were Aiden and Rob.

"Thank you, Justin, Aiden, Rob." She nodded at them in turn. "That was a timely arrival."

Justin crossed his arms and leaned nonchalantly against the building. "Fred's gettin' old now, but he was a terror in his day, and he's still no one to mess with, *Mizzz* Brandt. You might not want to be walking around here on your own at night, as I can't guarantee me and my mates will always be in the right place at the right time."

"I appreciate your concern, Justin."

The boy shrugged, back to being cool. "Not concerned about you, lady, just promised Jerry I'd keep an eye out. And I don't want Flora to have to bail Fred out again. She's got enough trouble, and fortunately for you she does make a damn fine seed cake."

"I hope to sample it one day. But about you calling Mr. Turnbull 'uncle'…"

Justin shrugged. "He likes us kids to call him that. Makes him feel big protector, I guess. Although I think he is a sort of cousin of my mother's or something."

The boys turned and walked away. Vivien figured she was in Justin's debt now, and that was probably the way he liked it. It would make up for what he saw as his weakness in confessing to her about helping his grandmother.

She quickly got in her car and headed home. As there was no immediate threat to her safety, she decided Geoffrey didn't need to know about this little contretemps. It would cause him unnecessary concern. But she would think twice about letting Becky go home early in future, and it might be worth talking to Inspector Torksey about her run-ins with Fred Turnbull since the aforementioned 'relationship' with the Bonners was obviously not of the friendly sort.

35

"Chuckling to herself, Nancy said aloud, 'Romance and detective work won't mix tonight!'"
— Carolyn Keene, *The Bungalow Mystery*

Vivien kept her head down the rest of the week, working a couple of days at the library and spending the others getting the house in order and trying to clean up the garden as much as possible before the gardening service came. The lowlight was her reacquaintance with the English nettle, but she greatly enjoyed unpacking the last boxes containing her treasures from home.

She was glad she had listened to her friends when they'd encouraged her to take all her most beloved tchotchkes with her. Her glass-fronted cabinet in the lounge was now full of mementos, including a clay drinking vessel bought at a Renaissance Faire and pewter figures of King Arthur and Queen Guinevere that her parents had given her as a birthday gift during her teenage obsession with T. H. White's *Once and Future King*.

The wall-to-wall shelving in her new library now contained

her most precious books and also Geoffrey's large collection of non-fiction. While Vivien preferred cozy mysteries, which generally satisfied her innate sense of justice, Geoffrey was more of a history fan, delving into the murky depths of the political mind. If Vivien ever decided to write a historical murder mystery, she was sure he would come in handy between his reading and his knowledge of chemistry.

Sydney, too, was happy with the new shelves, climbing as high up on them as possible to glare down at his keepers before Vivien chased him off them, only to take refuge on top of the lounge cabinet.

By Sunday, Vivien was going a bit stir crazy and Geoffrey suggested a shopping trip to York. It was drizzling sporadically, but Vivien was delighted with the idea and rushed to don her rain gear after they'd consumed a light breakfast of yoghurt, toast, and juice.

After parking near one of the medieval town gates (she always forgot which gate was where, so it was just as well Geoffrey was there to navigate them back to the car), the two of them wandered through various cobbled streets taking in the historic beauty of the city. They visited a hat shop creatively named 'The Hat Shop' where Vivien purchased a raspberry-colored woolen hat she in no way needed, then walked to the food court behind The Shambles, where she was delighted to find a place that made burritos to order. Vivien had often bemoaned the lack of good Mexican food in England over the decades of her visits, but of late she'd noticed more Mexican restaurants popping up. And while many of them were 'Tex-Mex', which was more pepper-based than the tomato-based Californian version she favored, it was usually enough to fulfill her craving.

After lunch she refused Geoffrey's suggestion to visit the minster. It was gorgeous, but she'd been several times before and didn't feel like paying the somewhat expensive entrance fee. Instead, Geoffrey offered to take her to one of his favorite places in the city, refusing to say more until they got there.

They walked down Goodramgate to an unassuming pair of wrought iron gates between a comic book shop and a clothing store. Fastened to the gates was a small sign identifying the location as Holy Trinity Church and listing the hours it was open. As they walked through the gates, Vivien noticed a blue plaque on the left wall declaring the church was where Anne Lister and her partner, Ann Walker, had their union blessed. She'd read some of Lister's nineteenth-century, five-million-word diaries which described everything from her bowel movements to her vast sexual exploits at a time when lesbianism was so unacknowledged it wasn't included in a Victorian law outlawing homosexuality. In addition, her diaries were the basis for an entertaining BBC television series called *Gentlemen Jack* that Geoffrey had suggested they watch. Vivien remembered reading that the plaque had originally described Lister as being of "non-conforming gender", but after protests the words were replaced with "lesbian".

She was enchanted as they traversed a small path between the surrounding buildings and found themselves in a leafy garden surrounding a church built of honey-colored stone. The rain having stopped, there were a few people milling about and relaxing on the benches, and she and Geoffrey absorbed the palpable feeling of tranquility in silence for a few moments before entering the building.

Inside the church, Vivien was delighted to see uneven brick floors and iron candleholders that must have been there for over a hundred years. Colored light filtered through stained glass windows that Geoffrey told her dated back to the fifteenth century. The raised wooden box pews had hinged doors for entering, like ones she'd seen on a visit to Whitby.

She stood in front of the altar, imagining the joy of those two ladies pledging themselves to one another in the face of almost universal disapproval. Behind the altar were old reredos boards featuring the ten commandments prefaced by Roman numerals. "Though shalt do no murder" was listed on the right, and Vivien felt an almost unbearable sadness well up inside her as she thought of Sebastian and the prejudice he had still faced over a century later. Had that really been a factor in his death, or were there other reasons someone felt they had to kill an innocent child? In that moment she rededicated herself to discovering the truth, even if she didn't yet know how it might be done.

She continued to muse on the matter as they drove home later that afternoon, and she noticed darkness was already descending thanks to the time change. Geoffrey had to stop for petrol and Vivien took the opportunity to grab a bag of Doritos in the accompanying mini-mart while he paid. The well-worn cash register pinged while they waited in line (*the queue!*) and Vivien nostalgically noted it was a model she'd edited the manual for in her previous life. She loved her new life, but she still felt a bit homesick when talking to her family, despite the fact that the day before they had once again called at the wrong time thanks to America not having switched to Daylight Saving yet. Ah well, she thought, next week they would all be in sync again. She gazed at the cash register, then at the darkened video monitor in the corner of the shop, and suddenly she had an idea who had killed Sebastian Bonner and how they'd got away with it.

The only remaining question was why.

36

"Crime is common. Logic is rare."
— Arthur Conan Doyle, 'The Adventure of the Copper Beeches'

Fulfilling her promise to Geoffrey, Vivien filled him in on her theory on the way home and was gratified when he couldn't find fault with it. They agreed there was one more conversation to be had before they went to the police, so as soon as they got home they ate a quick dinner and then headed over to the pub. As they'd hoped, Clive Foster was ensconced at the bar with pint in hand. He glanced up as they entered, then straightened and watched with narrowed eyes as they headed toward him. While Geoffrey ordered drinks, Vivien perched herself on the stool next to Clive and leaned over to address him *sotto voce*.

"We need to talk to you. Now. I think you have the key to catching Sebastian's murderer."

Clive looked at her dispassionately. "I do not want to get involved in any of this. I didn't murder anyone, and I don't know who did. I just want to be left alone, as I told the police earlier this week. So please, just stay away from me."

He turned back to his drink, but Vivien was not to be dissuaded when she felt she was so close to the truth.

"I'm not suggesting you killed anyone. Or even that you did anything wrong. But there's a secret you've been keeping, and I think it is at the heart of these events." She paused to take in Clive's crossed arms, the stone face, and softened her tone. "Please, Clive. I know you cared for Sebastian. I know you were his friend. Do this for him, and if it turns out I'm wrong, I swear your secret will never pass my lips. But if I'm right, there is someone out there who will do anything to keep people from knowing that secret, and that means you're on their list of people to kill."

For a couple of very stressful minutes, Clive considered her words. Then, with a sigh, he rose to lead them to a corner table. After they settled, there was a long silence as he struggled with where to start. Vivien decided to help him along.

"The reason you were let go from your position and from the church, it wasn't anything illegal, was it? In fact, it was due to a…shall we say, most inconvenient love." Clive nodded miserably, his eyes suddenly shining with unshed tears. Vivien allowed him time to compose himself before continuing.

"It was part of your friendship with Sebastian, sharing the truth of being homosexual. But if it had been Sebastian you fell in love with, you would have been arrested, since he was underage. So I'm guessing it was someone else?"

Clive gazed at her for a moment, his brow puckered. "You know, don't you? How?"

"It was something Sebastian said about the sins of the father. I thought he was just randomly quoting scripture, until I realized he might have meant it literally."

Clive nodded. "You called it inconvenient, and it was in fact the most inconvenient person possible. Worse still, it was Sebastian who saw me kissing his father in the church office one evening two years ago. He'd been sent by his mother to fetch Archie for dinner."

Geoffrey replied. "Ah. Indeed. Archie Bonner, politician, family man. A same-sex extramarital affair is not something he'd want to be generally known. But are you saying Sebastian outed you? That seems…surprising."

Clive shook his head. "No, we didn't even know he'd seen us at the time, but I can imagine how confused and upset he must have been. I think he was dealing with his own uncertain sexuality at the time and had no one to talk to about it. He eventually told me about seeing us, so at least I got a chance to tell him how sorry I was, and to be his friend."

"Did he confront his father as well?" Vivien asked, but the ex-vicar shook his head.

"Not that I know of. I don't think he wanted any more stress in his home life."

"He must have told somebody besides you, though, or none of this would have happened."

Clive's mouth was set in a firm line, but there was a guilty look in his eyes.

"He let slip something to his grandfather soon after it happened, thanks to the colonel sharing too much of his whisky. I figure it was Jay who told his daughter. But however Rachel found out about it, she went directly to my bishop and demanded I be punished for adultery and the seduction of a parishioner, claiming she had a witness who would swear to it if necessary. I didn't know then it was Sebastian, but I made it unnecessary by confessing, hoping to save everyone more pain. I think she also blamed me for Sebastian being gay, as if Archie and I had given him the idea or something."

"You told me you didn't really know the Bonners that well," Vivien commented.

"Well, it wasn't exactly anything I was going to brag about, now, was it? Besides, you have a habit of coming on pretty strong, Ms. Brandt, and I didn't see any need to satisfy your curiosity."

Vivien gazed at him for a moment before nodding. "Didn't Archie or anyone else speak up for you when you were punished?" she wanted to know.

"Archie's a lovely man, and cares about his constituency, but Rachel rules that particular roost. As for the rest of the community, they really didn't know what was happening, and I certainly didn't want to cause any more upset by sharing my story, not to mention it would be ruining Archie's career and disobeying my orders from the diocese to keep quiet about all of it. So it was put about that I was resigning my parish immediately, as well as my vocation, to pursue other interests. But I'm afraid I've had a harder time hiding my pain than I thought I would, so people have maybe figured out I didn't have much choice in the matter. Plus, of course, I haven't in the end managed to find any other interests."

"Wouldn't it have been easier to move away?" Geoffrey asked.

"Probably. But the fact is I still care for Archie, and this part of the country is my home. Even if I could afford to move, it seems I'm too weak to give up everything I love.

And that, ladies and gentlemen, is why I drink." He raised his pint glass and punctuated the sentence with a large swallow of lager.

Vivien leaned forward to squeeze his non-drink-bearing arm in sympathy. "I'm so sorry. I can't imagine how hard it's been for you. But I have to ask: did it never occur to you that the people who knew this secret of yours were being killed?"

Clive scanned their faces. "Of course it did. But out of the others who knew, Archie and Rachel were both alibied, and I'm pretty sure someone would have noticed a bishop skulking about the place murdering people. So I really couldn't see how there could be a connection. Plus, Colonel Jay's suicide seemed to put an end to the issue. I assumed he'd killed his grandson and then couldn't take the guilt. Admitting to everything at that point wouldn't have helped anyone."

He paused and cocked his head as he looked at them. "But I'm guessing since the two of you came to me directly on this, and seem to have figured out most of the story, you have a theory that links my past sins to this current horror?"

"We do indeed," said Vivien. "But we need to confirm it with the police before ruining anyone else's reputation. So I hope you'll forgive us if we wait a bit longer to reveal all until we can confirm our theory is, in fact...uh...fact."

Clive shrugged as he turned away to take another gulp of his drink, then stared into the empty glass. "Fine by me, I'm in no hurry to be universally reviled. But I would issue you the same caution you've given me. Now that you know the secret, you're going to be on the killer's list as well. You'd best take care."

37

"The study of crime begins with the knowledge of oneself. All that you despise, all that you loathe, all that you reject, all that you condemn and seek to convert by punishment springs from you."

— Henry Miller

Geoffrey and Vivien stopped by the police station after talking to Clive, only to discover DI Torksey was unavailable. They left him a note with some pertinent details and a request to get in touch as soon as possible. But there was no call that evening, and a reluctant Geoffrey had to go to work Monday morning to give an important presentation to his management team. Vivien promised her husband that when the detective called she would set up a meeting so they could convince him of the viability of their theory together.

In the meantime, Vivien continued to unpack and unwrap, satisfied that she was almost done with this momentous move. Shortly after ten, her cell phone (*mobile!*) finally rang.

"Ms. Brandt? This is Detective Inspector Torksey.

Apologies for the delay in replying to your message, I was dealing with some personal issues this weekend and our new duty sergeant has yet to grasp what is important to pass on. Do you have a moment to talk?"

Vivien settled into a nearby chair. "Indeed, Inspector. As we said in our note to you, Geoffrey and I made a couple of discoveries on Saturday, and we think they provide a motive for the murder of Sebastian and possibly Colonel Jay, as well as revealing the identity of the murderer. Could you come by this afternoon so we can discuss it with you?"

"Sergeant Martin and I do have a full day already scheduled, Ms. Brandt. Can you give me an outline of this information? If it sounds plausible, we'll try to drop by later."

Vivien paused. This was exactly the situation she'd described to Geoffrey, where the witness declares over the phone, "I know who the killer is and I will tell you anon!", only to be immediately murdered. She decided that wasn't going to happen to her, so Geoffrey would just have to forgive her for doing this without him. She took a deep breath and began to explain their theory to the inspector.

"Very well. We think there's a hole in Rachel Bonner's alibi for Sebastian's murder, namely a cash register—I mean till—that didn't automatically reset when the clocks went back, and we also think we know why she did it. It has to do with a secret love affair and everything that goes along with that."

There was a long pause on the other end of the line. "I appreciate the information on the alibi, Ms. Brandt, we will get onto that immediately. But I have to inform you, Rachel Bonner also has an alibi for her father's death, whether it was murder or not, and that one is cast iron. And though she was seen visiting him a few days before he died, multiple people drank from the whisky decanter after that, and she was away from home the entire day of his death, with multiple witnesses to attest to that fact. So if you believe the murders are connected by a single motive and the same person did both, it can't be her."

Bollocks! thought Vivien to herself. *Have we got it all wrong, then?*

Before she could reply to the detective, she heard the soft click of the front door opening and turned to find Rachel Bonner standing at the entrance to the living room. Rachel placed a finger over her lips in a shushing motion and then mimed putting the phone down. Vivien thought fast.

"Okay, Mom, it was good speaking to you," she said into the phone. "I've got to go now. I'm sorry cousin du Maurier has gotten out of hand, but I know you can deal with it. And of course I would love you and Dad to fly over and visit as soon as possible."

Torksey was immediately on alert. "Rachel Bonner is there?"

Vivien mentally offered a quick prayer of gratitude that she was working with a detective able to recognise an oblique literary reference to Daphne du Maurier's *My Cousin Rachel*. And to Sergeant Martin for having revealed his reading preferences.

"Exactly," she responded. "Do your best."

"We're close by and on our way. Try to keep her calm and talking." He slammed down the phone and Vivien was on her own. She put the mobile down on the table next to her, surreptitiously hitting the record button. There was no way to dial 999 with Rachel watching her so carefully. She wished

Torksey had at least left the line open or given the phone to someone so there would be a witness to whatever was about to happen. She would have to chastise him the next time they met, if there was one. But at least there would be a record this way.

"Hello, Rachel." Vivien plastered on a smile. "What a pleasant surprise."

Rachel was having none of it, her beautiful ice queen face contorted with hatred.

"Don't lie to me, you bitch. I know you've ferreted out my pathetic husband's disgusting affair with that supposed man of God. Someone ever so casually mentioned this morning that you and your spouse were seen conferring with Foster in a corner of the pub last night. They all know he made a laughingstock of me. What did he tell you? That Archie was driven into his arms by my domineering ways? That none of it was *his fault*?" She hissed the last words.

Vivien took a slow breath, hoping it wasn't going to be one of her last. "He didn't say any of that. He was simply reminiscing about his friendship with Sebastian."

"Friendship!" Rachel was close to shrieking at this point, and a vein in her usually perfect porcelain forehead had started visibly throbbing. So much for keeping her calm. "That pervert would never be satisfied by mere friendship with *anyone* in my family! He was out to ruin me from day one, especially when he saw I was becoming more prominent in the church than he was."

Well now, isn't that a bit of classic projection, thought Vivien. She tried not to panic, breathing through her nose as she'd been taught in her California yoga classes. Oh God, how she wished she was in California on a yoga mat right now, relaxing to tinkly chimes and looking forward to a mango smoothie after her workout. But no, she had to be here fending off a double murderer.

"Rachel, surely all that is ancient history now. Mr. Foster is out and you're in. Sebastian, bless his sweet soul, is no longer in pain. Let's put it behind us and try to heal, yes?"

Rachel stood there—her hair impeccably coiffed, her tasteful teal twinset complemented by a single strand of pearls—and glared at the woman seated in front of her. Then, ever so slowly, she reached into her designer handbag and removed a large kitchen knife.

"You have no future as an actress, Vivien," she hissed. "But maybe I can make you famous as a victim before I pay a visit to our dear Mr. Foster. Then I've only got to finish up by serving your husband a slow-acting poison at the next gathering, and people will sadly recall how he died from loneliness and the stress of being without you. It will all be very Romeo and Juliet."

A sickly smile formed on Rachel's face, and Vivien realized a calm Rachel wasn't any better than a manic one. The woman was either mad or hovering close to the edge of it. Especially if she thought she could get away with poisoning a world-leading pharmacological expert who worked with a whole bunch of other experts. Reason had just flown out the window and all Vivien could do now was to try to keep her talking until the police arrived.

"Oka-a-ay, but before all that happens, can you at least explain to me what happened with Sebastian? He was your son, Rachel, and I know you loved him."

The knife wavered for a moment, but not long enough for Vivien to take any action. Looking up she saw Rachel's eyes glittering with unshed tears.

"I did. Of course I did, even though he could be so difficult sometimes. I didn't mean to shoot him. I only took the gun to show him how serious I was, to convince him that I would have to take my own life if he shamed me in public by revealing what he knew. But he didn't care, he turned away from me, so I yelled his name and pointed the gun at my head, said I'd pull the trigger. He lunged toward me and...I don't know...it was just a reflex, I put my hands out to stop him and the gun just went off. And then he was dead and there was nothing I could do."

There was a strangled sob, but the knife stayed steady.

"But why did you confront him in my house, Rachel? Why not talk to him at home?"

Rachel straightened up and strengthened her grip on the knife, her face once again hard with renewed purpose. "Because it was all *your* fault. Encouraging his disobedience by giving him full access to your home, encouraging his mawkish sentimentality and feeding his selfish desire to be the center of attention. I saw him go into your house and suddenly I knew, if anything ugly was going to happen I wanted it to happen here, in this place of sin and depravity. He would still be alive if it wasn't for you, and for that you have to pay."

Rachel took a step forward as Vivien racked her brain for anything that would postpone the inevitable. She needed a miracle, and as soon as she thought it she heard the voice of God coming from the hallway. Or at least God's representative.

"Rachel, stop," the Reverend Jonathan Edwards pleaded as he appeared in the doorway. "This has gone too far. You can't keep killing people."

Rachel spun around to point the knife at him, even as her other hand rested gracefully on her hip, her handbag hooked over her forearm. She looked like a demented Stepford wife. Vivien saw her chance and started to rise out of the chair, but Rachel caught the movement and moved back slightly so she had them both in her sights as she replied to the vicar.

"Shut up, Jonathan!" she spat. "You're in this as deep as I am. If you'd had the balls to help me finish cleaning up this mess it could have all been done by now. Now you can't turn me in without incriminating yourself in dear Daddy's untimely demise, and we all know you're too much of a coward to do that. So just leave. Do it now. We're done. I never want to see your whiny face again outside of the pulpit, where you can play the hypocrite to your heart's content."

Vivien could see pain and confusion written clearly on Edwards' face, but he continued to act as if the woman in front of him was amenable to reason.

"Rachel, this isn't you. I've seen how loving you can be, and you know I love you. I'd do anything for you. Don't destroy everything we have. People will understand the pressure you were under. Sebastian was an accident. Give yourself up before it's too late."

He spread his hands in supplication and Rachel lunged forward, slicing his left forearm with the knife. Vivien saw blood well through the vicar's fingers as his right hand gripped the wound, his eyes widened with shock. Whatever dream world Edwards had been living in, it looked like he had woken up to a nightmare.

Rachel stepped back and looked down her patrician nose

at him. After an initial exclamation, Vivien stayed where she was, not wanting to give the woman cause to strike again at either of them.

"People know *nothing*!" Rachel yelled, her eyes darting back and forth between her two victims. "I was going to have it all. Archibald was on his way to being Prime Minister and I would have had everything I deserved: power, influence, and money. I could have made this country great if I wasn't surrounded by weaklings, men who put their own feeble passions above their duty to their family and their nation. But I can still do it. I'll start over once Archie is gone. I'll use my connections to find a new way in."

Vivien was wondering if 'gone' meant Archie was on Rachel's apparently lengthening list of future victims—if the woman had her way the entire village was going to be decimated—when she glimpsed a man ducking and running under the front window of the house toward the door. She suddenly realized she had to make sure Rachel and Jonathan didn't notice any errant noises; the faintest hint of a threat might trigger a violent reaction. It was time to play her part by drawing their attention.

"Really, Rachel," she loudly announced, "how great can a woman be who relies on men for her status and power? You should at least have the guts to run for office yourself."

As Rachel turned fully toward her, Vivien caught the snick of the front door opening. She hoped Rachel was too hyped up to have heard it. Edwards' attention was still focused entirely on his ex-beloved, his features constantly changing as they reflected his struggle to understand her betrayal.

"For myself," Vivien continued, "I certainly can't

recommend you for membership to the Power Chicks Club, so that's one influential group you definitely won't be joining."

There was a moment of silence as Rachel looked at Vivien with pure loathing. "You. Are. An. Idiot!" she screamed before moving forward, knife raised.

Vivien jumped out of her chair and quickly backed up to the fireplace when suddenly all hell broke loose in the form of a tan and black ball of fury that flew through the air and landed on Rachel's head. Screaming in pain, Rachel reached back to try and dislodge her attacker with her free hand, but she was hampered by the handbag hanging from her elbow. Sydney gave an unearthly howl and jumped to the floor as a shapely Viking arm encircled Rachel's neck. Sergeant Martin's other hand clasped the woman's wrist, whacking it repeatedly against the nearby doorframe until she was forced to drop the knife. Rachel struggled vigorously for a few seconds but was ultimately no match for the muscular sergeant. She slumped as PC Marsden stepped up to remove the handbag from her arm and help Martin handcuff her.

Torksey entered the room already on the phone requesting an ambulance for the vicar, who was sitting in the hall still holding his arm. Edwards did indeed look a little faint, so after hanging up the inspector went over to him and wrapped a handkerchief around the wound, tying it tightly. Vivien found herself inappropriately marveling that there were men who still carried handkerchiefs but was glad that Geoffrey didn't subscribe to the habit as it would add a 'yuck' factor to the laundry.

And as if her thought had summoned him, at that moment Geoffrey walked in. Vivien would discover later that he had cut his presentation short to return home and ensure his wife was safe and secure, but right then she just felt she'd never been so glad to see anyone. She gratefully registered the care and worry evident on his face and began to mentally grapple with how to explain yet another tragedy happening in their home. She wondered, not for the first time, if he would regret marrying her. Her husband, however, was made of sterner stuff, so when he opened his arms she simply stepped into them and hugged him close.

38

"If you cannot get rid of the family skeleton, you may as well make it dance."

— George Bernard Shaw

"And that's how I spent my weekend. What were you guys doing?"

It was the Saturday following Rachel's arrest and Vivien was on her regular call with her family. Despite the fact the US had now also set their clocks back an hour her parents had still managed to call at the wrong time, but Vivien was so glad to talk to them she didn't mind at all.

"So it was when you remembered the cash register didn't automatically reset for Daylight Saving Time that you knew Rachel was the killer?" her father asked admiringly.

"Well, I didn't know, but I suspected it might be the case, and the fact that the video monitor wasn't working meant Rachel could use the till receipt with the wrong time on it to give her an alibi. It was something to be investigated, anyway. And then Rachel gave the whole thing away because she got paranoid about us talking to the ex-minister. I think she really was getting quite overwrought at that point; it was only a matter of time before she broke."

Vivien's mother still had a face full of worry. "But Vivien, the danger you put yourself in! Did you not think about how we would feel if you'd been harmed?"

"I wasn't trying to make you worry, Mom, believe me, or to get myself killed. Geoffrey and I did what we could to share our theory with the police, but we had no idea Rachel knew about our talk with Clive. Things just snowballed very quickly, and Rachel's mental state turned out to be very unpredictable."

"Mental state, my butt. You mean she was so crooked that if she swallowed a nail she'd spit up a corkscrew, Sis," Melanie commented with her usual flair.

"And what about the current vicar, what's the deal with him?" her father asked.

"He's been released on bail and is holed up in the rectory, with the assistant vicar from a neighboring village taking on his duties in the short term. I really don't know what will happen to him, or how big a role he had in this whole thing. Rachel implied he had something to do with Colonel Jay's death, but the police are being very closed-mouth until after the first official hearing, when all the evidence can be documented for referral to the Crown Court. Inspector Torksey says he'll be able to tell us more after that."

"That poor old military man," Charlotte sighed. "I only hope he didn't realize he was poisoned by his own daughter, or her extramarital religious boyfriend."

"It is a shame," agreed Vivien, "but it does seem like Colonel Jay suspected Rachel early on and chose to protect her anyway. And Hayley has since discovered from one of his close friends in the retirement home that he had terminal cancer. It must have been a lot for him to deal with all at once."

"And what about the two of you?" her father asked. "Will you still want to live in that house, considering all that has happened there?"

Vivien sighed. "I've already spent so much time and energy on doing up the house, and I really do love it. I've got specialists coming in this week to do a final deep clean"—she didn't want to mention the word 'bloodstain' or that they were in fact replacing part of the floor, it would undoubtedly set her mother off—"and I'm hoping that and the passage of time will make us comfortable again. Heck, maybe I can even get some sort of supernatural cleansing going, I hear there's a coven in the village that might be able to help."

"Might as well. Can't dance, never could sing, and it's too wet to plow!" her sister enigmatically pronounced.

Geoffrey's face appeared over Vivien's shoulder and was greeted enthusiastically by her family.

"It's lovely to see all of you, too," her husband purred in his caramel company voice. "Melanie, those earrings are marvelous."

Vivien made vomiting noises as her sister smiled.

"I just wanted to let you know," Geoffrey continued, "I'm keeping a very close eye on your daughter, and between myself and Sydney, we're here to protect and to serve."

Charlotte's face cleared instantly, much to Vivien's disgust. "Thank you, Geoffrey, we're ever so glad you're there for Vivien. And Sydney is an absolute hero, of course!"

"Yes, Vivien has been complaining about him climbing the furniture, but now we're all glad he was there ready to defend his mistress when the time came."

"If that ain't a fact, God's a possum," Melanie contributed.

Vivien snorted. "I still think he was after the velvet bow holding up Rachel's hairdo, without a single thought for my safety."

"And I'm equally sure you're wrong, my darling. Sydney knows on which side his bread is buttered." He smiled at the screen. "I hope you will all be able to come out and visit soon. My daughter, Sara, is coming home in a few months and I'm sure she'd love to get to know you all. Plus, I know Vivien misses you. Check your calendars?"

Everyone but Vivien nodded happily as Melanie finished the conversation with a flourish. "Certainly sounds better than a poke in the eye with a sharp stick!"

39

"And the day came when the risk to remain tight in a bud was more painful than the risk it took to blossom."

— Anaïs Nin

Three weeks had gone by during which statements had once again been taken, documented, and signed, and village gossip began to die down. Vivien passed the time by planning a large Thanksgiving dinner and inviting Geoffrey's family over to introduce them to that very American holiday. She wanted to ask them to dress as pilgrims or Native Americans, but Geoffrey gently suggested everyone would be happier without buckled shoes and feathered headdresses.

Now, listening to the soothing sound of rain on a grey Saturday morning, Vivien admired the bedroom she'd created for her stepdaughter according to Sara's specific demands, which had been communicated via Skype from a warm, sunny Melbourne. She'd managed to source a purple color for the walls that didn't look gloomy even on such a day, and the room was lightened considerably by touches of teal, which was Sara's favorite color. Hearing her iPad ping in the library next door, Vivien walked over and opened it to find an email from Sergeant Martin.

"Ms. Brandt," it read, "I have Inspector Torksey's permission to send you the attached, as it is not included in the case evidence. We found it on Sebastian's computer, in a sort of online diary, and thought you might appreciate it. Thank you again for your assistance, and I hope we may one day meet in more felicitous circumstances. Oh, and say hello to Sydney, my new crime-fighting partner."

Vivien carried the iPad downstairs to sit on the daybed in her now-spotless conservatory. It somehow felt like the right place to deal with whatever this was. She opened the attachment and began reading.

We've got a new neighbour, called Vivien Brandt. She's American, and as brash and opinionated as you might expect.

Hey! Vivien thought. *Not fair!* Then she smiled. It might be a little bit fair. She read on.

But she also seems really nice and fairly smart. She's offered Lucius and me a job and a place to be together after school, and I can't see that she gets anything out of it except a badly painted shed. Pretty refreshing. I don't know her well enough yet, but I'm wondering if she might be the person I've been looking for, the adult who can keep secrets and give me good advice. Time will tell. Until then, she makes me laugh, and it's been a long time since I've done much of that. I look forward to talking to her some more.

Vivien put the iPad down and felt a prickle of tears. There was still an ache in her heart when she thought about Sebastian, and she suspected there always would be. She was sorry about Jay, but to some extent he'd made choices—or avoided them—that fed into the way events unfolded. And if he did know about the poison in his whisky, then she respected that drinking it had been one of those choices that were his to make.

Sebastian, on the other hand, hadn't had time to make many choices, and had everything to live for. His death was a bonafide tragedy, in Vivien's opinion.

"I'm so sorry, Sebastian, but thank you for being my friend," she whispered to the room. A rare shaft of November sunlight suddenly broke through the clouds and bathed the conservatory in a warm glow. Vivien felt oddly comforted.

Looking around the empty windowsills, she decided it was time to finish off the house decoration with some plant life as an homage to the boy who would never get to fulfil his dreams. She went to find Geoffrey and convince him to accompany her to the nearest garden center.

Geoffrey had taken a few days off to spend with his wife and make sure she was fully recovered from having her life threatened, as well as showing her how important she was to him by rarely leaving her side. She'd thought it was sweet at first, but the honeymoon was soon over. Or whatever you called the period following a trauma. Lemonmoon? Vivien was sure her sister would have a colorful phrase for it.

But despite being back at work full time, her husband still exhibited an outsized amount of excitement at the idea of picking out plants on his day off. Vivien knew from her English friends this was because a garden center was like

Disneyland to your average Brit. If an Englishman's house was his castle, then his garden was his personal Wonderland.

They wrapped up warmly to battle an increasing chill in the air and set off, soon arriving at a buzzing car park which they had to circle twice before finding a space.

They grabbed a shopping trolley and headed for the indoor plant section where they spotted Archie Bonner and Clive Foster ahead of them, laughing as the latter picked up a plant with a particularly frightening porcelain monkey climbing its small trunk and pretended to put it in the trolley in front of them. Archie, dressed in wrinkle-free tan slacks and a light blue polo shirt, looked as debonair as always, and even Clive seemed to have made an effort to spruce himself up, wearing dark blue jeans with a pink dress shirt.

As they approached, Vivien cleared her throat and gently said their names. Both men turned, their faces flushing, as if they'd been caught doing something illicit. Geoffrey smiled and nodded at them, receiving nods in return. For once Vivien wasn't sure what to say next, but she had her doubts the others would do any better, so she took the plunge.

"Archie, it's nice to see you again, and you too, Clive. I won't ask how you are, these past weeks must have been terrible, but I hope you know that, if there's anything we can do for either of you, you have only to ask."

Archie smiled sheepishly at her. "I've been meaning to come by, Vivien. I understand from the police that you were instrumental in getting justice for my son, and I just want to say that I'm very grateful. Nothing can bring Sebastian back, and it's certainly beyond comprehension that he was killed by his own mother…"

The man took an understandable moment to compose himself before continuing.

"...but I know eventually I will be glad it was resolved so quickly and without further bloodshed. Except for my poor father-in-law, of course."

Clive gave his friend a sympathetic pat on the back, to which Archie responded with a look that held gratitude and fondness before he turned back to Vivien and Geoffrey.

"I also want to say how sorry I am that I sided with Rachel and practically threw you out of Sebastian's funeral." He nodded at Geoffrey. "And to thank you again for your offer to help with the legalities. I should have known something was wrong when Rachel was so rude to the two of you. She usually exhibits an iron control over herself. But I thought it was merely the shock of Sebastian's death that caused her aberrant behavior."

"Well, in a way it was," Geoffrey replied. "Just not for the reasons we all assumed. Have you spoken to her since her arrest? Is she coping all right?"

"I haven't talked to her, though the inspector tells me she's already suggested several social activities for improving the prisoner experience. Which she has offered to organize, of course. I don't know if I will ever be able to forgive her for what she's done—to Sebastian, her father, as well as threatening others including yourselves—but the woman doesn't lack determination. I'm just sorry she was able to hurt so many people while I buried myself in my work."

"You don't have to apologize, we certainly don't hold you responsible for her behavior, and we hope you will consider us friends," Geoffrey assured him.

"Thank you. I have no idea what the future holds for me,

or if I will still be your MP after the next election. There are so many issues to work through, and decisions to be made, but that is good to know."

He looked shyly at Clive and a slight pink once again suffused his face. "Clive has been an enormous help and provided invaluable support. I don't know what I would have done without him these past weeks."

Vivien noted a look of pure happiness on the ex-vicar's face before the two men turned to continue up the aisle. She smiled at the thought that at least something decent might be salvaged from this horrible situation once grief had a chance to recede, and made a mental note to invite them both over for dinner soon.

"Oh, that reminds me!" Archie declared, turning back to Vivien. "I hear from the Masons that you have some experience in interior decorating. Would you be interested in helping me redecorate the house? I feel a brand-new start is in order, maybe something a bit more bohemian. I'm happy to pay for your time and recommend your services to others if all goes well, as I'm sure it will."

Vivien nodded happily. It crossed her mind that Archie might be hiring her out of guilt, but she was okay with that, there was no sense barring the door when opportunity knocked. Besides, she was sure Sebastian would have wanted her to help his father. Her start in Nether Chatby hadn't gone exactly to plan, to say the least, but maybe things were starting to get back on track. She mouthed a quiet *thank you* heavenward just in case Seb was listening. Or anyone else.

Vivien and Geoffrey proceeded to load up their trolley with lush greenery and brightly colored pots. She then spent the afternoon planting and arranging the new growth around the edges of the conservatory, replacing the memory of death with lush life and creating a space she knew would become a welcome retreat someday, when time had eased the pain.

40

"I realized as I walked through the neighborhood how each house could contain a completely different reality. In a single block, there could be fifty separate worlds. Nobody ever really knew what was going on just next door."

— Janet Fitch, *White Oleander*

It was a couple more weeks before DI Torksey and Sergeant Martin finally came by to catch them up on the case, once an initial hearing had been held. Sergeant Martin pleased Vivien enormously by admiring the new décor, and a newly mellowed Torksey didn't even object when Vivien asked if Hayley and Will could stay to hear about the aftermath of the arrests.

Once they were settled with the obligatory cups of tea and biscuits, Torksey got right to the point.

"You were correct, Ms. Brandt, about Mrs. Bonner's alibi. The till had not been reset when the time changed. The employee tasked with doing so over the weekend had called in sick, and we didn't think to interview the night staff about any irregularities. It had been set properly by the time we got there after Sebastian's murder, but by checking the opening receipts we could tell the systems were an hour ahead on the Monday, giving Rachel Bonner a false alibi for the time of the murder. It does seem odd that there's still technology that doesn't automatically reset in this day and age, but there you are. Well done for pointing out the possibility."

Vivien acknowledged the compliment with a nod. "If I hadn't edited the manual on that cash register, I mean till, I probably wouldn't have considered it either. But I specifically remember thinking the same as you did when I came to the chapter on resetting it for Daylight Saving Time, that it was outmoded. I had to confirm with the company that it was still true. That and the fact that the video system didn't seem to be working gave Rachel what she needed to construct her fake alibi."

Vivien saw a distinct flicker of annoyance in the chief inspector's eyes before he responded. "Apparently the video system hasn't functioned in months. As is too often the case, our murderer got lucky there, so to speak. Or, as you say, she may have noticed it wasn't working when she was there. And the attendant who identified Mrs. Bonner as having been at the station admitted he wasn't certain of the time when we presented him with the discrepancy on the receipt."

"It must have been the icing on the cake when she saw him enter my house and realized she could throw suspicion on me."

Torksey acknowledged her statement with raised eyebrows as he munched on his chocolate Bourbon.

"Well, I guess that closes the case on Sebastian's death,"

she continued. "That poor child, saddled with the unwelcome knowledge that both his parents were having affairs."

Vivien paused as she became aware of everyone's questioning looks and hastened to explain her comment.

"He was very unkind about Reverend Edwards when we last spoke, practically accusing him of hypocrisy. I figure it was because he knew about the man's relationship with his mother. Come to think of it, even if Sebastian had been religious, I think two lying ministers seducing his parents would have dented anyone's faith, and it also made his parents unlikely confidants. It's no wonder he finally resorted to hinting about the situation to his grandfather out of drunken desperation. Unfortunately, that also sealed Colonel Jay's fate. Or did it? Do you now know what happened with the colonel's whisky?"

"As I said, we knew Rachel wasn't the culprit there. Others drank out of the whisky decanter after she visited, without ill effects. To be fair, we weren't sure that Sergeant Hardwick—it seems the title of Colonel was adopted rather than earned—was even murdered. But since so many of his friends protested that it was out of character, we decided to investigate, as you know, and finding the poison in the decanter rather than just in his glass did suggest murder rather than suicide. Thanks to the lively curiosity of Hardwick's neighbors, it wasn't long before we had multiple reports that he was visited by Reverend Edwards on the day he died. Security cameras set up by the property management company—working this time, thank goodness—confirmed Edwards visited carrying a package, and his phone records revealed he made a call to Mrs. Bonner while exiting the property. We also found the original bottle of whisky in the bin with Edwards' fingerprints on the neck, probably from when he pulled it from the bag."

"So Edwards purposely killed the old man? What was his motive?" Vivien wanted to know. "Based on what I heard while Rachel was trying to kill me, I'm guessing Edwards was having an affair with her?"

"Indeed," Torksey confirmed, ignoring Vivien's dramatic description. "While being clear he is not absolving himself of responsibility, he claims she seduced him and he fell in love with her. He says she gave him the bottle of whisky to deliver to her father and suggested Edwards say it was a gift from himself to earn Hardwick's goodwill. Evidently, Edwards believed the man would someday be his father-in-law. He claims not to know the poison was in there and acknowledges his judgement was…skewed, to say the least. Hardwick must have poured the whisky into the decanter after Edwards left, as only his prints are on that."

"Is there any evidence to tie Rachel to this? She can't be getting away scot-free, can she?" said Hayley.

Torksey smiled. "While it looks like she was careful to wipe her prints off the bottle after adding the poison and resealing it, we managed to get one of hers off the paper bag containing the whisky, which was also in the bin. I'm sure a good barrister will be able to sow doubt about how it got there, but it's a solid case even so, thanks to her obvious motive, Edwards' confession, and the proof of their affair.

Vivien felt a deep sadness at the ruination of a man she had come to like and admire.

"I knew Edwards seemed troubled, but I never suspected anything that bad," she remarked wistfully. "What must he have been going through, wondering who had put poison in the whisky and when, not wanting to believe it was the woman he loved."

The detective inspector took a moment to shake his head at the perfidy of men in lust before continuing. "The fact that Edwards didn't avoid the cameras or turn off his phone does seem to back up his story that he didn't know—or didn't want to know—he was carrying poison. When we presented him with the evidence of his visit to Hardwick, he figured all that remained was the truth, as Mr. Holmes might say."

Vivien threw a dazzling smile at him for referencing the famous Victorian detective. It seemed to stun him momentarily, so a grinning Sergeant Martin took up the narrative.

"In fact, we were in the car headed over to bring him in for further questioning when you called that day, which is why we were able to get to you so quickly. We had an officer keeping an eye on him while we gathered all the evidence. He reported that Edwards was visiting Mrs. Bonner and then our officer left to attend to another call, knowing we were on the way to talk to him. But according to Edwards, instead of a lover he found an agitated Rachel who demanded help committing further crimes, namely killing you and Mr. Foster. Apparently, this finally snapped Edwards out of his delusion and he refused, at which point Mrs. Bonner went into the kitchen, returned with her handbag, and slammed the door on her way out of the house. I imagine Edwards spent a few minutes thinking back over their relationship and came to the realization that not only had his beloved probably killed her son, but she had left the murder weapon where it would implicate him. Then he decided he'd better check on you. Which was very fortunate for you, Ms. Brandt."

Geoffrey squeezed his wife. "And we are truly grateful. Will Reverend Edwards be charged for Colonel Jay's death?"

"We really have no way to prove he knew what was in the whisky beforehand, as I said," replied a recovered Torksey. "But he did withhold evidence once he knew the whisky was poisoned."

"Perverting the course of justice," the sergeant clarified.

Torksey nodded. "It was easy enough to find multiple people who had informed him about the poisoned whiskey, thanks to your village's incredibly efficient grapevine. And of course, it will be up to the Church what happens to his ministry."

Will, who had been quiet during these exchanges, suddenly piped up. "I'll tell you one thing, it seems like the Church of England needs a better human resources department to handle recruitment and interviews. They're zero for two in this village."

Hayley elbowed her husband in the side as Geoffrey responded. "Neither of them seem to be bad people, just weak in the face of certain temptations." He turned to address the inspector. "We would be glad to speak on Edwards' behalf at his sentencing hearing. He did refuse to kill for Rachel once he knew the truth, and he very likely saved my wife's life."

He punctuated the thought with another squeeze of said wife. Vivien was starting to worry about bruises, but then she thought about how she would use them later to garner sympathy and favors. *Marriage could be such fun.*

Torksey nodded. "I will let you know who ends up representing him and you can discuss that with them."

Vivien continued to be troubled about motive. "I know I provided some of the evidence, but I'm still struggling to understand how Rachel could have killed her own son. And her father. For what? To keep people from finding out her husband had an affair?"

"Murderers aren't always the most balanced people, Ms Brandt," said Torksey. "Archibald Bonner told us his wife held that secret over his head, forcing him to do as she wanted in everything from home repairs to campaign appearances. She needed him to be squeaky clean for his climb up the political ladder and convinced him he wanted that too. To add the stick to that carrot, she swore if he ever told anyone about his relationship with Foster she would ensure he was reviled by his friends, his family, his party, and his constituents. Bonner confided to us he was considering revealing all anyway, seeing Sebastian struggle with his own sexuality. In fact, if she suspected as much, that might have increased Mrs. Bonner's sense of being threatened.

"As for Sergeant Hardwick, he must have suspected his daughter was involved, it explains why he refused to say anything in his own defence after we arrested him. But he would have been better off if he'd shared his suspicions with us."

"He probably felt guilty about the pig," Vivien muttered, garnering more curious looks but no follow-up.

Sergeant Martin broke the awkward silence. "It seems Mrs. Bonner's ambition was a powerful motivator; she was willing to do just about anything to keep her position as the wife of an up-and-coming MP. There's no evidence that her actions were driven by homophobia or revenge or anything other than a desire for power and influence, as she revealed to you, Ms. Brandt. Fortunately, we get to leave that to the forensic psychiatrists to sort, and just be glad our work on this case is done except for testifying at the trial."

"I imagine it was constantly coming in second," Hayley interjected thoughtfully. "She was raised by a popular father who loved to hog the limelight."

Vivien snorted at the unintentional second pig reference, which fortunately Hayley couldn't hear as she continued on with her theory.

"Then she married a man whose career had to be protected above all else, and was forced to deal with all the traumas of a teenager with his own emotional issues. For someone as strong-willed and intelligent as Rachel, it must have been galling to constantly have to subsume her own ambition to ensure the success of the men in her life."

"Who exactly was forcing her?" Vivien protested.

Hayley shook her head. "Sadly, she must have either been taught to believe that was the proper way of things, or else she simply lacked the imagination to find a path to fame for herself other than as the dutiful daughter, spouse, and mother. And lover, I suppose. She probably seduced Reverend Edwards to ensure her power in the church community. She certainly ran campaign events and village festivals extremely efficiently, but that was never going to be enough for her."

They all sat quietly for a moment, contemplating another life gone so very wrong. Vivien felt a twinge of remorse for what she'd said to Rachel about never being a Power Chick. It must have really hit home. But then, the woman was a serial murderer and had been threatening her with a knife at the time, so she wasn't going to dwell on it.

"Did she try to use her alibi again?" she asked Inspector Torksey.

"Yes, but we've informed her it won't do, thanks to your information about the till. She may not have gone to your house set on murdering her son, but she did take the gun she'd stolen from her father. We suspect she wore gloves so as not to leave any fingerprints and, unlike Edwards, she turned her mobile off during that time, which was something she evidently rarely did. It will throw doubt on her argument that it was an accident. Plus, she tried to hide her actions using the petrol station receipt, and physically threatened you and Edwards. Of course, she continues to deny she had any role in the death of her father."

Geoffrey's brow was creased. "I still find it hard to believe Colonel Jay didn't taste the wintergreen oil, even in whisky that peaty."

Torksey shrugged. "He may have done, but you can see how it might have been hard for him to accept that his own daughter was trying to kill him, and by extension had killed his grandson. He may have simply decided drinking it was easier than facing the fact that he'd raised a murderer."

"Well, that and he was dying anyway from the cancer," Hayley said, and then flushed when Torksey stared at her. "What?" she squeaked. "I just found that out recently from his friend Maude. He told her the day before he died. Did I forget to mention it?" She lapsed into silence.

"We learned about the cancer from the autopsy, but thank you for revealing it was common knowledge. This really is a small village," Torksey said wryly. "Hardwick's state of mind aside, at least we've discovered where Rachel got the wintergreen oil. Susan Ramakrishnan came forward once Mrs. Bonner was in custody and admitted a jar of wintergreen oil was missing from her candle-making equipment. She was afraid one of her daughters had taken it and didn't want them mixed up in Colonel Jay's death if it turned out to be the poison involved. But she now recalls Mrs. Bonner visiting her at home a couple of days before Hardwick's death, and acknowledges Rachel was left alone long enough to have taken the oil."

Ah, thought Vivien, *that explains Susan's odd behavior at the funeral. Maybe she thought Samantha had stolen it to give to Justin.* Everyone did seem to suspect Justin of the worst things.

Inspector Torksey waved to get Hayley's attention. "And on the subject of knowledge, Mrs. Mason, while your brother has acquitted himself well in all this, it hasn't escaped our notice that you and Ms. Brandt were very well informed at times. It's one of the reasons we decided to share information with you ourselves, rather than expose anyone to too much temptation."

He paused as the two women did their best not to look guilty, then continued.

"All I ask is that you are mindful of PC Marsden's career, he has the makings of an excellent police officer and I wouldn't want to see him hauled up in front of the PTB for leaking confidential case details."

Hayley and Vivien looked at each other, eyes wide, before turning back to Torksey to exclaim simultaneously, "YOU watch *Buffy the Vampire Slayer*?"

Both Torksey and Martin smiled.

"I saw the DVDs in your house, Mrs. Mason, and yes, it remains some of the best writing on television," said Sergeant Martin.

"Ms. Gellar is a wonderful actor," Inspector Torksey deadpanned.

Will just groaned.

"Lastly," said Torksey, "on the topic of Mr. Turnbull, we've had a chat with him and we're keeping an eye out to circumvent further disturbances, as well as encouraging the library to get CCTV cameras installed for the longer term. But do let us know if there is any further trouble, Ms. Brandt."

Geoffrey finally pulled his arm back from around Vivien so he could shift sideways to give her a questioning look. Torksey, glancing between them and guessing Vivien hadn't told her husband about that particular adventure, threw his own cheeky grin in her direction.

"Gee, thanks," Vivien eventually mumbled.

At that moment there was a knock on the front door and a relieved Vivien jumped up from the sofa to answer it. She knew Geoffrey would want to know about the Turnbull business once they were alone, but any reprieve was welcome in the meantime.

"Hello," said the short, voluptuous woman on her doorstep. She was dressed in a flowing green tie-dyed skirt topped by a white peasant blouse that glowed against her coffee-colored skin. Her shoulder-length cornrowed hair had pink streaks in it and her dark brown eyes twinkled with humor. "I'm your neighbor, Tabitha. I'm sorry to be so late coming by to welcome you, but I've been away on a long holiday."

"Uh, lovely, and thanks for the welcome. Did you go anywhere nice?" Vivien asked. Sydney twined around her ankles and received a smile of appreciation from the visitor, who bent over to tickle him under the chin before straightening up to answer.

"Salem, Massachusetts. It was a bit of a work gig as well as holiday, I was attending the annual Wiccapedia conference.

I'm the leader of the local coven here in Nether Chatby. Anyway, I just wanted to say hello and hope your time with us is blessed."

Will must have been signing the overheard conversation for Hayley back in the living room because the latter could be heard loudly laughing as Vivien found herself speechless for the second time in five minutes. *Living here certainly isn't going to be boring*, Vivien decided.

References

As a fan of *Gilmore Girls* and *Buffy the Vampire Slayer*, I am something of a slave to casual pop culture references in my writing. It is my hope that if you made it this far you have recognized many of them, or at least that they did not mar your enjoyment of the book.

If, in fact, any of these references piqued your interest in the original source, here is where you can find out more, including where you can view/read/experience them for yourself.

Chapter 1
- *Upstairs, Downstairs* was a BBC production from the 1970s that followed the household of a Member of Parliament (MP) and his family and servants in the early twentieth century. It was a big hit in America after being shown on the PBS channel. Find out more at https://www.imdb.com/title/tt0066722/.
- The proposed names for Vivien's dream dogs—Lancelot, Percival, and Galahad—are names of knights in the King Arthur legend.
- Jeeves and Wooster are characters created by humorist P. G. Wodehouse in a series of novels. A television series was created

of his stories with Jeeves being played by Stephen Fry and Bertie Wooster by Hugh Laurie (of *House* fame in America). It's not currently available on any streaming platforms, but you can find out more at https://www.imdb.com/title/tt0098833/. Although I strongly advise you to go to your local library and read them first, all of his books are absolutely hilarious.

Chapter 2

- Lord Alfred Tennyson's phrase "red in tooth and claw" is from his poem "In Memoriam A. H. H.", 1850. You can find the poem at https://poets.org/poem/memoriam-h-h.
- Donna Reed was the star of *The Donna Reed Show*, a black-and-white TV series from the 1960s that featured the perfect American family. https://www.imdb.com/title/tt0051267/?ref_=fn_al_tt_2 has more information.
- Cate Blanchett is a film star, who played an elven queen in the Tolkien films and won an Academy Award for playing Katharine Hepburn in *The Aviator*. Learn about her at https://www.imdb.com/name/nm0000949/?ref_=nv_sr_srsg_0.

Chapter 3

- *Gone with the Wind* is a book by Margaret Mitchell about the American Civil War that was made into a very successful film starring Vivien Leigh as Scarlett O'Hara, Clark Gable as Rhett Butler, Olivia de Havilland as Melanie Wilkes, and Leslie Howard as Ashley Wilkes. Scarlett is jealous of her sister-in-law Melanie in the film, and Olivia de Havilland famously feuded with her sister Joan Fontaine for most of their lives, but Vivien's mother obviously wasn't considering these facts when naming her daughters.
- *Buffy the Vampire Slayer* was a movie (not great) and then a TV series (very great) that debuted in the late 1990s. It was created by Joss Whedon, who then went on to oversee the spin-off

series, *Angel*, and a space-western series, *Firefly*. He also directed the first two Avengers films. The episode with the discussion of kinds of parties is in Season 3, "Dead Man's Party". For a list of all episodes, see https://www.imdb.com/title/tt0118276/.

- *Murdoch Mysteries* is a Canadian television series that started in 2004 starring Yannick Bisson. It's about an enterprising police detective in early twentieth-century Toronto. If you like quirky detective series, see https://www.imdb.com/title/tt1091909/?ref_=fn_al_tt_1 for more information.
- Previous to *Murdoch Mysteries*, Bisson starred in *Sue Thomas: F.B.Eye*, about a deaf woman who works for the Federal Bureau of Investigation (FBI). See https://www.imdb.com/title/tt0329934/ for more information.

Chapter 4

- *Pretty in Pink* is a 1986 film in which a girl from the wrong side of the tracks must choose between dating her childhood friend or a sensitive rich boy. See https://www.imdb.com/title/tt0091790/?ref_=fn_al_tt_1 for more information.
- The Brat Pack was a name given to several stars of 1980s films such as *The Breakfast Club* and *St. Elmo's Fire*. It included Molly Ringwald, Emilio Estevez, Judd Nelson, and Ally Sheedy, among others. See https://en.wikipedia.org/wiki/Brat_Pack#Membership for more information.

Chapter 5

- *Downton Abbey* (https://www.imdb.com/title/tt1606375/?ref_=fn_al_tt_1) was an ITV 2004 series about the fictional Crawley family and their servants.
- The *Star Trek* episode "Mudd's Women" (https://www.imdb.com/title/tt0708439/) is about women who take a pill that makes them artificially beautiful so they can be sold to miners on an alien planet. What can I say, it was the 1960s.

- Dante Gabriel Rossetti was a member of the Pre-Raphaelite Brotherhood painters. He attached a verse from Goethe's *Faust* to the frame of *Lady Lilith*:

    "Beware of her fair hair, for she excels
    All women in the magic of her locks,
    And when she twines them round a young man's neck
    she will not ever set him free again."

    Make of that what you will.
- Yoda is a character from *Star Wars*. I'm betting you've heard of *Star Wars*, I'm just trying to be comprehensive.

Chapter 7
- Wonder Woman and Batman are characters in the DC Comics universe. Several movies and television series have been made about each.
- *Firefly* is another series created by Joss Whedon, about the crew of a piratical spaceship trying to make a living after being on the wrong side of an intergalactic war.
- Harry Styles is an English singer-songwriter who began his career as part of One Direction.

Chapter 9
- You can find out more about *Fruits Basket* Manga comics at https://www.goodreads.com/en/book/show/8192675-fruits-basket and about Manga in general at https://www.21-draw.com/what-is-manga-a-guide-to-japanese-comic-books/.
- Cecil B. DeMille was a Hollywood director in the first half of the twentieth century known for producing films featuring enormous numbers of actors.
- Eddie Izzard is a stand-up comedian who began as an 'action transvestite' and eventually changed gender. She prefers the name Suzy now and has always been incredibly funny.

- *Poltergeist* is a 1982 film about a haunted house. The exorcism mentioned really just makes the ghosts more pissed off. See https://www.imdb.com/title/tt0084516/?ref_=nv_sr_srsg_0 for more information.

Chapter 10
- The National Coal Mining Museum in Wakefield is well worth a visit: https://www.ncm.org.uk/.
- *he Count of Monte Cristo* is a novel by French writer Alexandre Dumas, and it is about a count who is locked up in an island prison after being betrayed by his friends. He escapes and spends the rest of his life wreaking revenge upon them.

Chapter 11
- "A Whole New World" is a song from Disney's 1992 film version of *Aladdin*.
- Lancelot (nicknamed Capability) Brown was a famous English landscape architect of the eighteenth century, responsible for designing the grounds of many English stately homes. So Vivien is making a joke upon his name by dubbing herself 'Incapability Brown'.

Chapter 12
- The Cheshire Cat is a character from *Alice in Wonderland*, originally a novel titled *Alice's Adventures in Wonderland*, by Lewis Carroll but later adapted into a 1951 animated film by Disney. There is a later mention of Wonderland that is also referencing that film and its portrayal of a giant garden.
- Loki, the Norse god of mischief, was the villain in the first Avengers film, 2012's *The Avengers*, and was played by actor Tom Hiddleston.

Chapter 13
- Miss Marple is a fictional elderly lady detective created by English crime writer Agatha Christie. If you don't know who Agatha Christie is, check her out, she's the original cozy crime queen and the best-selling author of all time with sixty-six novels to her credit.
- Jessica Fletcher is a fictional elderly lady detective and writer who was played by Angela Lansbury in the long-running American TV series *Murder She Wrote*. I can't wait to be an elderly lady myself so I can start detecting.

Chapter 15
- Cruella de Vil is a villain from Dodie Smith's novel *The Hundred and One Dalmatians*, later made into a Disney film.
- Sara Paretsky is a crime writer whose most famous series of books features female private eye V. I. Warshawski. Patricia Cornwell has similarly created a series featuring forensic coroner Kay Scarpetta.

Chapter 17
- *Gilmore Girls* was an American television series following a mother and daughter who live in the fictional Connecticut town of Stars Hollow. It is famous for its rapid-fire dialogue featuring many pop culture references and has had a big influence on my own writing.

Chapter 18
- The Kardashians are a celebrity family known for their wild antics and a reality television show. See https://en.wikipedia.org/wiki/Kardashian_family.
- The National Trust is a charity that preserves and maintains historic homes in the UK so people can visit them and learn about their history. Learn more at https://www.nationaltrust.

org.uk/. A similar charity is English Heritage: http://www.english-heritage.org.uk/.
- Charles Frederick Worth was a nineteenth-century clothing designer known for his lush fabrics and trimmings and his incorporations of historic dress.

Chapters 19 and 20
- *The King and I* is a 1956 Rodgers and Hammerstein musical starting Yul Brynner and Deborah Kerr. In the film, the King of Siam is very proud of the many English platitudes he has learned, and finishes many pronouncements with "Etcetera, etcetera, etcetera".

Chapter 22
- American television features the Hallmark Channel, which provides original programming including several series of mysteries featuring feisty female professionals who get stuck witnessing murders. Many of these films and series are currently shown on British digital channels such as Paramount and Great! Movies.

Chapter 23
- "Green and pleasant land" is from a poem called "Milton" by William Blake, which was set to music by Hubert Parry a hundred years later in the song "Jerusalem". Learn more at http://www.thisdayinquotes.com/2011/03/englands-green-and-pleasant-land.html.

Chapter 25
- *Outlander* is a 2014 American television series based on books by Diana Gabaldon. It is about a woman from 1940s England who accidently finds herself time traveling to eighteenth-century Scotland where she is forced to marry the unusually

sensitive and stunningly gorgeous James Fraser. See https://www.imdb.com/title/tt3006802/?ref_=fn_al_tt_1 for more information.

Chapter 26
- The story of the fake Lincoln quote in *Pollyanna* is mentioned in Hayley Mills' biography *Forever Young: a Memoir* and also here: https://www.moviemistakes.com/main7151.

Chapter 27
- "Empire" refers to the British Empire, which reigned over India and other countries for close to three centuries. More at https://www.britishempire.co.uk/.
- St. George is the patron saint of England, and thus also the name of the England flag, which has a red cross on a white background. This is different from the Union Jack, which is the flag for the whole of the United Kingdom: England, Scotland, Wales, and Northern Ireland.

Chapter 31
- Disney+ is a digital streaming channel that owns the rights to the Marvel films. For Disney fans, it's a must, although as a cat lover I dearly wish their vault included *The Three Lives of Thomasina*.

Chapter 32
- Hercule Poirot is Agatha Christie's creation, mysteries featuring Roderick Alleyn are by Ngaio Marsh, Eve Dallas and Roark are futuristic crimefighters in the *In Death* series by J. D. Robb, and the Miss Fisher mysteries are by Kerry Greenwood.

Chapter 35
- *Gentleman Jack* is the BBC series based on Anne Lister's

diaries. Suranne Jones is brilliant in the title role, although thank goodness the series doesn't go into details about Lister's bowel movements like the book does.

Chapter 37

- *The Stepford Wives* is a novel by Ira Levin about a community with suspiciously obedient and perfectly groomed wives, and it has twice been made into a film.

Acknowledgements

As Winston Churchill once said, writing a book is an adventure, starting out as a toy and amusement before becoming in turn a mistress, a master, and finally a tyrant. In addition to the dedication, therefore, my first thanks have to go to my husband Chris, who survived for over a year under this novel's tyrannical rule and always encouraged me to live my dream. He is my rock.

My sister Joanie has also been an unflagging cheerleader and one of the first to read and give feedback on a draft of the novel. Friends Jonathan Freckleton and Lorraine Lund followed as beta readers, their comments proving invaluable.

The Doncaster Writers Group stuck with me week after week giving magnificent guidance based on their experience. It is a much better book thanks to them. Thriller writer Mary Torjussen from Jericho Writers provide much-needed structure, and Troubador has been an excellent publishing partner.

My heartfelt appreciation also extends to everyone who has read and enjoyed this book. I don't write for the money (although I'm certainly not going to selflessly donate any that comes my way ENTIRELY to charity!), I do it because I love it, and because I hope it brings some happiness to others. If that is you, then bless, and thank you for reading.

About the Author

Gianetta Murray has spent most of her life, like Vivien, as a technical writer and editor and a librarian. She's had wonderful job titles including Information Architect and Knowledge Disseminator, but Author is her favorite so far.

Though she grew up in California she has now lived with her husband and two cats in South Yorkshire, England for almost twenty years. (Well, not the same two cats, but always at least two!)

She enjoys watching Hollywood musicals, *Buffy the Vampire Slayer,* and Scandi noir. She reads all sorts of things, and plays guitar, flute, drums, and ukelele. The ukelele may show up in future books in the series.

In addition to the Vivien Brandt series, she has published a collection of humorous paranormal stories called *A Supernatural Shindig* and is part of an international group of authors who publish an annual Paths anthology, of which the latest is *Spring Paths*. Both are available on Amazon.

For more information on Gianetta's work and life, join her email list at https://gianettamurray.com, or follow her on Facebook, Instagram, or YouTube.

Stay tuned for the next installment in the Vivien Brandt Mystery series:

Dug to Death